WITHDRAWN

W9-BWW-924

Large Print Gar
Gardner, Erle Stanley, 1889-
1970.
The case of the silent
partner

STACKS

The Case

of the

Silent Partner

Also by Erle Stanley Gardner
in Large Print:

The Case of the Lazy Lover
The Case of the Counterfeit Eye
The Case of the Crying Swallow
The Case of the Lucky Legs
The Case of the Perjured Parrot
The Case of the Sunbather's Diary
The Case of the Amorous Aunt
The Case of the Phantomed Fortune
The Case of the Buried Clock
The Case of the Stepdaughter's Secret
The Case of the Curious Bride
The Case of the Lonely Heiress
The Case of the Smoking Chimney
The Case of the Shoplifter's Shoe

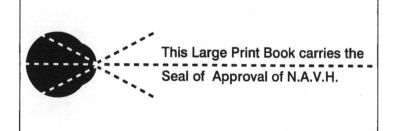

This Large Print Book carries the
Seal of Approval of N.A.V.H.

The Case
of the
Silent Partner

A PERRY MASON Mystery

Erle Stanley Gardner

Thorndike Press • Waterville, Maine

Copyright © 1940 by Erle Stanley Gardner

All rights reserved.

Published in 2003 by arrangement with
Hobson and Hughes, LLC.

Thorndike Press Large Print Paperback Series.

The tree indicium is a trademark of Thorndike Press.

The text of this Large Print edition is unabridged.
Other aspects of the book may vary from the original edition.

Set in 16 pt. Plantin by Minnie B. Raven.

Printed in the United States on permanent paper.

Library of Congress Cataloging-in-Publication Data

Gardner, Erle Stanley, 1889–1970.
    The case of the silent partner / Erle Stanley Gardner.
      p. cm.
    ISBN 0-7862-5047-X (lg. print : sc : alk. paper)
    1. Mason, Perry (Fictitious character) — Fiction.
  2. Large type books. I. Title.
PS3513.A6322C9 2003
  813'.52—dc21
                                  2002044837

The Case

of the

Silent Partner

NEWARK PUBLIC LIBRARY
NEWARK, OHIO 43055-5054

Large Print Gar
Gardner, Erle Stanley, 1889-
1970.
The case of the silent
partner   7543672

Cast of Characters

Mildreth Faulkner — A dynamic young lady executive, whose independent spirit started the fireworks 9

Harry Peavis — Her steamroller competitor, who believed in getting what he wanted, no holds barred 9

Lois Carling — Mildreth's clerk, beautiful and bitterly jealous 13

Della Street — Perry Mason's secretary, co-conspirator, and generally a good gal in a pinch. 15

Robert Lawley — Carlotta's gambling husband, who didn't know the stakes meant murder 16

Carlotta Lawley — Mildreth's sister, a heart case with death staring at her from more than one direction 17

Esther Dilmeyer — A glamorous gambling lure. Dissatisfied, she accepted orchids and a box of poison...... 28

Perry Mason — An easy-mannered but granite-eyed, rapier-minded lawyer who said, "Legality be damned," and turned up a murderer 47

Lieutenant Tragg — A keen-witted, rough-and-ready cop who almost out-guessed Perry Mason 57

Sindler Coll — A handsome and very frightened young man, of shady and nebulous profession 67

Harvey Lynk — A nightclub owner and gambler. The ante was too rich for his blood 90

Dr. Willmont — Who kept two witnesses alive for Perry Mason 108

Clint Magard — Lynk's partner, a fat and slippery character who had an alibi
. . . . 200

1

Mildreth Faulkner, seated at her desk in the glass-enclosed office of the Faulkner Flower Shops, selected a blue crayon of exactly the right shade. Clever at sketching, she used crayons to help her visualize just how flower groupings would appear. Now, with a rough sketch of the Ellsworth dining room at her left, she was trying to get something that would go nicely with the dull green candles Mrs. Ellsworth intended to use for illumination.

Someone tapped on the glass, and she looked up to see Harry Peavis.

She pushed her sketches to one side and nodded for him to come in.

Peavis accepted the invitation as he did everything else, without any outward indication of what his thoughts might be, without any change in pace. A big-boned man of hard muscle, his shoulders and hands showed the effects of hard toil on a farm in his early youth. Now that he had achieved wealth and a virtual monopoly on the city's retail flower business, he went to great pains to fit into the role of successful businessman. His suits were well tailored, and his nails carefully manicured and polished, striking a note of incongruity with the labor-twisted fingers.

"Workin' kinda late?" he asked Mildreth.

She smiled. "I nearly always work late. If it isn't one thing, it's another. Reports on the payroll, income tax, estimates, and a hundred things. Anyhow, it's only seven o'clock."

"You've been having it pretty hard since your sister's heart went bad, haven't you?"

"Oh, I'm getting along all right."

"How is she?"

"Carlotta?"

"Yes."

"She's a lot better."

"Glad to hear it."

"She's still in bed most of the time, but she's improving every day."

"You have three stores, haven't you?"

"Yes," she said, knowing that he was thoroughly familiar, not only with the stores and their locations but generally with the amount of business they did.

"Uh huh," Peavis said. "Well, I sort of thought it might be a good plan to invest a little money with you girls."

"What do you mean?"

"Some stock in your corporation."

Mildreth Faulkner smiled and shook her head. "Thanks, Mr. Peavis, but we're getting along all right. This is a very small, very close corporation."

"Perhaps it ain't as close as you think it is."

"Close enough," she smiled. "Carlotta and I have all of the stock between us."

His grayish-green eyes twinkled out at her from under shaggy brows. "You'll have to think again."

She frowned for a moment, then laughed. "Oh, that's right. There's a certificate of five shares which was given Corinne Dell when we incorporated — we needed three on the board of directors. That stock was just to qualify her as a director."

"Uh huh," Peavis said, pulling a folded stock certificate from his pocket. "Well, Corinne Dell married one of my men, you know, and — well, I took over the stock. You can transfer this certificate on the books, and issue me a new one."

Mildreth Faulkner frowned as she turned the certificate over in her hands.

"Reckon you'll find it all in order," Peavis said, "endorsement all okay an' everything."

She put the stock certificate down on the desk, looked up at him frankly. "Look here, Mr. Peavis, I don't like this. It isn't fair. I don't know just what you have in mind. You're a competitor. We don't want you snooping in our business. Corinne shouldn't have sold that stock. I suppose she couldn't very well have helped herself under the circumstances, but I just want you to know where we stand."

Peavis said, "I know — business is business. You overlooked a bet on that stock, and I didn't. I like you. I want you to like me. But any time you make a business mistake an' I can cash in on it, I aim to do it. That's business. You know we could work out a deal on the rest of that stock. You could stay on here and manage the business. I'd take fifty-one per cent and . . ."

She shook her head.

"You could make just as much money as you're doing now," he said, "and have unlimited capital back of you for expansion. I'd make a good partner."

"No, thank you. We're doing fine as it is."

"Well, just enter the stock transfer of those five shares."

"Just *what* are you trying to do?" she asked.

"Nothing," he said, with a guilelessness which was patently assumed. "I won't interfere with your work. I'll be sort of a silent partner. Go ahead and make a lot of money. Now that I have an interest, I like to see the executives workin' late."

He chuckled and raised his gaunt frame from the chair. Mildreth, watching him lumber down the aisle of the flower shop, knew that his keen eyes, under those shaggy brows, missed no detail.

For some minutes she sat in deep thought, then, putting away her sketches, said to Lois Carling, who was on duty at the front of the shop, "Close up at nine-thirty, Lois. I won't be back."

She paused for a moment to survey herself in the full-length mirror near the front of the store. At thirty-two, she had the figure of twenty-two, and the experience acquired through seven years of building up a remunerative business had made her alert mentally and physically, given her a certain aura of dynamic efficiency which kept her muscles hard, firm, and free of excess flesh. Only a worker could have had her alert efficiency and trim lines.

Lois Carling watched her out of the door, her eyes somewhat bitter and slightly wistful. Lois Carling represented dynamic youth, the explosive forces of new wine. Mildreth Faulkner had the mature individuality of a vintage wine. It was, perhaps, only natural that Lois Carling, possessed only of beauty, impatient of the "slow-but-sure" recipe for success, should ask herself the question, "What's *she* got that I haven't?" — only Lois asked it not as a query which carried its own answer, but as a groping attempt to define personality. But because matters philosophical were far removed from Lois Carling's mental environment, she opened a drawer in the counter, took out a box of candy which had been slipped her by Harry Peavis as he came in, and bit into a chocolate.

There was a telephone booth in the front of the garage where Mildreth Faulkner kept her car. While she was waiting for an attendant to bring it down, she acted on an impulse, and looked up the number of Perry Mason, the lawyer.

There was an office number, and below it a notation, "After office hours, call Glenwood 6-8345."

Mildreth Faulkner dialed the number, found that it was a telephone service which made a specialty of handling and sorting telephone calls for professional men. She explained that she wished to make an appointment with Mr. Mason on a matter of important business, and asked if it would be possible to see him that evening. The woman who was taking the call asked Mildreth for the number of the phone from which she was calling, told her to hang up, and she'd be called back within a couple of minutes.

Mildreth saw the attendant bringing her car up, opened the door of the telephone booth to motion him that she would be out in a minute. He nodded, swung the car off to the left by the gasoline pumps, and Mildreth stepped back into the booth just as the phone rang. She picked up the receiver and said, "Hello."

"Is this Miss Faulkner?"

"Yes."

"This is Della Street, Miss Faulkner, Mr. Mason's secretary. Could you tell me something of the nature of your business?"

"Yes, I have the Faulkner Flower Shops. It's a corporation. I have a business competitor who's managed to buy a few shares of stock, the only ones not controlled by my family. I think he's going to make trouble. I want to know what to do about it."

"Won't an appointment tomorrow be all right?"

"I presume so. I — well, to tell you the truth, I acted on impulse in calling just now. I've been worried ever since I learned about the transaction a few minutes ago."

"Will ten-thirty tomorrow morning be convenient?"

"Yes."

"Very well, Mr. Mason will see you then. Good night."

"Good night," Mildreth Faulkner said, and, feeling somewhat relieved, got into her car, and drove at once to Carlotta's house out on Chervis Road.

Chervis Road wound around the contours near the summit of the mountains which looked down on Hollywood from the north. Carlotta and Bob lived in a stucco hillside house which gleamed white by day, but now appeared as a grayish oblong of mysterious shadows, silhouetted against the twinkling cluster of city lights which lay far below.

Mildreth inserted her latchkey, clicked back the lock, and entered the living room where Bob Lawley was sprawled out in a chair reading a newspaper. A small, leather-backed memorandum book was in his left hand. A pencil was behind his right ear. He looked up, frowning at the interruption, then, as he saw Mildreth, managed a smile of welcome. She noticed that he hastily shoved the notebook into the side pocket of his coat. "Hello, Millie. I didn't hear you drive up."

"Where's Carla?"

"Upstairs."

"Asleep?"

"No. She's lying there reading."

"I'll go up for a few minutes," Mildreth said. "You aren't going out, are you, Bob?"

"No. Gosh, no. What gave you that idea?"

"I want to see you."

"Okay."

She paused in the doorway, turned, and said, "When you're figuring the race horses, Bob, don't think you have to fall all over yourself putting things out of sight just because I happen to walk in unannounced."

For a moment he flushed, then laughed, and said, somewhat sheepishly, "You startled me, that's all."

Mildreth climbed the stairs to where her sister lay in bed. Pillows propped against her back elevated her shoulders to a comfortable position. A rose-shaded reading lamp, fastened to the head of the bed, threw light over her left shoulder to the pages of the book she was reading.

She turned the shade of the light down

so that the room was filled with a soft, rosy glow, and said, "I'd about given you up, Millie."

"I was detained. How's everything today?"

"Getting better day by day, in every way," Carlotta said with a smile.

She was older than Mildreth, and her flesh had a bluish-white appearance. While she wasn't fat, the tissues seemed soft and flaccid.

"How's the heart?"

"Fine. The doctor said today that I can drive my car within a couple of weeks. It certainly will seem good to get out. I'll bet my little coupe has forgotten how to run."

"Don't be in a hurry," Mildreth cautioned. "Take it easy, particularly when you start moving around."

"That's what the doctor said."

"What's the book?"

"One of the new ones that's supposed to have a deep social significance. I can't see it."

"Why not try something lighter?"

"No. I like these. The other stories get me excited, and I have difficulty sleeping. Another ten pages of this, and I'll drop off to sleep without having to take a hypnotic."

Mildreth laughed, a low, rippling laugh.

"Well, I'm sorry I was late. I just ran in to see how you were getting along. I'll run down and talk to Bob for a little while and be on my way."

"Poor Bob," Carlotta said softly. "I'm afraid it's been pretty hard for him, having an invalid for a wife. He's been just simply splendid, Millie."

"That's fine."

"You don't . . . you never have really warmed up to Bob, have you, Millie?"

She raised her eyebrows. "Let's not talk about that now. We'll get along all right."

Carlotta's eyes were wistful. "He feels it, Millie. I wish you'd *try* and get better acquainted with him."

"I will," Millie promised, her lips smiling but her eyes purposeful. "I'll go down and begin right now. You take it easy, Carla, and be sure not to overdo as you start getting better."

Carlotta watched Mildreth through the door. "It must be splendid to be so vibrantly healthy. I wish you could give me some of your health for about an hour."

"I wish I could give it to you for longer than that, Carla, but you'll be all right now. You're over the worst of it."

"I think so. I know I'm lots better now than I was."

Carlotta picked up her book. Mildreth gently closed the door and walked quietly down the stairs.

Bob Lawley folded the newspaper. The pencil was no longer behind his ear. "Drink, Millie?" he asked.

"No, thanks." She sat down in the chair opposite him, accepted one of his cigarettes, leaned forward for his match, sat back, and looked at him steadily. "Don't you think it might be a good plan if we all three sat down and had a business chat?"

"Not yet, Millie."

"Why?"

"Carla shouldn't be bothered with business right now. I've talked with the doctor about it, and he says she's doing fine, but it's largely because she's accustomed herself to washing her hands of business. Why, what's wrong?"

"Harry Peavis was in tonight."

"That big clod! What does *he* want?"

"He wants to buy the business — a controlling interest in it."

"He would. Tell him to go peddle his papers."

"I did, but it seems he's a stockholder now."

"A stockholder!" Bob exclaimed, and she saw swift alarm on his face. "Why, how the devil could he . . ." He hastily averted his eyes.

"Corinne Dell. You remember she married a man who works for Peavis. I suppose her husband got her to turn over the stock. I should have picked up that stock before she left. To tell you the truth, I'd entirely forgotten about it. It's such a small block and . . ."

Bob seemed positively relieved. He laughed. "What can he do with that? It's only five shares. That's a drop in the bucket. Tell him to go to hell — put on assessments and freeze him out."

She shook her head. "Harry Peavis won't be pushed around. He wants something . . . I'm just a little afraid of him. He may be entitled to look over our books. Perhaps that's what he wants. I don't know. I'm going to see a lawyer in the morning."

"Good idea. Whom are you going to see?"

"Perry Mason."

"He doesn't handle that stuff. It takes a murder case to get him even interested."

She said, "If he gets enough for it, he'll be interested. This needs someone who can do more than just look in a law book and tell you what the law is. It needs a lot of legal ingenuity."

"Well, he's the bird to handle Peavis all right if you can get him to handle it," Bob Lawley admitted, "but you're making a mountain out of a molehill."

"I thought it would be a good plan to take up *all* of the stock certificates and the stock book. He'll want to see them."

"Oh, you don't have to do that," Bob said hastily.

"Well, he might ask for them."

Bob's voice was harsh with nervous impatience. "Gosh, Millie, I've got an important appointment in the morning, and that stock's in the safety deposit box. Tell you what you do. If he wants to see the stock, *I* can take it in to him later on. I don't think he'll want to. I have an appointment with an insurance company adjuster in the morning — confounded nuisance. I could cancel it, of course, if I *had* to, but I've had a lot of trouble getting him on the job."

"What was the accident, Bob? You never did tell me anything about it. I learned of it from Carla."

"Oh, just one of those cases of where some guy comes down the street, crocked to the eyebrows. I wasn't even in the car. I had it parked at the curb. I don't know how in the world he managed to smash it up the way he did. He must have skidded into it from the side."

"Did you get his number?"

"No. I tell you I wasn't there. The car was parked. A couple of people who saw it told me about it, but they were too dumb to get his license number."

Mildreth said, "Well, I guess I'm not really going to need the stock, although I'd like to have it. Couldn't you get down to the safety deposit box, Bob, and . . ."

"Absolutely not, Millie. I've got two or three appointments in the morning. I just can't cancel them now, but if he needs the stock, I'll bring it in later. You can get in touch with me. You don't need to have it there when you're talking with him. Don't be silly! Next week would be okay."

"Well, I guess it's all right," she said, and there was a note of weary dejection in her voice.

"You're working too hard, Millie. Can't you take it a little easier?"

"Oh, I'm all right. Business is pretty good, and there's quite a bit of detail work. . . . Well, I'll run along, Bob."

"Leave a message for me if you want that stock," he said. "I could pick it up day after tomorrow — but I can't imagine why he'd want to see the certificate."

"Look, Bob, can't you get into that box and . . ."

"Lord, no!" he interrupted, raising his voice. "You're getting to be an old woman. Stop that damned worrying."

"Bob . . . the stock's there, isn't it? It's all right? You . . ."

He got up out of the chair. "For Christ's sake, quit nagging! Don't I have enough on my mind without you running around yapping about your damned stock? I know you don't like me. You never did. You broke your fool neck trying to poison Carla's mind against me. Now . . ."

"Stop it!" she interrupted. "You're like a schoolboy. . . . And you're shouting. You don't want Carla to think we're quarreling, do you?"

He sat down wearily. "Oh, hell, what's the use? . . . If Mason wants to see that stock, tell him to ring *me* up. You give me the willies. If you don't want to quarrel, get the hell out of here."

She stalked wordlessly to the door, out into the evening.

Gliding along Chervis Road, Mildreth Faulkner was entirely oblivious to the charm of the clear, star-lit night. Why had Bob been so glib with detailed explanations of that automobile accident? Why was it so important to meet the insurance adjuster? Why had he had so much trouble getting him on the job? Why did the idea of producing that stock throw him in such a panic? She *had* been tactless about it. She didn't trust him. For weeks now she'd been trying to find some legitimate excuse for getting that stock certificate out of his hands. Carla had endorsed all her securities, turned them over to Bob. . . . Of course it was absurd to doubt his loyalty to Carla, yet she couldn't help being uneasy, and that story about the accident, with the *front* of the car smashed in.

"I suppose I'm an awful heel," Mildreth said to herself, "but unfortunately I know my brother-in-law altogether *too* well."

So she drove to the Traffic Department at police headquarters, made inquiries as to whether there had been any report on the accident, found that Bob's Buick sedan had been in a collision with another car, that Bob had been in the wrong.

A telephone call to the man who had been driving the other car elicited the information that Bob had not been alone in the Buick at the time of the accident. A blond young woman, rather attractive, had been in the front seat with him. The man had taken her name as a witness. Just a minute, and he'd . . . Here it was. Esther Dilmeyer. The address she'd given him was the Golden Horn nightclub. He believed she'd said she worked there, but he couldn't be certain. The man who was driving the car — Mr. Lawley — had been very nice. The accident was all his fault, and he was going to settle. There'd been another man in the back. No, the settlement hadn't been made yet, but Mr. Lawley was to call at eleven o'clock tomorrow morning. "Would you mind telling me who you are, Ma'am?"

She said, quickly, "I'm with the Workman's Compensation Fund. We understood Miss Dilmeyer was injured."

Her informant said, "I was the only one that was hurt. I got shaken up pretty badly. There was another man in the car with Lawley. You could use him as a witness if you had to. His name was . . . wait a minute. Here it is. Sindler Coll."

"Had they been drinking?" Mildreth asked.

"No, but they were going plenty fast."

Mildreth said, "Thank you," and hung up.

Why did Bob go to such elaborate means to mystify everyone concerning the traffic accident? The car was insured, and the in-

26

surance company would take charge. . . .
But the insurance company quite obviously hadn't. Bob was meeting the other
party at eleven o'clock in the morning to
make an adjustment. Apparently, the insurance company knew nothing whatever
about the accident.

Mildreth Faulkner wanted to get back to
that floral design, but right now she felt
something else was more important.

Evidently Bob had no intention of explaining the presence of the nightclub
hostess in his car.

2

An expression of bitter disillusion on Esther Dilmeyer's features made her seem suddenly old.

All about her was the gaiety of the night-club, a forced, hectic hilarity which needed the constant flow of alcohol to keep it at the high level which would declare dividends for the management.

The orchestra ground out melodies with swinging rhythm. A master of ceremonies radiated synthetic enthusiasm as he announced the numbers of a floorshow through a microphone. Waiters, moving back and forth among the tables, carefully followed instructions that food must not be brought too soon after cocktails. Those who had drunk too much were being served watered drinks; those who seemed "sourpuss" were having a special visit from the head waiter with the virtues of the wine list extolled.

For those who were properly vouched for, there was a more quiet but sinister activity in the thickly carpeted suite of rooms above the nightclub.

The management was extremely careful about the list of patrons who were permitted to pass through the door marked PRIVATE in the rear of the hat-check room, climb the flight of stairs to the rooms where the whir of the roulette wheel mingled with the hum of well-modulated conversation.

On the lower floor the management encouraged laughter and drinking. On the upper floor, all this was changed. The management let it be known that it much preferred to have the patrons of the tables in formal evening attire. Everywhere the subtle suggestion of quiet refinement was impressed upon those who wooed the Goddess of Fortune. Thick carpets muffled the sound of footfalls. Heavy drapes, subdued indirect lighting, and a drawing-room atmosphere of sumptuous richness encouraged well-bred quiet.

A man who has lost more than he can afford in a place where alcoholic beverages flow freely and there is boisterous excitement, is quite apt to make what is known, in the parlance of the game, as a "beef." A man who feels just a little out of his element, who is forced to don formal attire, who is surrounded by external evidences of wealth, will be inclined to accept his losses with dignity and make a quiet exit. Not until he has divested himself of his formal attire, and seen his environment in the pitiless glare of daylight, will remorse and self-condemnation make him realize that a loss is a loss. Then he is quite apt to realize that taking losses "like a gentleman" is a racket fostered by those who profit — but by then it is too late.

Esther Dilmeyer didn't understand the full significance of the psychology, but she knew enough to realize that when she was called on to perform in the nightclub as a part of the floorshow or to pinch-hit for some entertainer who hadn't shown up, she was expected to sway her body in syncopated rhythm, to make a direct personal appeal to the audience, get them out of themselves and "in the mood."

On those occasions when she moved among the tables on the upper floor, she comported herself in the dignified manner of a lady. Here there was no loud laughter, no swaying of the shoulders, no swinging of the hips.

As a rule, women regarded Esther Dilmeyer with cool suspicion. Men could always be counted on to give her a second look, to make a play for her whenever she gave them the least encouragement. Esther understood men with the familiarity which engendered contempt. She realized that she knew women hardly at all.

Esther Dilmeyer, her thoughts carefully masked, sat at a table alone, toying with a glass which contained ginger ale and charged water, designed to make it appear to the uninitiated as a champagne cocktail. Habit twisted her lips into a mechanical half smile. At sharp variance with the implied invitation of her attractive appearance was her mood of black depression.

How many hours had she sat like this waiting for suckers? Always it was the same story. Men would drift past. Those who were with their wives would look at her enviously, make a mental resolution to come back some other night when they were alone. Men who were unescorted would try any one of the five standard brands of pick-up technique which Esther had learned to know and to classify just as a chess player can tell what opening his opponent is going to use as soon as the first pawn is advanced on the board.

Well, she thought, it served her right. She could have made something of her life. Instead, she'd dropped into this, capitalizing on her appearance, on her youth.

31

Men fell for her. She let them buy her drinks. If they were interested only in pawing, she would casually look at her watch, mention that her husband would join her in ten or fifteen minutes; or tip a wink to one of the waiters, and be summoned to the telephone, returning after a few minutes with the same message.

If the men had money to spend, she encouraged them to spend it, and if they seemed to be just the proper type, she would make tentative references to the activities which went on upstairs. If the man still seemed interested, she arranged for a card and would escort him up to the roulette table.

The croupiers could place a man in the first few plays; the plunger, the cautious man, the tightwad, the seasoned gambler, and, occasionally, best of all, the man who hated to lose, who would figure that the game owed him money after the few losses.

There was a code system of signals between Esther Dilmeyer and the croupier. If the sheep had lots of wool to be cut, she stayed around and supervised the shearing. Otherwise, she would drift back to the nightclub, looking for more prospects.

She looked up as Mildreth Faulkner approached her table.

Mildreth met her eyes and smiled.

Esther Dilmeyer braced herself. Did this have to come now, on top of everything else? Probably some woman whose husband had broken down and told about meeting the blonde at the nightclub, the visit upstairs to the gambling place, the resulting loss of money. She hated men like that, men who were eager for adventure, then ran whimpering home, who confessed with a great show of repentance, shed crocodile tears, berated themselves — and who promptly repeated the experience at the first available opportunity.

Mildreth pulled out a chair and sat down. "Hello," she said.

One of the waiters hovered cautiously in the distance, waiting for a signal from Esther Dilmeyer. The place didn't encourage scenes.

"Good evening," Esther Dilmeyer said with chilling formality.

Mildreth sighed. "I saw you sitting here alone," she said, "and I'm alone. What's more, I'm lonely, and I'm completely, absolutely, and entirely washed up with men. I sat down and tried a cocktail, and three men smirked at me before I'd finished. How about letting me buy you a drink, and then I'll go?"

Esther Dilmeyer felt a surge of relief. It wasn't a beef then after all. She beckoned to the waiter.

"Another champagne cocktail?" Mildreth asked.

The blonde nodded.

"Make it two," Mildreth said.

"Take this one away," Esther told the waiter. "It's stale," and with a laugh at Mildreth, "I was brooding too much to drink, I guess."

It was a situation which called for a little tact. Esther couldn't make any profitable connections sitting there with Mildreth Faulkner at her table. On the other hand, there was no harm in letting Mildreth buy one drink.

Esther looked at her watch. "My boy friend," she said, "is late."

"Oh, you have a date. I should have known it. Well, I won't detain you."

"It's all right. Sit down. We've loads of time for that drink. He keeps me waiting lots of times . . . damn him!"

Mildreth said, "Haven't I met you somewhere before? Your face is familiar."

Esther Dilmeyer shook her head. "I don't think so. I don't remember you."

"I saw you somewhere. . . . Oh, wait a minute. Weren't you in an automobile accident, a Buick sedan? Yes, you were, I remember now. I remember seeing you in the car."

"Did you see that smash?"

"Yes. I was walking along the street. If your boy friend was the one who was driving that car, he's worth waiting for."

"Him?" Esther Dilmeyer asked contemptuously. "He's good looking, but he's a sap. The other one was my boyfriend. His name's Sindler. He certainly is good looking, and he knows it, damn him. What do you do, or is it any of my business?"

"Oh, I have a little business of my own, running some stores. I have three of them."

Esther Dilmeyer said wistfully, "God, it must be nice to be in business for yourself and be independent. If I'd started in working and got some real business experience, I might have had something to look forward to instead of this racket."

"Racket?" Mildreth asked.

"I'm a hostess."

"Oh, I see."

"No, you don't. You couldn't unless you'd tried it. It's a lousy business."

"Why don't you leave it and get into something else?"

"How can I? I don't know shorthand or typing, haven't any business experience, and am damned if I'll go out and scrub floors and do housework for some woman who wants to keep her hands pretty so she can waste the afternoon playing bridge."

"There are lots of jobs open to a woman who has a pleasing personality and good looks."

"Yeah, I know. You see the want ads in the paper every once in a while. I followed up a couple of *those* leads. That's a worse racket than this."

Mildreth studied her and noticed the bitterness, the first faint lines about the eyes and lips. "I didn't mean that," she said. "There are jobs that are on the square. I hire girls every once in a while, girls who are attractive, pleasing, are able to keep their tempers, and know how to handle the public."

There was sudden hope in Esther Dilmeyer's eyes as she looked up at the woman across the table, then the hope faded. "Yeah, I know," she said. "Some people buy tickets on the sweepstakes and get their pictures in the paper. It happens every little while."

"That's a beautiful gown you have," Mildreth said.

"Like it?"

"Very much."

"It isn't so expensive. When you're in this game, you have to keep looking well, but you don't have a fortune to throw away on clothes. After a while, you learn how to shop."

"An orchid corsage would go wonderfully well with that color."

"Yes, probably it would. However, people don't send me corsages very often, and I'm not buying any orchids."

"I've got some I'm going to send over for you," Mildreth said.

"You have?"

"Yes. Some orchids I ordered for a customer who came down with the flu and couldn't use them. Are you going to be here for a while? If you are, I'll send them up."

"That'll be swell. Thanks a million. . . . You're sure it wouldn't bother you?"

"Not at all. I'll be glad to. What name do I put on them?"

"Esther."

"Simply Esther?"

"They know me here. Well, you could make it Esther Dilmeyer. What's your name?"

"Mildreth."

"That's a pretty name."

"Thanks."

The waiter brought their drinks. "Here's luck," Mildreth said over the rim of the glass.

"I'm going to need it."

Abruptly Mildreth said, "How badly do you want to get out of here, Esther?"

"You mean out of this racket?"

"Yes."

"Plenty bad. Oh, I'll give you the low-down. I've played it for what it was worth. I've been at it five years. I sit up nearly all night, drinking too much, smoking too much, and not getting enough fresh air. I'm beginning to show it. That's when it hurts."

Mildreth nodded.

"You look at other people and you can see that they are showing signs of age, but you just don't think that could ever happen to you. Then, all of a sudden, the boy friend throws you over for someone a little younger. . . . Nuts! I'd chuck this racket in a minute if I could get a decent opportunity."

"You seem pretty bitter about it."

Esther Dilmeyer sipped her cocktail. "Know why?"

"No."

"My boyfriend, the one you saw me riding with in the car, is friendly with the boss. Lately, he's picked up someone else. He tried to keep me from finding out about it, but I finally took a tumble just this afternoon. He's trying to get this new girl into *my* job, and ease me out of the picture.

"They think I don't know about it. I'm sitting here working while they're going around behind my back. Sindler Coll's out with her right now. Harvey Lynk, one of the men who runs the place, has gone out to a little cabin he has in Lilac Canyon. By one or two o'clock in the morning, it'll all be fixed up. Can you blame me for feeling bitter?"

Mildreth Faulkner shook her head.

"Show me a chance to make an honest living so that I can beat 'em to the punch, and I'd walk out of here so fast it would make your head swim," Esther said vehemently.

"How would you like to work in a flower shop?"

"Gosh, that would be swell. Is that what you do?"

"Yes. I run the Faulkner Flower Shops."

Esther Dilmeyer had been raising her glass to her lips. She lowered it again to the table. "Then you're — you're Bob's sister-in-law. You knew him all the time . . . that accident."

Mildreth met her eyes and said, "Yes, I came here to try and find out something about what was going on. I intended to try and pump you, but after I saw you, I realized that you weren't an enemy of mine — just a woman trying to get along in the world."

"Then you were stringing me along about that offer?"

"Don't be silly, Esther."

"How do I know it isn't just a scheme to try and pump me?"

"Because, you goose, I told you my name. Otherwise, I'd have handed you a line and tried to get what I could."

Esther Dilmeyer fumbled with a cigarette.

"Yes," she admitted, "that's right."

"Do you want to work for me?"

"What do I have to do in order to get the job?"

"Just give the business the best that's in you, try and get along with the customers, build up goodwill and . . ."

"No, I mean how much do I have to tell you?"

"Not a thing unless you want to."

Esther Dilmeyer thought that over for a few seconds, then said, "No, that wouldn't work. I've been mixed up in giving you a double cross. I could never work for you

40

unless I told you the whole thing and you said it was all right after you knew what had happened."

"Do you want to do that?"

"I'm not particularly crazy about doing it, but it's the only way I could ever go to work for you."

"Well, if you want to do it, you can have the job. You can have it without that."

"No. I'd come clean."

"Do you know where Lynk is right now?" Mildreth asked abruptly.

"Yes, at his cabin waiting for that little trollop to . . ."

"But do you know where the cabin is?"

"Sure," she said, and laughed bitterly. "I've been there. All of the girls who worked here went there."

Mildreth said, "I have to go telephone. While I'm gone, make a note of the address of the cabin and give it to me, will you?"

Esther nodded.

Mildreth went over to the telephone booth and once more put in a call for Mason's night number.

"I think you can get him at his office if you call right now," she was advised. "He said he was going to be there for a couple of hours, and that was only about an hour ago."

41

Mildreth dialed Mason's office, heard Della Street's voice on the other end of the line. "This is Miss Faulkner again, Miss Street. I'm in a very precarious position. I *have* to see Mr. Mason tonight."

"Tonight?"

"Yes."

"I'm sorry. Mr. Mason is working on an important brief right now, and won't finish the dictation until midnight. He simply can't see anyone."

"Could he see me after midnight?"

"I'm afraid not. He has to sleep, you know."

"Listen, this is *very* important. I'm willing to pay any amount within reason. I'm afraid that tomorrow morning may be too late."

"Why? What's the matter?"

"I've just learned that my sister, who's an invalid, has turned over all of her securities to her husband. Apparently he's put those up as security on some gambling debts. Among these securities is a block of stock in the flower stores I operate. I'll know a lot more about it by midnight, and . . . Oh, couldn't you please persuade Mr. Mason . . ."

"Just a minute," Della Street said. "I'll see what I can do."

She came back on the line after a thirty-second interval. "Mr. Mason won't finish dictating until around midnight, then he'll go out for a cup of coffee. If you want to be here at one o'clock, he'll meet you."

"Thank you *ever* so much! Now listen, I'm working on a witness. Her name is Esther Dilmeyer. Please make a note of that. I'm going to try and get her to come in. If she does, please hold her there and be nice to her. She knows all the facts. I doubt if I can get anywhere without her."

Della Street said, "I'll have to bill you for this appointment whether you keep it or not. If you'll give me your name and address . . ."

"Mildreth Faulkner. I run the Faulkner Flower Shops. My address is 819 Whiteley Pines Drive. I have a telephone. If you wish, I can send you some money before midnight."

"That won't be necessary," Della Street said. "Mr. Mason will see you at one o'clock."

Mildreth Faulkner hung up the telephone. Her face was resolute as she walked back to the table where Esther Dilmeyer slipped her a folded piece of paper.

She said, "What time do you get off work here, Esther?"

"Oh, I can leave any time after one o'clock."

"I want you to do something."

"What?"

"Go to the office of Perry Mason. He's my lawyer."

"When?"

"At one o'clock."

"You mean Perry Mason, the lawyer who solved the Tidings murder case?"*

"That's the one."

"Gosh, he's — he's a *big* shot. I always said that if I ever committed a murder, I was going to hold up a bank at the same time and get enough money to have Mr. Mason get me off." She laughed.

Mildreth said, "Then how about meeting me at Mr. Mason's office at one o'clock?"

"He won't be at his office then."

"Yes, I've made an appointment."

"Why do you want *me* there?"

"Because I want to get Bob Lawley out of my business. I'll need your help to do that — and if you're going to be working for me, you won't need to mind what any of these people think."

"Okay, I'll do that little thing. Listen, it

*See *The Case of the Baited Hook.*

44

may be about five or ten minutes after one."

"All right, and I'm going to send you some orchids."

"Oh, don't bother."

"It isn't any bother. I really do have some orchids that were left over on an order. They'd go fine with that dress, and I'm going to send them up."

Esther Dilmeyer leaned toward Mildreth. "Listen," she said, "if you talk with Lynk, watch your step. And don't mention that I spilled anything. I swore I'd never rat, but you caught me when I was pretty low and that offer of a job — well, that's one of the few times anyone ever offered to give me a break. How did you know about Lawley getting milked dry and about me?"

"I tried to get him to bring up some securities . . . Oh, well, never mind. Now you'll have to forget all about this, Esther. You mustn't ever mention to anyone that I was talking to you."

"I'll say. And don't you let on to Lynk that I know he has the skids greased for me. I want him to think I'm walking out under my own power. He won't want visitors tonight, either. You'll have to watch your step with him. And as for Sindler Coll and that baby-faced little bitch he's bringing in . . ."

She blinked her eyes again, then forced a laugh, and said, "Oh, well, what do I care?"

Mildreth looked at her watch. "You don't. I'll have to be moving now. I have lots to do between now and one o'clock. I want to see Lynk."

"Watch Lynk," Esther said. "He's bad if you try to crowd him. He has a nasty temper. If he isn't ready to talk turkey, don't crowd him — and don't threaten him with Perry Mason."

Mildreth smiled. "Thanks. I'll be tactful."

Suddenly Esther called her back. "Listen, I want to play fair with you. When I work for anyone, I give them all I have, but . . ."

"Yes?" Mildreth prompted.

"Look, Lynk thinks he's going to double-cross me on some private stuff, but I'm going to see that I don't get gypped here."

Mildreth said, "Fair enough, but let me return your own advice: Be careful and watch Lynk."

Esther smiled. That smile changed her whole face. "Don't think I don't know how dangerous a game I'm playing — and don't think Lynk won't suspect me, but I've got a way around all that. . . . Nuts! What do you care about *my* grief? See you at one o'clock — perhaps just a shade later."

46

3

At eleven-thirty, Perry Mason unlocked the door of his private office, held it open for Della Street. "No need for you to wait, Della," he said. "That brief took less time than I thought it would. I'll sit around and read the advance decisions until one."

"I want to wait."

Mason hung up his hat and coat. "There's nothing you can do. I'll talk with her and . . ."

"No," she interrupted. "I have to stay now. I just had a cup of coffee. That means I can't sleep for an hour and a half."

Mason stretched himself in his swivel chair. His motions held none of the awkwardness characteristic of many tall men who have long bones and rangy figures. And many a witness, misled by Mason's casual manner, fabricating a story on the witness stand with every assurance that his prevarications were completely concealed, suddenly found himself facing a pair of granite-hard eyes, and realized only too late the savage belligerency with which Mason could bear down on a perjurer, the rapier-like thrusts of his agile mind.

But, for the most part, it pleased Mason to assume a good-natured, easy-going attitude of careless informality. He disliked the conventional ways of doing things, and this dislike showed in his manner and his handling of lawsuits.

Della Street, his secretary, had learned to know his various moods. Between them existed that rare companionship which is the outgrowth of two congenial people devoting themselves to a common cause. When the going got rough, they were able to function with the perfect co-ordination of a well-trained football team.

Mason tilted his swivel chair back, and crossed his ankles on the corner of the desk.

"You should have let her call during office hours," Della said. "You've had a hard day, and then with all that dictation on top of it . . ."

Mason disposed of her comment with a gesture. "Not this case. She sounds as though she's in real trouble."

"Why, how do you know? You didn't even listen over the telephone."

"I saw your face," he said.

"Well, she *did* impress me, but even so, I don't see why it wouldn't keep until tomorrow."

"A lawyer is very much like a doctor," Mason pointed out. "A doctor devotes his life to easing a person's body. A lawyer devotes his to easing their minds. The machinery of justice is very apt to get out of gear if it isn't kept well oiled and running smoothly. Lawyers are the engineers."

Mason took a cigarette, offered Della Street one, and they lit them from the same match. Mason, tired from the hard day, settled back in his chair and relaxed in the luxury of complete silence.

After some five minutes, he said musingly, "One of the first things a professional man has to learn is that the person who makes the most urgent demands on his time is usually the one who doesn't intend to pay. But I don't think this will be one of those cases."

"You mean that's a general rule?" Della Street asked.

"Absolutely. The man who expects to pay a lawyer for his time wants to get off as cheaply as possible. Therefore, he never calls on the lawyer for extraordinary services unless it's absolutely necessary. The man who doesn't intend to pay doesn't give a hoot about the size of the bill. Therefore, he's perfectly willing to call the lawyer at all hours of the night, ask him to give up a golf game on Saturday afternoons, or come to the office on Sundays. It's always the same."

"Well, if she's like that," Della Street said, "we'll just send her a bill for five hundred dollars."

Mason said, "Let's try to get her on the phone, tell her I finished with my brief earlier than I expected, and that if she wants to advance the appointment by an hour, it'll be all right with us."

The telephone rang, just as Mason finished talking.

Della picked up the receiver, said, "Hello. . . . Yes, this is Mr. Mason's office. . . . Can't you speak more clearly? . . . Who is it? . . . What's that name?"

She turned to Perry Mason and cupped her hand over the mouthpiece. "She's drunk," she said.

"The Faulkner woman?" Mason asked.

"No. Esther Dilmeyer."

"Oh, yes," Mason said. "The witness. Let me talk with her."

Della handed him the phone.

Mason said, "Hello. What is it, Miss Dilmeyer?"

The voice that came to him over the telephone was so thick that it was with difficulty he could understand what she was saying.

"Promised come your office . . . Can't . . . Poisoned."

"What's that?" Mason asked sharply.

"Poisoned," the voice said wearily. "They got me."

Mason's eyes glinted. "What's that? You're poisoned?"

"Thash right."

"You're not drunk?"

"Not tonight. . . . Thought I was smart. . . . They got me first."

"Where are you?"

The words came with an effort, interspersed with intervals of heavy breathing. "Apartment . . . Box of candy . . . ate . . . sick . . . Can't . . . Can't . . . Please send help . . . Get police . . . Get . . . Get . . ." The conversation terminated in a crash as though the telephone had been dropped to the floor. Mason said, "Hello. Hello," and heard nothing. Then, after a moment, the receiver clicked into place at the other end of the line.

Della had dashed from the office the minute Mason said, "Poisoned," to plug in on the switchboard and ask the exchange operator to trace the call, but she was too late. The receiver had been hung up at the other end before Della had finished explaining what was wanted. She waited at the switchboard long enough to learn that there was no possibility of tracing the call, then came back to Mason's private office.

"What was it?" she asked.

"She says someone sent her a box of candy, that she ate the candy, and was poisoned. She certainly sounds sick or drunk. Now the question is, what's her address, where is she? See if there's a Dilmeyer listed in the telephone book."

Della thumbed through the pages of the telephone book.

"No, there isn't."

Mason looked at his watch. "That Faulkner woman should know where she is. See if you can get her on the phone."

Mildreth Faulkner was listed at her residence address, and the Faulkner Flower Shops were listed. Della finally got a response on the residence phone. A somewhat sleepy high-pitched voice said, "Hello. What is it?"

"Is this Miss Mildreth Faulkner's residence?"

"Yes. What do you want?"

"I want to speak with Miss Faulkner. It's very important."

"She ain't here."

"Do you know where I can reach her?"

"No."

"When do you expect her in?"

"I don't know. She don't tell me when she's coming in, and I don't ask her."

"Wait a minute," Della said. "Don't hang up. Do you know a Miss Dilmeyer — Esther Dilmeyer?"

"No."

"It's very important we find out her address."

"Well, I don't know. And don't ring me up at this hour of the night to ask foolish questions."

The receiver banged indignantly.

Della shook her head at Mason.

Mason said, "Miss Faulkner isn't due until one?"

"No."

"We've got to locate that Dilmeyer woman. That call sounded genuine to me." He pushed the papers he had been using in dictating his brief to one side and said, "Police headquarters, Della."

A moment later, when she had headquarters on the line, Mason said, "This is Perry Mason. I had a call a few minutes ago from an Esther Dilmeyer. She said that she was at an apartment. I presume it's an apartment where she lives, but she didn't say so. I don't know the address. I don't know anything about her, except that I had an appointment with her for one o'clock this morning. She was to be at my office. She's a witness in connection with some matter. I don't know just what it is.

"Now get this straight. She said over the telephone that someone had sent her a box of poisoned candy. She sounded very ill. Her speech was thick, and apparently she either fell over or the telephone slipped from her hand as she was talking. Then the receiver was dropped back into place. She seemed to think she'd been poisoned to keep her from talking."

"You can't give us an address?"

"No."

"Well, we'll try and look her up. We'll see if she's registered as a voter. That's about all we can do."

Mason said, "Call back and let me know if you find anything, will you?"

"Okay, but if we haven't got an address, there's nothing we. . . . Where are you?"

"I'm at my office."

"You'll be there until we call?"

"Yes."

"Okay, we'll call back."

Mason hung up the telephone, pushed back his chair, got to his feet, and stood with his hands pushed down deep into his trousers pockets. "This thing's goofy, Della," he said. "I don't think the police are going to do anything. Of course, they may find her in the voters' register. . . . Miss Faulkner didn't say what she was a witness to?"

"No."

"Think back on that conversation. See if you can . . ."

"Wait a minute," Della said. "She was calling from a nightclub somewhere. I could hear the sound of an orchestra. It . . . Wait a minute now. I remember hearing the background of music. It was . . . Chief, I'll bet it was Haualeoma's Hawaiians. I could get the background of Hawaiian music, and they were playing an Island song that I heard a couple of weeks ago when they were on the radio."

"Well, it's a lead," Mason said. "How could we go about finding out where they're playing?"

She said, "I think I can find out. I'll go out and play tunes on the switchboard. See if you can think of any other way of getting the address."

Della went out to the switchboard. Mason hooked his thumbs through the armholes of his vest, and paced the floor, his head dropped forward in thought.

Della came running into the office within little more than a minute. "Got it, Chief," she said.

"Her address?"

"I think we can get it."

"What is it?"

"The Hawaiians are at the Golden Horn. That's a nightclub. I rang up the club and asked if they knew an Esther Dilmeyer. The hat-check girl said she did. She said that Esther Dilmeyer had been there this evening, but had left early, saying she had a headache. I asked her if she knew a Miss Faulkner, and she said she didn't. I asked how we could find Miss Dilmeyer's address, and she said she didn't know, that she thought Mr. Lynk, one of the proprietors, knew where she lived, but Mr. Lynk is out tonight, and couldn't be reached."

"You told her it was important?"

"Yes, I told her it was a matter of life and death."

Mason said. "Okay, Della. Get me police headquarters. See if you can get . . . Let's see . . ."

"Lieutenant Tragg?" she asked.

56

"Yes, they've just put him on Homicide, and he's a live wire."

"Weren't you responsible for Holcomb's transfer?" she asked as she put in the call.

A smile twisted the corners of his mouth. "Holcomb was responsible for that himself," he said. "A damned, opinionated, obstinate . . ."

"Here's Lieutenant Tragg on the line."

Mason said, "Hello, Lieutenant. This is Perry Mason."

"Well, well, this is a surprise! Don't tell me you've discovered another corpse."

"I may have at that."

Lieutenant Tragg's voice became crisply businesslike. "What is it?"

Mason said, "I had an appointment for one o'clock with an Esther Dilmeyer. She's a witness in a case. I don't know exactly what it is. I've never met her. She rang up about ten minutes ago, and could barely talk over the telephone. She said she'd been poisoned. Someone had sent her poisoned candy. She certainly sounded about ready to pass out. Evidently the telephone either slipped from her hands and fell, or she keeled over while she was talking to me. Then the receiver was hung up before I could trace the call."

"You don't know where she is?"

Mason said, "I'm coming to that. Della Street, my secretary, did some fast thinking and some good detective work. I won't take time to tell you about it, but the result is that she got a lead into the Golden Horn. That's a nightclub. Esther Dilmeyer is known there, and was there this evening, but apparently the underlings don't know her address. Lynk, who runs the place, does, but he's out. That's the story in a nutshell. What do you say?"

"Sounds like quite a bit of smoke," Lieutenant Tragg said. "There may be some fire. But we haven't a heck of a lot to go on."

"Well, don't say I didn't tell you," Mason said. "If someone finds her body tomorrow morning, and . . ."

"Wait a minute," Tragg interrupted. "Hold your horses. Where are you now?"

"At the office."

"Want to take a run around to the Golden Horn?"

"Do you?"

"Yes."

"Okay."

"I'll be by for you in about five minutes," Tragg said. "If you can be waiting down on the sidewalk, it'll save that much time."

"Think we can do anything by telephone?"

"I doubt it," Tragg said. "It won't take over a few minutes to get there. Be all ready to jump in when you hear the siren, because I'll cut her loose."

Mason said, "I'll be down there," hung up the telephone, ran to the coat closet, and grabbed his hat and coat. "Okay, Della," he said, "you hold down the office. I may call in a little later."

It took a minute or two for the elevator to get up to Mason's floor. The night watchman dropped him to the street level, and Mason had less than a minute to wait at the curb before he heard the scream of a siren, saw the blood-red glare of a spotlight, and then Lieutenant Tragg was skidding a police sedan in close to the curb.

Mason jerked the door open and jumped in. Tragg accelerated the car into such swift speed that Mason's head was jerked back as the machine lurched forward.

Lieutenant Tragg said nothing, but concentrated on driving traffic. He was about Mason's age. His features stood out in sharply etched lines. His forehead was high, his eyes keen and thoughtful, an entirely different type from Sergeant Holcomb. Mason, studying the profile as the car screamed through the streets, realized that this man could be a very dangerous antagonist indeed.

"Hang on," Tragg warned as the car screamed in a turn.

He was, Mason saw, enjoying the excitement of tearing through traffic with siren screaming and motor roaring, but, with it all, the man was as cool and detached as a surgeon performing a delicate operation. His face showed complete concentration and an entire lack of nervousness.

Tragg slid to a stop in front of the Golden Horn. The two men debouched from the car and ran across the sidewalk. A big doorman, resplendent with uniform, barred their way. "What's it all about?" he asked, his drawl a contemptuous challenge to their haste.

Tragg promptly shouldered him to one side. The doorman hesitated a moment as though debating whether to try to detain the officer, then dashed for a speaking tube built into the wall. He whistled three times sharply.

Tragg led the way into the nightclub.

"The hatcheck girl knows something," Mason said.

Tragg moved over to the counter, showed her his star. "Esther Dilmeyer," he said. "Where can we find her?"

"Gosh, Mister, I don't know. Someone

was asking over the telephone awhile back."

"You know her?"

"Yes."

"Does she work here?"

"Well, in a way. She hangs out here."

"Gets a commission on business she develops?"

"I wouldn't know."

"Who would?"

"Mr. Magard or Mr. Lynk."

"Where are they?"

"Mr. Lynk is out tonight, and I don't know where Magard is. I tried to locate him after the young woman telephoned, but I couldn't find him."

"This place supposed to run without anyone in charge?"

"Ordinarily, one or the other of them is here. Tonight it just happens they're both out."

"Who else would know? The cashier? Some of the waiters?"

She shook her head. "I don't think so. I've made inquiries. I tell you who I think would."

"Who?"

"Sindler Coll."

"Who's he?"

"Her boy friend."

"Living with her?"

The hat-check girl shifted her eyes.

"Come on, sister. Don't be coy. You heard what I said."

"No, I don't think so."

"Where do we find Coll?"

"I think the cashier has his address. He cashes a check here once in a while."

Lieutenant Tragg said, "Thanks. You've got a good head on your shoulders, sister, as well as a pretty one. Come on, Mason."

They skirted the dance floor, and pushed past the crowded couples moving slowly to the rhythm of the music. Tragg asked directions from a waiter, and walked on to find the cashier in a cage between the dining room and the nightclub.

Tragg showed her his star. "You know a Sindler Coll?"

She stared at him, hesitating, apparently debating on a course of action.

"Come on," Tragg said. "Look alive. Do you know him?"

"Y-y-y-yes."

"Where can we find him?"

"I don't know. What's he done?"

"Nothing, so far as I know."

"What do you want him for?"

"Listen, sister, I haven't got time to give you a bunch of history. I want Coll, and I want him fast. What's his address?"

"He's at the Everglade Apartments."

"What apartment?"

"Just a minute."

She opened a drawer and took out an address book. Her fingers trembled nervously as she turned the pages.

"Don't happen to have the address of Esther Dilmeyer in there, do you?"

"No. The hat-check girl was asking a few minutes ago. What's the matter?"

"Nothing," Tragg said, "just give us Coll's address, and make it snappy."

"It's on the second floor, Everglade Apartments, 209."

"Got a telephone?"

"I don't know. I haven't his number here."

"You know him when you see him, do you?"

"Oh, yes."

"He hasn't been in here tonight?"

"No."

"Would you have seen him if he had been?"

"Yes."

"Do you usually see the customers that come in here?"

"Well . . . Not all of them, but . . ."

"I see. Coll's someone in particular, eh?"

"Well, he drops in once in a while," she

said, her cheeks showing color beneath the patches of rouge.

Tragg said to Mason, "Well, we'll try Coll at the Everglade Apartments. . . . Listen, sister, who's running this place?"

"Two men, partners, Clint Magard and Harvey J. Lynk."

"Know where either of them are?"

"No. Lynk has a little cabin somewhere. He goes there for relaxation."

"Relaxation, eh?" Lieutenant Tragg said, glancing at Mason. "Where is it?"

"I wouldn't know. It's up in Lilac Canyon somewhere. . . . And Mr. Magard isn't in right at present."

"You don't know where Magard is?"

"No. He should be in any minute."

"When he comes in, have him call police headquarters and ask for Sergeant Mahoney. Have him tell the sergeant all he knows about Esther Dilmeyer — don't forget. I'll call back in a little while. What number do I call?"

"It's Exchange 3-40 . . ."

"Write it down," Tragg said.

She scribbled the number on a piece of paper.

"Okay, I'll call you back. Have Magard call headquarters."

Tragg nodded to Mason.

As they walked out, Mason said, "I've never before fully appreciated the handicap of being merely a private citizen."

"Getting sarcastic?" Tragg asked.

"No, merely making an observation."

"You have to handle 'em like that or they'll start swapping gossip with you and you'll never get anywhere. People seem to forget we have emergency calls pouring in in a steady stream. We haven't time to dillydally, or let other people take the lead. You have to keep 'em on the defensive to ever get anywhere."

They squeezed past the dance floor, and on the stairs leading to the sidewalk Tragg asked, "Know anything about this joint, Mason?"

"No. Why?"

"I have an idea it's a phony. Some day I'll knock it over."

"Why?"

"That doorman. In the first place, he's a professional pug."

"How do you know?"

"The way he handled himself. Notice the way he swings his left shoulder forward when he thinks there's going to be trouble. He made a dive for a telephone when we started in. Gave a signal which had been agreed on in advance to warn of a police raid. Notice the cauliflower ear — his left."

The big doorman regarded them with cold hostility as they came out. Tragg, walking past him toward the car, suddenly whirled and jabbed an extended forefinger into the man's chest. "You're big," he said. "You're tough. And you're fat! You're not as fast as you used to be. What's more, you're dumb. I didn't know there was anything wrong with the joint until you tipped me off to the lay. You might tell your boss that. When I knock the place over, he'll have you to thank. . . . If you don't tell him, I will. Next time you see me, salute. Good night!"

He strode on past to the car, leaving the big man in his resplendent uniform staring with bewildered eyes and a mouth that sagged slowly open.

Tragg laughed as he snapped on the ignition. "Just giving him something to think about," he said, and spun the car in the middle of the block, roaring into speed as he kicked on the switch which sent noise pouring from the siren on the front of the car.

The Everglade Apartments had originally been designed for a clerk, a switchboard operator, and elevator boys. The pinch of the economic shoe had converted it into automatic elevators, and a lobby used purely for purposes of ornament.

Lieutenant Tragg pressed his thumb against the button opposite Sindler Coll's name on the outside of the big glass door through which could be seen a part of the lobby.

"No luck?" Mason asked after several moments.

"No dice," Tragg said, and pushed the button marked MANAGER.

At the third ring, an indignant woman in nightgown, slippers, and kimono pushed open the door of one of the lower apartments, and came shuffling across the lobby to the door. For a long moment, she stood staring at them through the plate glass, then, opening the door a crack, she asked, "What is it?"

Tragg said, "We want Sindler Coll."

Her face darkened with indignation. "Well, of all the nerve! . . . There's his bell. Go on and ring it! . . ."

"He doesn't answer."

"Well, I'm not his keeper!"

She started to slam the door. Tragg pulled back his coat and gave her a glimpse of his badge. "Take it easy, Ma'am. We have to find him. This is important."

"Well, I haven't the faintest idea where

he is. I'm running a respectable place here, and . . ."

"Sure, you are, Ma'am," Tragg said soothingly, "and you wouldn't want to get in bad by refusing to co-operate with the police when they wanted a little something. The way things are now, the place has a nice reputation, and we have you marked as a law-abiding citizen who's on the side of law and order."

Her expression softened. "Well, I am."

"Sure, you are. Oh, we keep the places pretty well pegged, and know what goes on. We know whom we can depend on, and whom we can't. And lots of times banks and mortgage companies that are looking for apartment-house managers give us a ring and ask us what sort of a record the party had in the last job. You'd be surprised how careful the bigger people are to get managers who are friendly with the police."

"Well, I can understand that," she said. The hostility had left her voice. She seemed so eager to impress them that she was all but simpering. "The way things are now, people can't be too careful. Now, if there's anything *I* can do for you — anything."

"We'd like to find out something about

Coll — not about his habits, but where we could locate him. Do you know anything about him, who his friends are, or anything of that sort?"

"No, I don't. I can't give you a bit of help on that. He's a quiet chap, but I know he's very popular. There are quite a few people come to call on him."

"Men or women?"

"Mostly . . . well, *some* women. We don't bother our tenants as long as they're quiet."

"Do you know an Esther Dilmeyer?"

"No, I don't."

Tragg said, "We have to get Coll as soon as he comes in. Would you mind dressing and waiting here in the lobby until you see him come in? Then call police headquarters, ask for Lieutenant Tragg. That's me. If I'm not in, get Sergeant Mahoney on the line, and he'll tell you what to do."

"I'll be glad to," she said. "It'll only take me a minute." Gathering her robe about her, she shuffled rapidly across the lobby to vanish through the door of her apartment.

Tragg turned to Mason and grinned. "Doesn't it feel pretty strange to you to be co-operating with the police?"

Mason's answer was prompt. "No. The

69

strange thing is to feel that the police are cooperating with me."

Tragg threw back his head and laughed, then, after a moment, said, "Well, tell me about the case, Mason."

"What case?"

"Didn't you say Esther Dilmeyer was a witness?"

"Oh, yes. It's a civil case, and I can't give you details without my client's consent. I'll say this much. A Mildreth Faulkner, who owns the Faulkner Flower Shops, rang up and made an appointment for one o'clock."

"Afternoon?" Tragg asked.

"No, morning. First, she called for an appointment at ten-thirty in the morning. Then she rang up again, very much excited, and said she simply had to see me sometime tonight. I was working on a brief. My secretary told her I wouldn't be finished before sometime after midnight, and we offered her a one o'clock appointment, thinking that would make her back out. She grabbed at it and told me to be on the watch for an Esther Dilmeyer who was an important witness. I gathered that she wouldn't have much of a case without Dilmeyer's testimony."

"Then it's a fair inference that someone

knew about it, and poisoned Dilmeyer to keep her from talking."

Mason nodded.

Tragg said, "Let's start working from the other end, then. Find out from Mildreth Faulkner who the adverse parties are. We'll start putting screws on them."

"We can't get Miss Faulkner. Della Street, my secretary, has been trying to get her. She's up in the office still trying."

Tragg jerked his head toward a telephone booth. "Give her a ring."

Mason entered the telephone booth and called his office. Tragg stood with his arm extended, the hand resting on the edge of the folding door of the telephone booth, his weight propped against the arm.

"Hello, Della," Mason said. "Anything new?"

"Haven't been able to get a thing," she said. "I find there are three branches of the Faulkner Flower Shops, each with a separate phone. I've been calling them in turn."

"No answer?"

"No answer."

"Well, we've got a lead on a man by the name of Coll, but we can't locate him. I left word that Magard, Lynk's partner, was to call as soon as he came in."

"I'll keep one of the trunk lines free for

incoming calls, and use the other one for my own calls."

Mason said, "If you get an address, call police headquarters direct."

"Tell her to ask for Sergeant Mahoney," Tragg said.

"Ask for Sergeant Mahoney," Mason went on. "Tell him to rush some radio officers out to her apartment, and break in the door if they have to."

Mason hung up. "Suppose there's any use calling the Golden Horn?" he asked. "After all, Magard might not have telephoned."

"Better let me do it," Tragg said.

He waited for Mason to emerge from the booth, then Tragg entered and dialed the Golden Horn. Mason, standing outside the telephone booth, looked down and saw something white under the bench on which the telephone rested. He stooped down and picked it up.

"What you got there?" Tragg asked.

"Handkerchief," Mason said. "Woman's handkerchief. I'll give it to the manager. There's an initial on it. . . . The letter 'D' . . ."

Lieutenant Tragg's arm emerged from the telephone booth, beckoning Mason frantically. The lawyer hurried over. Tragg,

72

with his hand over the mouthpiece, said, "Magard came in just now — according to what the girl says. He may have been there some time, and decided not to bother with a call. I'm having her put him on. . . . Hello, Magard. This is Lieutenant Tragg of headquarters. I left word for you to call headquarters. Why didn't you do it? . . . Well, it's funny you got in *just* as I was telephoning."

There was an interval during which the receiver made noises while Lieutenant Tragg winked at Mason.

"Well," the officer interrupted abruptly, "never mind all the explanations. I want to know where Esther Dilmeyer lives. She has an apartment somewhere, and I want to get there right away. . . . What's that? . . . Well, get the safe open and look it up."

Tragg again pushed his hand over the mouthpiece. "I *know* he's covering up something now," he said. "He was pouring explanations and apologies into the telephone. That's a sure sign. I think we're on the right track. . . ." He jerked his hand away, said, "Yes. Hello. Isn't she working for you? . . . Well, where *can* you find out? . . . You're sure about that? . . . Now, listen, this is important, and I don't want any run-around. . . . All right, all right, you

73

haven't any idea . . . Now, wait a minute. Does she have a social security number? . . . I see. . . . Now listen, I may want to get you again. Don't leave the place without leaving a telephone number where you can be called."

He hung up the telephone, turned to Mason, and said, "That's damned strange."

"He doesn't know where she lives?"

"No. He says she claims a girl can be a hostess in a nightclub, and keep her self-respect only as long as no one knows her home address. Sounds goofy to me."

"Me too," Mason said.

"Anyway, that's his story. He says she'd never give it to them, that she works on a commission basis, so he doesn't consider her an employee."

The door from the manager's apartment opened. The manager, wearing a house dress, came toward them. Her face, which had been given a generous application of rouge somewhat unevenly applied, was decorated in the unchanging smile of one who has made a practice of ingratiating herself with strangers. She said, "I . . ." and turned toward the door. The men followed her gaze. Through the plate glass they saw a slim-waisted young man run up the porch stairs, and jab a key into the lock of the door.

The manager had time to say, "This is Coll now," before the door opened. Tragg waited until the man was well on his way toward the elevator, noticing the half-running pace, the excited tension which seemed to grip him.

"Puttin' out a fire?" Tragg asked.

The man apparently saw them for the first time, jerked to a standing stop, and stared.

The manager said, ingratiatingly, "Mr. Coll, this is . . ."

"Let me handle it," Tragg interrupted, stepping forward and jerking back the lapel of his coat so that Coll could see his star.

Coll's reaction was instantaneous. He half turned back toward the big plateglass door, as though about to run. By an effort, he caught himself and turned a white face to Tragg.

Tragg was ominously silent, watching Coll's countenance begin to twitch.

Coll took a deep breath. Mason could see the hands clenched into fists. "Well, what is it?" he asked.

Tragg took his time about answering. Both men studied Coll: A small-boned, slim-hipped individual whose coat was heavily padded at the shoulders. The even tan of his face indicated that he habitually went without a hat and was much in the open. His hair, black and glossy, waved back from his forehead with a rippling regularity that suggested the touch of a professional hairdresser. Despite his five feet ten inches, the man weighed not much more than a hundred and thirty pounds.

Tragg's voice had the rasping belligerence of a police officer dealing with a law violator. "What's the hurry?" he asked.

"I wanted to get to bed."

"You certainly were steamed up about it."

"I . . ." The lips clamped into a thin line of silence.

Tragg said, "We want some information."

"What do you want?"

"You know an Esther Dilmeyer?"

"What about her?"

"We're trying to locate her. We got a lead to you."

"That's . . . that's all you want?"

"Right now," Tragg said.

The look of relief on Coll's face was almost comic. He said, "Dilmeyer . . . Esther Dilmeyer . . . Hostess at a nightclub, isn't she?"

"That's right."

Coll took a notebook from his pocket, started to thumb the pages, but, seemingly realizing Tragg's interest in the shaking hand which held the notebook, he abruptly closed it, put it back in his pocket, and said, "I remember now. The Molay Arms Apartments."

"What's the apartment number?"

Coll frowned as though concentrating. "Three-twenty-eight."

"When did you see her last?"

"Why . . . why, I don't know offhand."

"A week ago, an hour ago?"

"Oh, probably yesterday sometime. She's at the Golden Horn. I drop in there once in a while."

"Okay," Tragg said, "go on to bed," and to the manager, "We shan't need you any more. Thanks for your co-operation . . . The Molay Arms is on Jefferson Street, isn't it, Coll?"

"I believe so, yes."

Tragg nodded to Mason. "Come on, let's go."

The Molay Arms Apartments was a little walk-up. Here again they encountered a locked door, a series of mailboxes and call bells. When there was no answer at Esther Dilmeyer's bell, Tragg again summoned the manager, ordered her to follow them

77

up to the apartment with a passkey. They climbed two flights of stairs and walked down a narrow, thinly carpeted corridor, redolent with stale smells, and the dank emanations which fill a poorly ventilated place where people are sleeping.

Three-twenty-eight was on the southeast corner. A light showed over the transom. Tragg knocked, received no answer, and said to the manager, "Okay, open it up."

She hesitated a moment, then inserted a passkey. The door clicked back.

The figure of a blond woman, dressed in a tweed skirt and jacket, light woolen stockings and rubber-soled gold shoes, lay sprawled near the door. The telephone had been knocked from a small spindly-legged stand to the floor. A box of chocolate creams was open on the table, and some wrapping paper in which the box had evidently been tied folded itself loosely around the edges of the box. The cover lay slightly to one side. On the cover was a chocolate-smudged card, saying, "These will make you feel better," and signed with the initials, "M.F." The chocolates were cradled in little paper cups. A blank space in the upper tray furnished the sole clue as to the number which had been eaten. Mason, making a swift survey, estimated that eight or ten were missing from the top layer of the box. The lower layer seemed untouched.

Tragg bent over the woman, felt her pulse, said to the manager of the apartment, "Go downstairs. Call Sergeant Mahoney at headquarters. Tell him Lieutenant Tragg has found the Dilmeyer girl and the candy, that she's evidently been poisoned. Tell him to rush out fingerprint men and an ambulance."

Mason dropped to one knee to look down on the unconscious figure. "Should we straighten her out?" he asked.

Tragg felt her pulse again.

The face was slightly congested. Her breathing was slow and seemed labored. The skin was warm to the touch.

Mason said, "Looks more like a drug than an active poison. Perhaps we can bring her out of it."

"We can try," Tragg said. "Get her over on her back. Okay. See if you can find some towels, hot and cold. We'll start with the cold."

Mason turned cold water into the washbowl, sopped a bath towel, wrung it out, and tossed it to Tragg. Tragg sponged off the woman's face and neck, and started gently slapping her in the face with the cold towel. After a moment, he raised her blouse, pulled down the top of her skirt, and applied the cold towels directly to the bare skin over the pit of her stomach.

There was no slightest sign of returning consciousness.

"Want a hot one now?" Mason asked.

"Yes, let's try that."

Mason turned on the hot water, found a clean bath towel in the lower drawer of a cabinet, and got it steaming hot. He tossed it to Tragg, received in return the cold towel, and held that under the cold tap in the bathtub.

For five minutes Tragg worked alternately with hot and cold towels.

"No use," he said. "That ambulance should be here." He looked at the telephone and said, "I don't want to touch that. Be careful about touching things, Mason, particularly that candy or the wrapping paper."

Mason nodded, shut off the water in the bathroom. Tragg got to his feet. Mason walked over to peer in the wastebasket. Then he opened the door of the clothes closet, and looked inside.

There were half a dozen expensive-looking evening gowns with shoes to match. By comparison, the clothes for daytime wear seemed somewhat shabby and few in number.

Tragg said impatiently, "I don't know whether she got the call through to Mahoney or not. I guess we'd better go down and . . ." He broke off as a siren sounded.

"This," he said, "will be it. We'll let them take the responsibility."

Mason said, "One thing I want, Tragg. I want to get my own doctor working on this."

"Why?"

"Your emergency surgeons are all right, but she won't get the complete care, particularly on follow-up treatment in an emergency hospital, that she will under my doctor. I want this woman taken to the Hastings Memorial Hospital, put in a private room, and I want Dr. Willmont to cooperate with whatever doctor is called in."

"Willmont, eh?"

"Yes."

"Who's paying for it?"

"I am."

"Why?"

"Because I'm interested."

Lieutenant Tragg indicated the note on the card. "I noticed the initials 'M.F.' on that card," he said.

"Well?"

"Mildreth Faulkner."

Mason said, "Nuts. A person wouldn't

81

send another a box of poisoned candy, and then put a card in with the candy for the police to find."

"You can't always tell," Tragg said. "Rules don't mean anything except on a general basis. And even then, they don't mean anything when you're dealing with crimes of women."

Mason said, "And, therefore, you think I don't want her to die simply because I'm protecting the poisoner. A person who isn't even a client, whom I don't know and haven't seen; but with whom I have an appointment in . . ." he glanced at his wrist watch, "exactly fifteen minutes."

Tragg laughed and said, "Well, when you put it that way, it *does* sound goofy. I guess there's no objection to taking her to the Hastings Memorial Hospital — if you can get Dr. Willmont on the job."

"I can try," Mason said. "I think there's a telephone in the manager's apartment."

He walked rapidly toward the stairs, met two white-garbed men carrying a stretcher in the corridor.

"Down at the end of the corridor, boys," Mason said. "Wait for me at the door of the apartment house. I'll tell you where to take her."

4

Perry Mason latchkeyed the door of his private office. Della Street was sitting over by a corner of the desk, Mason's desk telephone pulled over close to her.

"Hello," Mason said. "I'm about ten minutes late. Heard anything from our client?"

"No."

Mason said, "I guess it was a stand-up after all. That cures me of night appointments at the office."

"How is Esther Dilmeyer?" Della asked.

"She's at the Hastings Memorial Hospital. I got hold of Dr. Willmont on the telephone. He's rushing right out to meet her when she's unloaded from the ambulance. Looks like some drug, but it's too early to tell. Sometimes a drug which will induce sleep is given to cover the effects of some other poison. However, I'd say we got her in time, and she'll pull through."

"Did you," she asked, "throw a scare into Magard?"

"I'll say we did — that is, Lieutenant Tragg did."

"He sounded thoroughly subdued."

"Did he ring up?"

"Yes. He called, said that he understood you had been at the Golden Horn with an officer looking for information, said he'd given the officer the information he wanted, and inquired if there was anything else he could do for you."

Mason chuckled. "What did you tell him?"

"I thanked him and told him it would be all right."

Mason looked at his watch. "Well, I guess we'll be on our way and charge this to experience. . . . Wait a minute. Here's someone coming."

They could hear the rapid click-clack . . . click-clack . . . click-clack of heels in the corridor.

Mason opened the door.

Mildreth Faulkner said, "Thank you so much for waiting, Mr. Mason. I'm sorry I was late. I just couldn't make it any sooner."

Mason looked her over carefully, said, "Come in. Miss Faulkner, my secretary, Miss Street. This chair please. You're breathless and excited. How about a ciga-rette?"

"No, thanks. I have to work fast, Mr. Mason."

"What's wrong?"

She said, "It's a long story. I hardly know where to begin."

"Well, begin right in the middle," Mason said, "and keep moving."

She laughed. "It's this way: My sister Carlotta and I started the Faulkner Flower Shops. That was before Carla was married. We each had half of the stock except a small block of five shares which we gave to one of our employees to qualify her so there'd be three on the board of directors.

"Harry Peavis is a big competitor. He controls the bulk of the retail flower business here. I've always liked him. He's rather naïve in some respects, but a shrewd businessman, hard-boiled, occasionally somewhat tactless, and with a great deal of native ability."

"Where does he come into the picture?" Mason asked.

"He managed to pick up the five shares of stock which had been given to our employee."

Mason frowned. "Why? Does he want to pry into your business?"

"I thought so at the time. When he handed over the stock for transfer, he joked about being a silent partner, but I think there's something far more sinister back of it."

"Go ahead."

"My sister married a little over a year ago — about eighteen months ago."

"Whom did she marry?"

"Robert C. Lawley."

"What does he do?" Mason asked.

She made a little gesture which was more expressive than words, and said, "He manages my sister's money."

"Is that enough to keep him busy?"

"It was when there was more of it."

Mason smiled. "I take it things haven't gone so well under his management."

"No."

"What does your sister say to that?"

She said, "Carla developed heart trouble about a year ago. She didn't go to a doctor as soon as she should have. She kept on in a mad round of activity, and by the time she had to give in to it, she was pretty far gone. The doctor says it will take a long time before he can bring her back to normal. In the meantime, she isn't to be excited, or worried."

"She knows the true state of her finances?" Mason asked.

Mildreth Faulkner said, with feeling, "I

hope to God she does."

"But you've never asked her?"

"We don't talk about her husband," she said. "I never did like him. Carla thought I was prejudiced."

"She loves him?"

"Crazy about him. He's smart enough to keep her that way. A little flattery and those little attentions which women crave are all that's necessary. You know how it is with a man when the wife has the money. It's a shame more men can't learn that lesson, but it seems that only the ones who are in a position to profit financially ever do it."

"I take it you didn't approve of the match in the first place."

"I certainly did not. I always thought Bob was a weak sister, a fortune hunter, and a fourflusher."

"And I take it he knows that?"

"He does. Oh, we've tried to be civilized about the thing. We've gotten along all right. Occasionally, before Carla's heart got bad, we'd go on week-end trips together, and Bob would be so nice to me that butter wouldn't melt in his mouth. Then Carla would look at me as much as to say, 'Can't you see how perfectly swell he is, Millie?' "

"And what would you do?" Mason asked.

She said, "I'd try to be just as oily and smooth as he was, but I was burning up inside. I don't mind a man who's frankly on the make, but I do hate mealy-mouthed hypocrisy."

Mason said, "Well, that's the background. What comes next?"

"Bob has Carla's complete confidence. When her heart went bad, Bob started managing all of her affairs. When she'd ask questions, he told her it was no time to bother with business details, that things were going simply grand."

"And you didn't believe that?"

"I knew it wasn't true."

"How?"

"Well, about a week ago, Bob was in an automobile accident. No one would have thought anything of it if it hadn't been for the way he started making glib explanations. When you get to know Bob, he's like an open book. If he's going to lie, he'll rehearse it so carefully that the pieces all fit together so smoothly that — well, it's just too good to be true. It's like a gilded lily or a painted rose."

"So he lied about the automobile accident?"

"Yes . . . when I asked him about it."

"And you started checking up on him?"

She flushed slightly, and said, "When Peavis came in and asked to have that stock transferred on the books of the corporation, I began to do a lot of thinking. I realized suddenly that if someone controlled that five shares of stock and then could get Carla's block of stock, he'd have complete control of the corporation. I suppose it was very foolish of us, but we never thought of anything like that because it was all a family affair. I'd even forgotten about those five shares of stock, because we just went ahead with the business and did what we wanted. We never do have a directors' meeting, and there hasn't been a stockholders' meeting for three years. Well, anyway, that five shares of stock represent the balance of power."

"I presume," Mason said, "you're leading up to telling me that your brother-in-law has managed to get control of the stock your sister held."

"That's exactly it, only it's worse than that. Bob evidently has been plunging pretty heavily. Carla has unlimited confidence in him. She gave him a complete power of attorney, and endorsed all of her securities in blank when she got sick. The doctor said she wasn't to be bothered with business affairs. I always did think that Bob had a finger in that pie somewhere, and got the doctor to say that. It would have been rather easy to do, telling the doctor that Carla worried a lot about business."

Mason nodded. "Any idea where the stock is?" he asked.

She said, "It's apparently in the hands of a man by the name of Lynk who is one of the owners of the Golden Horn. The girl with whom my brother-in-law was riding at the time of the accident is a glamour girl who acts as decoy for — She's supposed to be here. She's the one I telephoned about. I'm expecting her any minute."

Mason said, "She isn't coming."

"What do you mean?"

"Someone sent her a box of poisoned candy. She rang me up about eleven-thirty, and could hardly talk. She apparently collapsed while she was talking over the telephone."

"Sent her poisoned candy!" Mildreth Faulkner exclaimed.

Mason nodded.

"But who on earth could have done that?"

Mason said, "There was a card on the candy box. It said, 'These will make you

90

feel better,' and was signed simply with the initials 'M.F.' Do you know anything about that?"

She looked at him, her eyes getting round. "Why, Mr. Mason — That card — Why, *I* sent it!"

"With the candy?" Mason asked.

"Good heavens, no! Understand, Mr. Mason, I started doing a little detective work. That automobile accident was my clue. I realized after Peavis called on me what an awful fix I'd be in if Bob had done something with that stock. I knew Carla had endorsed it and given him a power of attorney."

"But I thought it was Lynk who had the stock."

"I think Peavis either put him up to it, or Lynk is in touch with Peavis."

"I see. Tell me about that card."

"Well, as soon as Bob started talking about the accident with all those glib explanations, I realized at once that if there was anything wrong, that automobile accident would have something to do with it. I knew that there was something about that accident he didn't want me to find out. So I investigated. I could do that very easily because the other party had reported it to the Traffic Department. It seems that at the time of the accident, Bob had just left the Golden Horn and had a man named Sindler Coll, who I think is a gambler, and Esther Dilmeyer in the car with him.

"I don't think Bob would deliberately surrender the stock in order to get money to gamble, but I think they'd persuaded him his credit was good, and he'd plunged pretty deeply and had some bad luck. They'd given him something that was supposed to be a sure thing, and he wanted to collect a lot of winnings before he had to pay out his losses."

"All right, what about the card?"

She laughed. "I do seem to be getting all involved in explanations, don't I? Well, anyway, I went to the Golden Horn and managed to get acquainted with Esther Dilmeyer. She was feeling pretty low tonight. I gathered that she and Sindler Coll had been — well, pretty sweet on each other, and apparently he'd . . ."

Mason said, "All right. How about the card?"

She said, "I sent her some orchids."

"When?"

"When I left. She was feeling blue, and I told her I was in the flower business."

"She told you about the stock?" Mason asked.

92

"Not about the stock, but generally what was going on."

"Would Peavis surrender that stock if you threatened to sue?"

"Not Peavis," she said. "When he once gets his hands on anything, he hangs on until the last ditch. We might get the stock back, but we'd have five years of litigation doing it — and we might as well sell him control of the company as do that. But tell me, Mr. Mason, how did it happen that you thought *my* card was in the candy? That card was on the orchids."

Mason said, "Someone got it from the orchids and put it in the candy. How did you send the orchids?"

"By Western Union messenger."

"Were they wrapped?"

"Yes, they were in a box."

"About the size of a candy box?"

"Yes."

"Where did you send it?"

"To the Golden Horn."

"And it was addressed to her?"

"Yes."

"How?"

"What do you mean?"

"Pencil, pen and ink, typewriting, or . . ."

"Oh, pen and ink. I wrote her name on

the outside of the box — that is, on the wrapper, you know."

"The box was about the size of a three-pound candy box?"

"I guess it was."

"Someone," Mason said, "could very readily have taken that box at the Golden Horn, promised to take it to Esther Dilmeyer, then taken out the orchids and put in the drugged candy."

"I suppose so."

Mason said, "That could have been done all the more readily in case the person who received it was in a position of some responsibility."

Mildreth Faulkner studied the tips of her gloved fingers. She said, "I remember telling the boy he didn't need to make a personal delivery, but to be certain they would reach her. . . . I can't imagine . . ."

"He probably delivered 'em to the doorman," Mason said. "The doorman's rather officious."

"That may have happened."

"How much is that stock of yours worth?" Mason asked.

"A great deal — more than the real intrinsic value. You know how it is. I have three shops. They're all making money. I'm my own boss. I control the business policies. I'm making a good living out of the business, and the business is building up all the time. That's worth a great deal more to me than the book value of the stock. In other words, every thousand dollars' income that I'm making out of the place on a setup like that, I figure is the equivalent of a twenty-five thousand dollar capital investment. But, of course, I couldn't sell out on that basis."

Mason said, "I *may* have to pay out a little money. How high can I go?"

She said, without hesitation, "Go to ten thousand dollars if you have to."

"But not more than that?"

"N-n-no. Well, not without consulting me anyway."

Mason said, "I don't think I'll have to pay out a cent. If I do, it won't be very much, but — well, I'll do the best I can.

"Della, call up the Golden Horn. See if Magard will give us the address of Lynk's hide-out."

Mildreth Faulkner opened her purse, took out a folded slip of paper, hesitated, started to put it back, realized the lawyer's eyes were on her, and said, "I have it here — the address of the Lilac Canyon cabin."

"Where'd you get it?"

"From Esther Dilmeyer — but don't give her away."

"All right, I won't. Della, you take a taxi home and get some sleep. I'll call you in an hour or an hour and a half, Miss Faulkner."

Mason walked over to the hat closet, put on his hat and coat, grinned cheerfully at his worried client. "Now, take it easy," he said, "and don't worry. Things are going to be all right. Those men are running a gambling place in connection with the Golden Horn, and there are half a dozen weak points in their armor. One of them is Mr. Magard, Mr. Lynk's partner. I was at the Golden Horn with Lieutenant Tragg of the Homicide Squad. The doorman started getting officious, and Tragg put him in his place. By the time Magard got back, he knew that the police had been there. He'll fall all over himself trying to square things up."

Mildreth Faulkner said, getting to her feet, "I feel better now than I have at any time in the last few hours. This thing hit me an awful blow."

"Well, we'll do the best we can," Mason promised.

"You're — you're so thoroughly capable," she said with a little laugh. "I feel that everything is all settled right now. You're going out to the Golden Horn personally?"

"No, I'm going to Lilac Canyon, if Lynk hasn't returned to the Golden Horn."

"Well, no matter what happens, win, lose, or a draw, you'll call me just as soon as . . . well, call me by three o'clock anyway. I'll be waiting."

Mason said, reassuringly, "Sure, I'll call you. Close up the shop, Della, and put out the lights. I'm on my way."

5

The road up Lilac Canyon wound like a sinuous snake, twisting and turning. Side roads meandered off the main highway, following the contours of the steep hillsides to secluded little cabins, places almost within a stone's throw of the city, yet still distinctly rural and rustic.

At one time, before the city had entered upon its phenomenal spurt of growth, Lilac Canyon had been the hinterland. It was devoted to week-end cabins, little hideouts, places where city dwellers could spend quiet Saturday afternoons and Sundays.

Then the city had expanded. Lilac Canyon was still too precipitous, too brushy, and too rural to lend itself to real estate subdivision, but the lots were pounced upon by those who wished relatively cheap hillside property within commuting distance of the metropolitan district.

Mason had some trouble as he threaded

his way along the winding pavement of the main road, locating the names of the roads which turned off. Eventually, however, he found Acorn Drive and turned off, following the road along the contours until he rounded the shoulder of a mountain from which he could look down on the valley, and see the long lighted lines which marked the location of boulevards; in the distance the bright blotches of the suburban cities.

Mason slowed down, looking for house numbers, but the houses were back from the roadway, crowded up or down on the hillside, screened wherever possible by the scrub oak which was native to the hillside.

Abruptly Mason saw the red light of a car parked ahead. Just beyond was another car, and beyond that still a third. Up from the road to the right, was a small cabin with lights ablaze. A group of men gathered on a porch which stretched from the front around to the side of the house. They were smoking, and the little pin points of red light made by the tips of their cigarettes glowed into alternate spurts of brilliance like stationary fireflies.

The front door of the house was open. Across the illuminated oblong, men moved back and forth, men who kept their hats on. It might have been a Hollywood party, but there was no hilarity, no sounds of merriment emanating from the lighted building.

Mason swung his car so that the headlights fell on the license plate of one of the parked cars. He saw that it held an "E" within a diamond, the sign of a police car.

Abruptly, Mason changed his course and drove on past the group of parked automobiles.

Three hundred yards beyond, the road ended in a paved circle which gave Mason barely enough room to turn around.

Headed back toward town, he ran his car in close to the curb where there was a straight stretch free of parked automobiles. He switched out the lights, turned off the ignition, and climbed the two flights of stairs which led from the street, up the steep declivity to the porch.

One of the men seated on the porch recognized him, came forward, took his arm, pushed him slightly to one side. "How about it, Mr. Mason? Got a story for us?"

"On what?" Mason asked.

"On the murder. How do you come in on it? Are you retained, and, if so, by whom? What's it all about?"

Mason said, "I think you are one up on me."

"On what?"

100

"On the murder."

"You didn't know about it?"

"No."

"Then what are you doing here?"

"I wanted to get in touch with Lieutenant Tragg," Mason said. "I tried to reach him at headquarters. They told me I'd find him here. They didn't say what was wrong. You say a man was killed?"

"Yes. Shot in the back with a thirty-two caliber revolver."

"Do they know who did it?"

"No."

"Who was it?"

"Harvey J. Lynk is the name."

"Lynk," Mason said, "means nothing to me. What did he do?"

"Big time stuff. One of the owners of the Golden Horn, a nightclub. There's an upstairs above that nightclub."

"Rooms?" Mason asked.

"Roulette, craps, stud poker."

"What was this place? A love nest?"

"No one knows — yet."

"You say he was one of the owners. Who's the other?"

"Clint Magard."

"Has he been advised?"

The newspaper man laughed. He said, "The police have advised him, and every newspaper in town has sent a man to ask him for a statement."

"Why all the commotion?" Mason asked.

"Looks like a swell story. There's a woman in the case somewhere. A woman's overnight bag and some stuff are in there. Powder spilled on the dresser, a cigarette end with lipstick on it. . . . Tragg has a couple of leads he's working on. Have an idea we can make it a nice, juicy scandal-killing before we get done. Sweet young thing fighting to save her honor, finally pointing a gun. Lynk grabbed her. There was a struggle. She has no recollection of pulling the trigger. She heard an explosion. Lynk fell backward. Dazed, she dropped the gun and ran, afraid to tell anyone because . . . Hell, I should go ahead and outline a perfect defense for you. You'll probably be the attorney representing her and get ten thousand dollars for thinking up the stuff I'm giving you for nothing."

Mason chuckled. "Well," he said, "if Tragg is as busy as all this, I won't bother him. I'll catch him some other time."

"Want me to tell him you're here?"

"No. Don't tell him anything about my being here. I have something to take up with him and don't want to tip my hand. I'd prefer to walk in on him without having him know I'm looking for him."

"Figure on pulling a little surprise?" the reporter asked.

"Not exactly, but there's no reason why he should waste a lot of time speculating over why I want to see him and what I want to see him about."

"Something to that. And you can't give us a story?"

"No."

"Anything in what you want to see Tragg about?"

"Nothing you'd care to publish."

"You don't know whether you're going to get in on this case?"

Mason laughed. "I didn't even know there was a case. I've never seen Lynk in my life, and had no idea he'd been killed."

He turned back toward the stairs. "Well, so-long. I . . ."

A man's form loomed in the doorway of the house, cast a shadow along the porch. Lieutenant Tragg said, "Well, dust the whole damn thing for fingerprints and — Where's that photographer? I want a photograph of . . ."

He stopped midsentence as he saw Perry Mason halfway down the steps. "Hey, *you!*" he shouted.

Mason paused and looked back.

"What the devil are *you* doing out here?"

"Come down to the car," Mason invited.

"No. I'm too busy. Talk right here . . ."

Mason jerked his thumb toward the cluster of lighted cigarettes which marked the little group of reporters.

Tragg said, "You may be right at that."

He followed Mason down the stairs to where the lawyer had the car parked.

"Okay," Tragg said, "What did you want to see Lynk about?"

Mason smiled ruefully. "To tell you the truth, I thought I'd steal a march on you, but I see you beat me to it."

"How do you mean, steal a march?"

"Well, I wanted to know more about Esther Dilmeyer, who her friends were, wanted to get a line on anyone she'd been going with, wanted to find out whether her folks were living, whether she had much mail."

"You thought Lynk could tell you?"

"Yes, I had an idea he could."

"What gave you that idea?"

Mason said evasively, "I don't know."

"Why didn't you talk with Magard? He was at the office where the information would be more readily available."

Mason said, "I was going to talk with them both."

Tragg regarded him thoughtfully. "Holcomb," he announced at length, "always claimed you played dirty pool, Mason. I could never see it that way. I figured that you were on one side, Holcomb on the other. It was a fair fight. You moved a little faster than Holcomb could follow. At times, your hands were quicker than the eye — Holcomb's eye, anyway."

"Well?" Mason asked.

"Right now, I can appreciate just about how Sergeant Holcomb felt. You aren't strong on giving out information, are you?"

"I can't afford to be."

"Why?"

"I protect my clients."

"Yeah. I want to talk with you about that client. What do you know about her, and what did she say when she came in?"

"Came in where?" Mason asked.

"Your office. Didn't you say you had a one o'clock appointment?"

"Oh, that," Mason said, as though just placing what Tragg was talking about. "That was a minor matter. Well, I don't suppose she'd object if I told you, Lieutenant, but . . . Well, as a lawyer, I can't tell you about her affairs."

Tragg said, "Your appointment was for one o'clock."

"That's right."

"Let's say that took twenty or twenty-five minutes. . . ." He looked at his watch thoughtfully. "You hot-footed it out here and didn't waste a great deal of time doing it. How'd you get this address?"

"How," Mason asked, "did you know Lynk had been murdered?"

"How," Tragg countered, "did you?"

"A newspaper man told me."

"Headquarters told me. I was ordered to get out here."

"But don't you know how the murder was discovered?"

"No. Someone rang up headquarters, said to rush a car out here right away."

"Man or woman?"

"Woman."

"And they sent the car out?"

"Yes. She pretended to be telephoning from this cabin, said there was a prowler on the outside."

"Where do you get that pretended stuff?" Mason asked. "That probably was Lynk's little playmate. There was a prowler."

"Lynk had been dead quite a while before that call came in," Tragg said dryly.

"Why are you so sure of that?"

"The doc's word, not mine. Coagulation of blood, rigor mortis, and a lot of tech-

106

nical stuff. They fix the time of death as right around midnight, and they aren't going to be a hell of a long way off. It's a good thing we got here when we did. Tomorrow morning they'd have had to fix the time of death somewhere between ten o'clock and one o'clock. The way it is now, they can split it down almost to a few minutes one way or another. Figure it midnight on the nose, and you won't miss it far."

Mason said, "You haven't anything new on that Dilmeyer case, have you?"

"No. I had to drop that to work on this. I understand she's going to be all right. You're sure you didn't have an idea that perhaps Lynk wasn't in the best of health?"

"And came out here to discover the corpse?" Mason asked. "No, thanks. I've had my share of that."

Tragg studied the lawyer for a moment, then scratched his hair over his left ear. "You see your client and beat it out here. A guy would almost think Esther Dilmeyer was one of your witnesses, Lynk another, and that it's open season on the witnesses in that case of yours. Looks like someone doesn't want you to win that case."

Mason said, "If you find any angle on this that ties in with the Dilmeyer case, will you let me know?"

"I suppose you'll let *me* know what *you* find."

Mason said, "Well, there's no harm in trying. See you later."

"You will at that," Tragg assured him grimly.

Mason was careful to start his car in a leisurely manner, nor did he step on the throttle until he was a good half mile from the mountain cabin.

An all-night restaurant on the boulevard had a telephone, and Mason called the Hastings Memorial Hospital to ask for Dr. Willmont.

Mason had a wait of more than a minute before he heard Dr. Willmont's voice on the line.

"Mason talking, Doctor. What did you find with Esther Dilmeyer?"

"She'll pull through."

"The candy was poisoned?"

"Yes. Every piece had been tampered with."

"What was the poison?"

"Judging from the patient's symptoms," Dr. Willmont said, "and from the best guess I can make from tests we've carried out, it's one of the barbituric derivatives, probably veronal. The drug has a mildly acrid taste which is pretty well disguised in the bittersweet chocolates.

"It's a hypnotic, but there's a wide range between the medicinal and the lethal dose. The official dose is five to ten grains. That's usually sufficient to bring on sleep. Death has occurred after a dose of sixty grains, but, on the other hand, there's been a recovery after a dose of three hundred and sixty grains. There have been numerous recoveries with around two hundred grains. We haven't been able to analyze the candy definitely, but, judging from taste and other factors, there's probably five to seven grains in the centers of each of the chocolates. She evidently ate them slowly enough so there was an interval between the first ten or twenty grains and the rest of the ingestion, which gave the drug a chance to work before she'd eaten enough to bring about a fatal result."

"You're sure that's what it is?" Mason asked.

"Pretty sure, both from an examination of the candy and from the condition of the patient. Her face is congested, respiration's slow and stertorous. There are no reflexes. The pupil is somewhat dilated. There's a temperature rise of a little over one degree.

Personally, I'd say veronal, and I'd figure about five grains to a candy center. That would make about fifty grains she'd taken. That makes a recovery almost certain."

Mason said, "All right, keep on the job. See that she has the very best of care. Keep a special nurse on duty all the time. Watch her diet. I want to be damn certain that no one slips her any more poison."

"That's all taken care of," Dr. Willmont said dryly.

"When will she be conscious?"

"Not for some time. We've cleaned out her stomach, made a lumbar puncture, and drained off some of the fluid. That will expedite things a lot, but she has enough of the drug in her system so she'll be sleeping for quite some time. I don't think it's advisable to try to hurry that any."

"Let me know when she wakes up," Mason said, "and be sure to fix things there so nothing else happens."

"You think something's going to?" Dr. Willmont asked.

"I don't know. She was coming to my office to give me some information. She's a witness. I don't know what she knows. Someone evidently went to some pains to see that I didn't find out."

"Give her another twenty-four hours,

and she can tell," Dr. Willmont said.

Mason said thoughtfully, "It may be that whoever sent her that drugged candy didn't want to kill her, but simply wanted to keep her from telling me what she knows for twenty-four hours. In other words, it may be too late then to do any good."

"Well, nothing else is going to happen to her," Dr. Willmont promised. "No visitors are to be admitted without my permission. I have three nurses working on the job in shifts — and all of them have red hair."

"Okay, Doctor. I'm leaving it up to you."

Mason hung up the telephone and made time to Mildreth Faulkner's house on Whiteley Pines Drive.

Here also he was on a steep slope over-looking the city. The house was on the slope below the road, one story on the street, three stories on the back.

Mason touched the bell gently, and Mildreth Faulkner opened the door almost at once.

"What," she asked, "did you find out?"

Mason said, "She's going to pull through all right. Some drug, apparently veronal. You certainly are up in the air here."

She laughed nervously, leading the way into the living room. "Yes, I bought this house about six months ago, after Carla

111

got sick. I wanted to be near her."

"And are you?"

"Yes. She lives on Chervis Road. That's over around the shoulder of the hill."

"How far?"

"Oh, not more than five minutes' walk. I'd say about — Oh, I don't know. Perhaps a quarter of a mile."

"Just a hop, skip, and a jump in a car?"

"That's right. Tell me, why was she poisoned? Or was it an overdose of sleeping medicine?"

"No. She was poisoned. That is, the candy was poisoned. The chemist for the Homicide Squad says that every piece has been tampered with. They haven't made a complete analysis yet."

Mildreth Faulkner walked over to the grid over a floor heater, and said, "Sit down. I'm cold."

Mason dropped into a chair, and watched her as she stood over the grille, the upcoming draft of hot air agitating her skirt. "What's the matter?" he asked. "Did you get chilled?"

"I guess so. It's been a strain. Well, go ahead and tell me about it. What's the use of stalling? I suppose it's bad news."

He nodded.

"I was afraid of that. Lynk isn't the sort

who will scare easily."

"What made you think it was bad news?"

"You'd have told me when you first came here if it had been all good. How about a drink? Want one?"

"A short one," Mason said.

She opened a little parlor bar, brought out Scotch, ice cubes, and soda.

"Rather neat gadget that," Mason commented.

"Yes, it's really a little electric refrigerator, makes its own ice, keeps the charged water cold. Well, what did Lynk say? He hasn't turned the stock over to Peavis already, has he?"

"I don't know."

"Wouldn't he tell you?"

"He wasn't able to talk," Mason said.

"Wasn't able to? You mean he was drunk?"

She was pouring whiskey from the bottle, and her hand trembled enough so that the neck of the bottle chattered against the rim of the glass. Mason waited until she had finished with the whiskey, and had reached for the bottle of charged water.

"Lynk," he said, "was murdered, about midnight."

For a moment, it seemed that the words

meant nothing to her. She continued to trickle charged water from the siphon into the glass, then suddenly she gave a convulsive start, depressed the lever, and squirted liquid up over the rim of the glass. "You mean — Did I hear you right? Dead!"

"Murdered."

"At midnight?"

"Yes."

"Who . . . who did it?"

"They don't know. He was shot in the back with a thirty-two caliber revolver."

She put down the bottle of charged water, brought his drink over to him. "Where does that leave me?"

"Out on a limb perhaps," Mason said.

"At midnight?"

"That's right."

"Well, anyway, *I* have an alibi." She laughed nervously.

"What is it?" Mason asked.

"Are you serious?"

"Weren't you?"

"No."

"Well, let's be serious then. Where were you?"

"Why," she said, "I was . . . Why, how utterly absurd! Nothing could have suited me less than to have anything happen to him before I — we got that stock."

She paused in front of the little bar, then took out a bottle of cognac. "Scotch is all right," she said, "as a sociable beverage, but I'm cold and this has been a shock to me. I'm going to have a good jolt of brandy. Do you want to join me?"

"No," Mason said, "and I don't think you're going to have any brandy."

She had been about to pour the liquor. Now she whirled to stare at him. "You don't think *I'm* going to?"

"No."

"Why not?"

"Because," Mason said, "if you take a swig of brandy, and then that Scotch, in about twenty minutes or half an hour, you're going to be just a little warped in your judgment. You'll think you can get away with things that you can't."

"What in the world are you talking about?"

"Where," Mason asked, "is the fur coat that you had on when you came to the office?"

"Why, in the coat closet."

"There in the hall?"

"Yes."

Mason put down his drink, got up, and walked across to the door she had indicated. He opened the hall closet, and took down the hanger which held the silver fox coat she had worn to his office.

Suddenly she ran toward him. "No, no! Put that back. You can't . . ."

Mason slid his hand down in the right-hand side pocket of the coat and brought out a thirty-two caliber revolver.

"I thought," he said, "there was something heavy in your pocket when you came to the office."

As though his discovery had deprived her of the power to move, she stood motionless and silent.

Mason broke open the gun, saw that one shell had been fired. He smelled of the barrel, closed the gun, hung up the fur coat in the closet, carefully closed the door, walked across to his chair, and dropped into it. He placed the gun on a taboret by the side of the chair, picked up his drink, and said to Mildreth Faulkner, "Here's how."

She walked back to the place where she had left her Scotch and soda, without once taking her eyes from him.

Then she moved over to stand over the floor heater. "Can I . . . Can I drink this?"

"Sure," Mason said. "Go ahead. That will do you good. Just don't overdo it."

She drained a good half of the glass, kept

watching him with wide, frightened eyes.

"It *is* rather cool for this time of year," Mason said. "I've noticed when the days are warm and dry, there's usually a wind in from the desert, and that makes the nights cool off rapidly. Your fur coat should have kept you warm."

She said, "I got frightfully c-c-cold. I'm having a nervous ch-ch-chill right now."

"The whiskey will warm you up," Mason said casually. "How long have you had the gun?"

"Two years."

"Got a permit for it?"

"Yes."

"Buy it here in the city?"

"Yes."

"Do you know what ballistics experts are able to do with bullets?"

"No. What?"

"Every bullet fired from a gun bears an unmistakable identification which can be imprinted on it only by that one weapon."

"Are you trying to tell me that as — as my lawyer so you can warn me . . ."

"I'm not your lawyer."

"You're not? Why, I thought . . ."

He shook his head. "Not on this case."

"Why not?"

"I don't know enough about it. I don't go

117

around selling myself. My brains aren't a commodity like a motor car which anyone can buy who has the price. A person can buy a bulletproof car and use it to help hold up a bank, but he can't buy my knowledge of law to use in committing a crime."

"Mr. Mason, you aren't serious? You don't think I killed him?"

"I don't know. Even if you did, it might be justifiable homicide. All that I'm telling you is that I'm not going to represent you until I know the facts."

"You mean . . ."

Mason looked at his wrist watch impatiently and said, "I mean the police will be here almost any minute. If I'm going to represent you, I should know it before then. If there are any weak spots in your story, a little rehearsal wouldn't hurt any. Go ahead."

"I don't want you to represent me."

"You don't?"

"No. I want you to represent Carlotta, my sister."

"What's she got to do with it?"

Mildreth was silent for several seconds, then said, quickly, "Listen, Mr. Mason, if you're Carlotta's lawyer, and I tell you the whole story, they can't ever make you tell, can they?"

Mason said, "Anything you tell me, goes no farther."

"But is it legal? If I tell you something, and you're Carla's attorney . . ."

"Legality be damned," Mason said. "Don't stand there and quibble. If I'm going to do anything, I have to know what the hell it's all about."

"Well," she said, "the story is simple. I ran over to see Carla and Bob tonight. I had a talk with Bob, and told him I wanted to get that stock in the morning, that Peavis had shown up with the five shares. And Bob was so casual about the whole thing, but had so many reasons why he just couldn't get me that stock, that I became suspicious and — well, I'm not certain. I think perhaps Carla was listening from the head of the stairs."

"Go ahead," Mason said. "Make it snappy."

"Well, you know what must have happened. Bob had pledged that stock. He had to get it back just to show me anyway. He must have rushed out to see Lynk."

"What makes you think he did?"

"I . . . this gun."

"What about it?"

"Well, I got to thinking things over and decided to have another talk with Bob after

119

what I'd learned from Esther Dilmeyer. I thought it would simplify matters a lot if I could walk into your office and tell you just what the situation was, and . . ."

"Never mind what you thought. What did you *do?*"

"I went out to see Bob."

"What did he say?"

"Nothing. He wasn't there."

"Where was Carla?"

"She wasn't there."

"Perhaps they both went out."

"No, no. You don't understand. Carla has been confined to the house for months. She's been in bed for more than two months. Now she's getting around the house a bit, and occasionally she goes for a ride."

"Perhaps Bob took her for a ride."

"No. Her own car's gone."

"You think she drove it?"

"I'm sure she did. No one else ever drives it."

Mason said, "Bob went some place. You think he went to see Lynk. Now where do you think your sister went?"

"I think she followed him."

"You think Bob killed Lynk?"

"I think Carla . . . I don't know what *did* happen."

"All right, where did you get the gun?"

"Well, when I went there the second time and found they were gone, I looked around some. I found this gun on Carla's dresser."

"I thought you said it was your gun."

"It is, but I let Carla have it two months ago. She was left in the house alone quite a bit, and I wanted her to have some protection."

"Bob was going out?"

"Yes. You couldn't expect him to give up everything and become just a stay-at-home because Carla was an invalid. No one expected that, and — well, you know how it is. I suppose he . . . well, he . . ."

"Played around?" Mason asked.

"Yes."

"Was the gun on the dresser when you were there earlier in the evening?"

"No. And — well, a few of Carla's things were gone. I didn't notice them right at first, but I got to looking around and some of her medicines and a few of her clothes were gone."

"What do you think happened?" Mason asked.

Words poured out in hysterical rapidity. "I think that she followed Bob out to Lynk's place. I think Bob had my gun and killed him. I think Carla knows it. Good Heavens, I wish I knew where she was! I'm worried absolutely sick about her. It was bad enough for her to get out of bed and drive her car, but the shock of finding out about Bob, of knowing about the murder, of . . . it's awful."

"Then you think she came back to the house?" Mason asked.

"Yes."

"About when?"

"I don't know. I left there about quarter to one. That's why I was a little late getting to your office for the one o'clock appointment. I arrived about twenty minutes to one, and wasted a good five minutes looking around and trying to find what had happened. Then I decided to rush to your office. Then you told me about Esther Dilmeyer being drugged and — and you said you were going out to see Lynk, and I thought — well, I tried to persuade myself it was all right."

"Then you had an idea Lynk was dead before I went out there?"

"Well, I didn't know. I knew the gun had been used."

"How did you know that?"

"Because I looked at it, and found an empty shell in it."

"Then," Mason said, "you got your fingerprints all over the gun?"

"Yes, I guess so."

"And slipped it in the pocket of your coat?"

"Yes."

"Now you say you think Bob killed him?"

"That's right."

"And that Carla knew about it?"

"Yes."

"And that Carla came home and packed up some things and left?"

"Yes."

"Do you think Bob came back with her?"

"No. I think Bob must have just kept right on going. You know, I don't think Bob would have nerve enough to face anything like that. I think he'd kill a man and then run away."

"Then," Mason said dryly, "if we are to follow your reasoning to its logical conclusion, after Bob killed him, Carlotta got the gun with which the murder was committed."

She bit her lip and turned away so that he couldn't see her face.

"Is that right?" Mason asked.

She said, "I g-g-guess so."

123

"That isn't logical," Mason said. "You know it."

"Well, what is logical?"

"I don't know, but I want to find out where I stand. You want me to represent your sister?"

"That's right."

"But not you?"

"No. I can take care of myself."

Mason said, "Don't be too sure. If that's the murder weapon, it's in your possession. It has your fingerprints on it."

"I tell you I can take care of myself. They can't pin anything on me. I'm strong and healthy. They can question me, and it won't hurt me. They can't prove a thing."

"Where were you at midnight?"

"I was . . . I was at my store in the office trying to figure things out so I could see just how much money I could raise in case we had to buy that stock."

"And you want me to represent your sister?"

"Yes, please. I want you to stand back of her."

Mason said, "No one needs to know anything about her having gone out. If her husband killed him, that won't involve her."

"You don't understand. If you knew

124

about her condition, if you could see her. This must have been a terrible strain. If they should start questioning her, or the newspaper men should get after her and ask her questions about Bob and about where she was, and about how she got the gun and those things — well, it would undo all the good that her treatment has accomplished. She'd either die, or her heart would be so bad it never would get better."

Mason said, "Who's going to pay me for representing her?"

"I am."

"If I'm representing her, I'll be representing her alone."

"Of course."

"Her interests would come first."

"That's what I want."

"If yours get in the way, you'd be in the position of an adverse party. I'd smash you just as quickly as I would a total stranger."

"That's the way I want you to do."

"Did you ever hear of the paraffin test?" Mason asked abruptly.

"The paraffin test? What are you talking about?"

"For telling whether a person has fired a gun recently?"

"What's paraffin got to do with that?"

"Whenever a gun's fired, an invisible spray of powder particles backfire, and embed themselves in the skin of a person's hand. They're microscopic particles, invisible to the naked eye, but they *always* fly back and are imbedded in the skin.

"The Scientific Crime Detection Bureau has worked out a new technique for telling whether a person has fired a gun. They pour melted paraffin over the suspect's hands, reinforce it with a thin layer of cotton, and then cover it with wax. After the paraffin has just about set, the whole thing is rolled back from the hand. The little bits of powder which buried themselves in the skin of the hand are caught by the paraffin and adhere to it when the mold is taken from the hand. A chemical reagent is poured on the paraffin. That reacts on the nitrates in the powder so that it brings about a chemical change that makes the specks visible to the naked eye."

"I see," she said, her voice holding a slight quaver.

Mason said, "If Carlotta *didn't* fire that gun, it would be a lot better for her to go to the police right now and tell them her story, whatever it is. Then, before it's too late, the police could subject her hands to a paraffin test and prove that she didn't fire the gun. That would clear her."

"But . . . but . . . suppose she did?"

"In that event," Mason said, "with one shot fired out of the gun, with the police able to prove that the gun had been in her possession, with a paraffin test showing that she had recently fired the gun, and with the ballistics experts showing that the bullet which killed Harvey Lynk came from that gun, your sister would be headed for the gas chamber at San Quentin.

"And," Mason went on dryly, "the fact that Harvey J. Lynk was shot in the back isn't going to help a self-defense plea any."

Mildreth Faulkner slowly walked across to where the gun reposed on the taboret by Mason's chair. "I suppose I shouldn't have got *my* fingerprints on it."

"That's right," Mason said.

"Couldn't we wipe them off?"

"*I* couldn't."

She grabbed up the gun, crossed over to her purse, took out a handkerchief, and started scrubbing vigorously away at the metal.

Mason sat calmly at ease, sipping his Scotch and soda, watching her frantic motions.

"Careful with that gun," he warned.

"You have your finger inside the trigger guard."

A siren sounded close at hand, rising to a scream, then fading to a low, moaning sound as a car pulled up at the curb outside.

Mason said, "Unless I'm greatly mistaken, that will be Lieutenant Arthur Tragg of the Homicide Squad, and when he finds that gun absolutely devoid of fingerprints, he'll . . ."

"Look out. . . ."

Mason jumped up from the chair, lunged toward her, grabbed for her wrist — and was too late.

The revolver roared into noise. The bullet, sailing through a plate-glass window, sent tinkling fragments of glass dropping to the cement porch.

In the interval of startled silence which followed, the doorbell rang insistently. Knuckles pounded on the panels. Lieutenant Tragg called, "This is the police. Open up, or I'll smash the door in."

"That," Mason said calmly, "is the pay-off." He walked back to his chair, settled down in the cushions, picked up the drink, and lit a fresh cigarette. "It's your party now."

Mildreth Faulkner stood staring at the

gun. "Good Heavens! I had no idea it was going off. My handkerchief caught on the hammer and pulled it back. My finger was on the trigger, and . . ."

"Better let Lieutenant Tragg in," Mason interrupted. "I think he's getting ready to smash in a window."

She stooped and slid the gun along the floor under a davenport at the corner of the room.

Mason tolerantly shook his head at her. "Naughty, naughty! Lieutenant Tragg won't like that."

She went rapidly through the door to the reception hallway, started to run the last few steps, and opened the door. "What is it?" she asked.

"Who did the shooting just now?" Lieutenant Tragg asked, pushing his way into the hallway. "And is that Perry Mason's car out there? Is *he* here?"

"Yes, he's here."

"Who did the shooting?"

"Why . . . er . . . was there shooting?"

"Didn't you hear the shot?"

"Why, no, I can't say that I did. I heard something that sounded like a backfire."

Lieutenant Tragg made a sound which was midway between a sniff and a snort, and walked on into the living room. "Well,

129

Mason," he said, "*you* certainly get around."

"Travel," Mason told him, "is broadening. As you doubtless know, this is Miss Faulkner. Lieutenant Tragg, Miss Faulkner. You'll find that Miss Faulkner has excellent taste in Scotch whiskey, and, for your further information, *I'm* not representing her."

Tragg stood staring down at Mason. "You're *not* representing her?"

"No."

"Then what the devil *are* you doing here?"

Mason said, "Paying a social call and sipping a very delightful whiskey and soda."

"You fired that shot?"

"No."

The lieutenant's eyes moved rapidly around the room. He saw the hole in the plate-glass window, and walked across to examine it.

"For Heaven sakes," Mildreth exclaimed. "It's a bullet hole in the glass! Then it *was* a shot. Someone must have shot at me, Mr. Mason."

"Through the window?" Tragg asked.

"Yes."

"You didn't hear it?"

"No. I heard your car coming up. That

is, I guess it was your car, and I thought there was a backfire. I had no idea it was a shot."

"I see," Tragg observed calmly. "Then someone must have shot at you from outside."

"Yes."

"Well, let's see. Here's a hole in the drapes, and here's a hole in the glass. That gives us the line taken by the bullet. Now, sighting along that line, you can see that — Here. Pull that drape to one side. Now you can see my car parked at the curb. The line runs just in front of the car."

"That's right, it does."

"Then someone must have stood directly in front of my car and fired the shot. He must have been standing on stilts some fifteen feet high."

"You didn't shoot, did you?" she asked.

Tragg ignored the question. "Furthermore," he said, "by the time you've had as much experience with bullets as I have, you'll be able to tell the direction in which they're going when they go through glass. And there's the odor of smokeless powder in the room. I'm afraid, Miss Faulkner, that I'll have to look around."

"You can't. I forbid you to do it."

"Well, I'm going to just the same."

"He can't do it without a warrant, can he, Mr. Mason?"

Tragg said, "Mason isn't representing you."

"I know, but he can tell me that."

Mason sipped his Scotch and soda, pulled placidly at his cigarette, and said nothing. Lieutenant Tragg said, "You know, Miss Faulkner, we're going to quit playing horse right now, and get down to brass tacks. If you'll tell me who fired that shot and what was done with the gun, I won't take you down to police headquarters, have you searched, and have detectives come out and go through the house. . . .

"Wait a minute. You must have been standing about here. You heard me coming in the car. You must have fired that shot just as I was bringing my car to a stop. Now, figuring the angle of that shot . . . I was ringing the doorbell. Well, the natural place for you to have concealed the gun would have been under the cushions of this davenport."

He calmly walked over to the davenport and started raising the cushions.

"You can't do that," she said, grabbing his arm.

Tragg pushed her to one side. "Don't act up, sister," he warned, "or I'll have the place crawling with cops inside of twenty minutes."

"But you can't. You . . . Oh . . ."

Tragg dropped to his knees, placed his head down close to the floor, peered under the davenport, and said, "Oh-oh!"

Mason heard the grind of a car motor coming up the steep incline of a cross street. He carefully pinched out his cigarette, dropped it in the ash tray, stretched, yawned, and said, "Well, if the lieutenant will pardon me . . ."

"The lieutenant won't pardon you," Tragg said, sliding his left arm under the davenport.

"Meaning you're going to try to hold me?" Mason asked.

"Meaning I'm going to find out what you have to say about this before you go anywhere," Tragg said.

The car was coming closer now.

Mason said, "Sergeant Holcomb never liked to have me present when he was trying to get a statement from a suspect. He always thought that I was a disturbing influence. Funny thing about me that way. When I'm in the room, I simply can't keep from advising a person about constitutional rights, warning about traps, and so forth."

133

Tragg said, "You win. Get the hell out of here."

Mason smiled reassuringly at Mildreth Faulkner. "Be seeing you. Don't bother to let me out. I know the way."

As Mason turned from the living room into the corridor, Lieutenant Tragg said, "All right, Miss Faulkner. Tell me about the gun. Why did you fire it?"

"It was an accident."

Mason opened the front door.

"Were you perhaps taking a shot at Mason, or was he trying to take the gun away from you, or . . ."

Mason gently closed the door behind him, and stepped out to the porch.

A coupe had stopped just behind Tragg's sedan. A woman was getting out of it. Mason held up his hand, motioning for her to stop, and walked rapidly toward the car.

The woman said, in a rather flat voice, "What's the matter? What's . . ."

"You Mrs. Lawley?" Mason asked in an undertone.

"Yes, I'm Mildreth Faulkner's sister. What's . . ."

Mason said, "Get in your car, turn around, and drive back down the road until I catch up with you. Make it snappy.

Be quiet about it. The police are in there, and . . ."

She caught her breath. "You're Perry Mason, the lawyer?"

"Yes. Your sister wants me to represent you."

"To represent *me?* For Heaven sakes, what for?"

"I don't know," Mason said, "but unless you want to be dragged down to police headquarters while they try to find out, you'd better turn that car around and get started."

He walked over to his own car, switched on the engine, made an excessive amount of noise, backing, turning, clashing gears, and racing his motor. When Carlotta Lawley had her car safely turned around and was headed back down the grade, Mason snapped his car into gear, ran rapidly along behind her, and, some two hundred yards from the house, drove up alongside, and signaled her to stop.

"Were you," he asked, "going home?"

"Why, I . . . you see, I . . ."

Mason said, "Don't go home. Go to the Clearmount Hotel, register as Mrs. Charles X. Dunkurk of San Diego. Be sure you spell it D-u-n-k-u-r-k. Go to your room, get into bed and stay there. Don't go out, don't read the papers, don't listen to the radio. Simply stay there until I come to see you, and that won't be until sometime tomorrow — or rather later on today."

"You mean I'll have to wait there . . ."

"Yes," Mason said. "I don't want to attract attention by coming in to call on you at three or four o'clock in the morning. I have some work to do between now and the time I see you."

"And you don't want to talk with me now — to ask me any questions, to . . ."

"I do not," Mason interrupted. "I have more important things to do right now, and I want to get you under cover."

"I . . . my husband . . ."

"Forget him," Mason said, "and get started for the Clearmount Hotel. You know where it is?"

"Yes."

"Well, get going. Lieutenant Tragg isn't a fool. He's all excited now about finding a gun in Mildreth's possession, but it won't be long before he realizes that I made an awful lot of noise backing my car and turning around."

Without another word, Carlotta Lawley slipped her car into gear and shot ahead.

6

Left alone with Mildreth Faulkner, Tragg waited until the sound of Mason's car had died away in the distance, watched her eyes fight back the expression of panic and become defiant. There was nothing of the quitter about her. She stood, with her chin up, fighting for control. Excitement brought added sparkle to her eyes, color to her cheeks. She was, Tragg admitted, a beautiful woman, quite evidently accustomed to masculine deference — and she was trapped. It remained only for him to close the jaws of that trap.

Because he had her so thoroughly in his power, and because she was so naïvely unaware of the danger of dealing with an experienced police detective, he hesitated for a moment, then, putting admiration of her courage aside, he said abruptly, "Miss Faulkner, I'm going to ask you two questions. The answers to those two questions will determine our whole future relationship. If you tell me the truth, I may be able to help you."

"What are they?" she asked, in a voice which was as harsh and strained as the crackle of static on a radio.

"First, did you send Esther Dilmeyer the poisoned candy?"

"No."

"Second, did you kill Harvey Lynk?"

"No."

Tragg helped himself to a chair, made himself at ease. "Very well, I'm taking you at your word. If you had killed Lynk or sent Esther Dilmeyer the poisoned candy, I would have been the first to advise you to stand on your constitutional rights and not answer my questions."

A note of contempt crept into her voice. "In other words, if you'd asked me if I sent Esther Dilmeyer the poisoned candy, and I'd said, 'Yes,' you'd have been very magnanimous, and said, 'Now, Miss Faulkner, since you've told me the truth, I advise you not to answer any questions because you might incriminate yourself.'"

He grinned. "Hardly. I didn't expect you would admit it if you *had* been guilty. Not in so many words. But I could have told from your manner."

"Do you mean to say that you can ask a person a question like that, and tell from the manner in which the reply is given whether the answer is true?"

"Not all the time, but I can get a pretty good idea."

"Then," she said, still with that note of contempt in her voice, "having ascertained that I didn't commit either crime, you have done your duty, and there's no need to waste any more of your valuable time here."

"Not so fast. In the first place, I didn't say that I had decided you weren't guilty. In the second place, if you aren't guilty, you may have some information which will be of value."

"Oh, so you haven't cleared me yet?"

"No."

"I thought you said you had."

"No. I said that if you had been guilty, I would have been the first to advise you not to answer questions. Now I'm going to explain that a little, Miss Faulkner. If you are guilty, don't answer my questions because, *if you are guilty, I'm going to trap you!*"

"Well, I'm not guilty. And even if I were, I don't think you could trap me into admitting it."

"I think I could," he said. "Say, nine times out of ten."

Her silence was significant.

"Now remember, Miss Faulkner, if you

are guilty, please don't answer these questions. Simply say that you won't answer them."

"I'm not guilty."

"All right, with that understanding, you can answer questions, but remember, I've warned you."

She said hotly, "Since seven o'clock tonight I've been faced with a very difficult and trying business situation. I'm endeavoring to extricate myself from a difficulty — and I'm not going to tell you what that difficulty is or what I did with my time. I don't have to. I don't . . ."

"All right, all right," he interrupted. "Let it go at that. Can you tell me anything at all of the nature of your business difficulty?"

"No."

"Was it perhaps because your brother-in-law had turned over stock in your company to Coll as security for a gambling debt, and Coll, in turn, had turned it over to Lynk, and Harry Peavis, your competitor . . ."

He stopped at the expression on her face.

"How did you know that?" she asked.

"As it happens, I learned it from Mr. Magard, Mr. Lynk's partner."

"Then he was in on it?"

"No. He told me that he learned of it only this afternoon. He and Lynk had words about it. Magard told Lynk he'd buy him out, or Lynk could be the one to do the buying, but the partnership was finished."

"How did Magard find out about it?"

"He began putting two and two together, and finally called for a showdown with Lynk and forced Lynk to tell him."

"I see no reason for me to say anything."

"Why?"

"How do I know you aren't trying to trap me? You've been good enough to warn me that you intended to."

"The point is well taken," he said. "Now, I'm going to ask you to help me uncover some of the facts."

"What?"

"Did you know Sindler Coll?"

"No."

"You've heard your brother-in-law speak of him?"

"Yes."

"What did Lawley say about him?"

"He said that he wanted to bring Coll up to the house some night when my sister got better."

"Your sister is an invalid?"

"That's right — temporarily."

"Did Mr. Lawley mention anything about betting or horse racing in connection with Mr. Coll?"

"No. He just said that he thought we'd like Coll."

"What did you say?"

"I said nothing."

"Do I understand that you and your brother-in-law don't get along very well?"

"Oh, he's all right, but — well, you're asking me what I said, and that's what I said — nothing."

"And your sister?"

"I've forgotten. I think Carla said it would be very nice."

"Now," Tragg said, "I'm going to give you a few words, Miss Faulkner, and I want you to be thoroughly relaxed and at ease and tell me what each word calls to your mind."

"Another trap?" she asked.

He raised his eyebrows slightly. "My dear young woman, I told you that if you were guilty, I was going to trap you. The way you keep harping on the subject leads me to believe that you *are* — oh, well, skip it."

She said, "Just because you're a police officer who comes barging in here at two-thirty in the morning, I suppose that if I'm

142

not guilty, I'm to sit up all night and play charades with you."

"Hardly that. I'll take only a few minutes more of your time. Please remember, Miss Faulkner, that what I'm trying to do is to uncover the facts. If you're afraid to have me learn the truth, don't co-operate. If there's no reason why you wish to keep me from learning the truth, your co-operation will be appreciated."

"You've said all that before."

"So I have."

"Go ahead. What are the words? I suppose this is one of those association tests."

"Not exactly," Tragg said. "The association test calls for a lot of psychological stuff, holding a stop watch on a person to see how long it takes to answer. I'll be frank with you, Miss Faulkner. It's a trick which is sometimes used by psychologists. A lot of innocent words are given until the average reaction time of the witness is noted. Then words are given which might bring up a guilty train of thought. The person naturally wants to guard against betraying himself, and therefore his reaction time is a little longer on all these words."

"I see," she said, "but I'm fairly well informed. You don't need to explain elemental psychology to me."

143

"That makes it easier then for me to explain exactly what I *do* want. I want you to try and give me one word which is called to your mind by the words I will give you."

"Very well."

"And I want you to give me that word without any delay whatever. In other words, the minute I speak of a word, you come back fast with the word which you think of."

"Very well, go ahead."

"Home," Tragg said.

"Run," she snapped back at him with a slight glitter of malicious triumph in her eyes.

"Flower."

"Customer," she snapped, before the word was hardly out of his mouth.

"Orchid."

"Corsage."

"Faster," he said. "Come back at me just as fast as you can."

"Aren't I doing all right?"

"Just a little faster if you can."

"Go ahead."

"Coupe."

"Sister," she said, her voice slightly higher pitched.

"Gun."

"Accident," she almost shouted triumphantly.

Tragg's expression didn't change. "Stock."

"Transfer."

"Competitor."

"Peavis."

"Police."

"You."

"Paraffin."

"Test."

Lieutenant Tragg settled back in his chair and smiled at her. "I told you I'd trap you, Miss Faulkner," he said quietly. "Now hadn't you better sit down and tell me about it."

"I . . . I don't know what you mean."

"Oh, yes, you do. You know of the paraffin test for determining whether a person has fired a gun. Mr. Mason told you about it. It's fresh in your mind. You were so anxious to give the right answer when I came to the gun part, which you were smart enough to know I was leading up to, that you let down the bars of your vigilance just a bit after that, and walked into the trap on that paraffin test."

"Does a person have to be guilty of murder to know about that?"

"No," he said, "but when a woman has a

gun in her possession which has probably been used to commit a murder, when I find a noted criminal attorney closeted with her at two-thirty in the morning, and when, as soon as a police car drives up, she discharges the revolver, and when the first word which comes into her mind in connection with paraffin is the word 'test,' then I have pretty good reason to believe that the lawyer told her about the paraffin test, that she is a woman of intelligence, and realizes that the only way to protect herself is not by trying to get the powder *out* of her hand, but by having a perfectly legitimate excuse for showing powder *in* her hand.

"You see, Miss Faulkner, if a policeman were asked what word he associated with paraffin, he might very well say 'test,' but for a woman who is in the business of selling flowers to the public to associate paraffin with the nitrate test — well, it's just a little *too* much."

"So you think I killed him?"

"I don't know. I do know that that gun which you tried to conceal under the davenport has recently been fired twice. I know that the second shot was fired deliberately. I know that Perry Mason was here talking to you shortly before that shot was fired. It's a fair inference that he warned you that if you had fired that revolver recently, the paraffin test would furnish proof. And you were sufficiently ingenious to know what to do.

"I thought for a moment that it might have been Mason's idea, but the adroit manner in which you anticipated the simple traps which I set for you, and the swiftness of your mental reactions convinces me that you're a very clever woman, Miss Faulkner, and that you thought it up yourself."

She said, "I'm not going to make any statement. You're being unfair. I suppose now you'll arrest me."

"No. I'm not making an arrest right now. First, I'm going to check this gun for fingerprints. I'm going to compare a test bullet fired through the barrel of this gun with the fatal bullet which killed Lynk."

"You've already said it's the murder weapon."

"I think it is. You see, a ballistics expert found the bullet which had gone completely through Lynk's body. He was able to tell me the caliber, the make of shell, and certain other facts about the ammunition. I find this weapon in your possession loaded with exactly that same ammunition. *Now*, perhaps you'll tell me where you got the gun."

"At a sporting goods store."

"No, I mean tonight."

"Why — why couldn't I have had it with me all the time?"

Tragg said, "Miss Faulkner, you're trying to protect someone, either someone you love, or someone to whom you feel obligated."

"Why not myself?"

"Or," he admitted, "perhaps yourself."

"Well?" she asked.

Abruptly, Lieutenant Tragg got to his feet. "You're a very intelligent and a very clever woman. I've got just about all the information out of you I'm going to get, at least for the present. I'm taking that gun with me. By the time I talk to you again, I'll know a lot more than I do now."

"I suppose," she said sarcastically, "that in addition to my business worries, I can look forward to regular visits from the police."

"Miss Faulkner, I'll see you just once more. At the end of that next interview, I'll either exonerate you or arrest you for first-degree murder."

For a moment her eyes wavered.

He said quietly, "God knows I hated to do this. I warned you — not once but several times."

She was silent.

"I don't suppose," Tragg said, "there's any chance of getting you to look on me as a human being. After all, I'm only trying to find a killer. If you didn't kill him, you shouldn't fear me. I don't suppose there's any chance that we could be — well, friends?"

She said haughtily, "I am inclined to pick my friends for reasons other than that they happen to have been given employment on the police force."

He turned toward the door without another word.

Her eyes were frightened as she watched him, carrying the gun by a string looped through the trigger guard, quietly open the front door.

"Good night, Lieutenant," she said as he passed over the threshold.

He closed the door behind him without a word.

She stood there for a moment until she saw his car drive away, then she dashed to the telephone and frantically dialed the number of Carlotta's residence.

There was no answer.

7

Mason shamelessly used the prestige resulting from his association with Lieutenant
Tragg. The manager of the apartment house,
summoned once more to the door in the
small hours of the morning, strove to conceal her natural irritation.

"Oh, yes," she said. "The police again."

Mason smiled. "Well, *I'm* not. That is,
I'm not calling in an official capacity, although I'm trying to solve the case."

He acted as though there could be no
possible doubt of his welcome, and, en-
tering the lobby of the apartment house,
said, "I want to go up to see Coll for a
minute, and I don't want him to know I'm
on the way. You might get me a key. Then I
won't have to bother you."

Her face was swollen with sleep, her hair
stringy, her skin still greasy with make-up,
but she smiled coyly. "A key — to Coll's
apartment? I'm afraid . . ."

"Just the outer door," Mason said
hastily.

"Oh, that will be easy. I have quite a few extras. Just a moment and I'll get one."

As she walked into her own apartment, shuffling along in heelless slippers, Mason closed the door of the apartment house, and consulted his watch. He was fully conscious of the rapidity with which the precious minutes were ticking across the dial.

She returned with the key.

"Thank you," Mason said, taking the key. "I'll run up and see if he's in now. What's that apartment number?"

"Two hundred and nine."

"Oh, yes. And thank you very much. I'm quite certain we won't have to bother you but once more."

"Once more?" she asked.

"Yes," Mason said with a smile. "I think my associate, Lieutenant Tragg, will be here shortly. I'm afraid that we've pretty well disrupted your beauty sleep."

"Oh, that's all right," she said, with synthetic sweetness. "I don't mind at all. It's a pleasure to cooperate with the police — particularly when they're so nice about it."

She was getting wider awake every minute, and quite evidently enjoying her role of unofficial assistant to the police. Minutes were too precious to indulge her so Mason merely smiled his thanks and took the elevator to the second floor.

He found two hundred and nine without difficulty. A light was coming through the transom.

Mason tapped gently on the door, and almost instantly heard the sound of a chair being pushed back and of feet on the carpet. Coll opened the door. It was quite evident he had been expecting someone else. The sight of Mason disconcerted him.

"What do you want?" he demanded. "I gave you her address. It's the only one I have."

"I want to ask you some questions."

"Well, this is a hell of a time to be doing it. Who let you in the front door? Who are you? Are you a dick, too?"

"The name is Mason. I'm a lawyer."

Instantly, the man's face became absolutely void of expression. It was as though he had been able to shift a lever which threw out a clutch somewhere in his mental processes and divorced his features from any mental reaction. The look of annoyance vanished, leaving him like a graven image.

"Yes?" he asked tonelessly.

The lawyer was tall enough to look over Coll's shoulder to glimpse a part of the apartment through the half-open door. As far as he could see, there was no one else in the apartment.

Mason said, "It's going to be rather inconvenient asking questions here in the hallway."

"And it's going to be rather inconvenient having you in my apartment at this hour. Suppose you let it go until around noon."

"These questions won't wait," Mason said. "Do you know who killed Lynk?"

The eyes narrowed for a moment, then slowly widened. They were so dark that, in the light which came from the hallway, it was impossible to see any line of demarcation between pupil and iris.

"What is this, a gag?"

"You didn't know that Lynk was dead?"

"And I don't know it now."

"He was murdered, killed about midnight."

Coll, his eyes still wide, said, "What's *your* interest in it, Mr. Mason?"

Mason went on smoothly, "I am primarily interested in finding out who poisoned Miss Dilmeyer."

"Poisoned her?"

"That's right."

Coll said, "Are you crazy, or is this your idea of a joke?"

"Neither. Miss Dilmeyer's at the Hastings

Memorial Hospital right now." Mason, studying the expression of frozen surprise which was on Coll's face, added a melodramatic embellishment. "Hovering between life and death."

"How — how did it happen?"

"Someone shot him with a thirty-two caliber revolver — in the back."

"No, no. Esther."

"Oh, Miss Dilmeyer. Why, someone sent her a box of poisoned candy. Now what I want to find out is when that candy was received. Was it after she left here, or did she have it with her when she was here?"

Coll's eyes ceased to show surprise. "What do you mean," he asked, *"when she was here?"*

Mason said, "We know she was here earlier in the evening."

"About what time?"

"I can't give you the exact time. It was before eleven-thirty and after ten o'clock. We hoped you could help us on that." And Mason, with the air of a man producing credentials, took from his pocket the handkerchief which he had found in the telephone booth.

Coll stretched forth his hand mechanically, picked up the handkerchief, looked at it.

"That's her handkerchief, isn't it?"

"How should I know?"

"But you *do* know, don't you?"

"No."

Mason raised skeptical eyebrows.

"That is," Coll said, "I'm not going to identify it. It looks like the way she embroiders her initials on some of her things. I don't manage her wardrobe, you know."

"I understand," Mason said.

He heard the metallic click of the switch on the automatic elevator. The lighted cage made noise as it slid down the shaft. Coll looked over Mason's shoulder, said hurriedly, "Well, I'm sorry I can't help you any more than that. If you'll excuse me, Mr. Mason, I think I'll get to bed. I'm not feeling quite myself, and . . ."

"Oh, certainly," Mason observed. "I'm sorry that I bothered you. I can assure you I only did it because it was imperative . . ."

"That's all right," Coll interrupted hastily. "I understand. Good night, Mr. Mason."

Mason said, "Just one more thing. Do I understand you don't know whether Miss Dilmeyer was here tonight?"

"That's right."

"Then *you* weren't here in *your* apartment?"

155

"Not all the time. Look here, I'm not going to be questioned on my own personal affairs."

"When was the last time you saw Miss Dilmeyer?"

"I don't know. . . . I can't be bothered with all that stuff now, Mr. Mason. I tell you I can't help you. I don't have any idea who sent her poisoned candy. Now, if you'll excuse me, Mr. Mason . . ."

He made an attempt to close the door, but Mason's shoulder blocked him.

Coll said, with cold anger, "Mason, I don't want to get tough about this, but *I'm going to bed!*"

He put force against the door.

"Why, certainly," Mason said, abruptly withdrawing his shoulder and letting the door slam shut.

Mason walked rapidly down the corridor. The elevator was rattling upward in the shaft.

Instead of standing in front of the elevator, Mason walked some twenty feet beyond, to stand in the dimly lit hallway, flattened against the wall.

The elevator came to a stop. The doors slid smoothly open. A short, chunky man in full dress with dark overcoat and silk hat stepped out into the corridor with the rapidity of a man going some place in a hurry. He turned to the right, walking quickly down the corridor, looking at the numbers on the doors. He stopped at the far end of the corridor, looked back over his shoulder, then tapped on Coll's door.

As the door opened, light streamed out to give Mason a good view of the man's face. He had the thick neck and heavy features which go with broad shoulders and a beefy build. Mason heard Coll say, "Come in."

8

Mason tapped at the door of Mrs. Dunkurk's room in the Clearmount Hotel and went in. Morning sun, streaming through lace curtains, splashed pale orange on the counterpane. Through the open windows drifted the muffled sounds of distant traffic. Within the room, the labored breathing of the woman on the bed dominated all other sounds.

Mason said, "Good morning, Mrs. Lawley."

She managed to smile.

"How are you feeling?"

"Not . . . not good."

"You have some medicine?"

"Yes."

"Some that you took from the house?"

She nodded.

"And some clothes?"

"A few."

Talking was evidently an effort. She had held up well under the excitement of the night before, but now reaction had set in. There were dark circles under her eyes.

The lids were a bluish gray. Her lips were distinctly blue.

"Did you sleep?" Mason asked. She shook her head.

Mason said, "I'm going to get you a doctor."

"No, no. I'm — I'll be all right."

"I have one I can trust."

"He'll know who I am."

"Certainly he will. You're Mrs. Charles Dunkurk of San Diego. You're here to consult me on a very important matter. The excitement has undermined your health."

Mason crossed over to the telephone and called Dr. Willmont's office. He found the doctor was at the hospital, and left word for him to call Mrs. Dunkurk's room at the hotel. Then he went back to talk with Mrs. Lawley. "Feel up to telling me what happened?" he asked.

She said, "I had a shock."

Mason's nod was sympathetic. "Don't talk any more than you have to. I can tell you most of it. There are only one or two details I need to have you fill in."

"What are they?"

Mason said, "Your sister came to your house last night. She said enough to make it seem your husband had been in some rather serious difficulties. He raised his voice in an angry denial, and you heard him, got out of bed, and started downstairs."

"No," she said. "I was eavesdropping. Millie and Bob never did get along. I always felt that she . . ."

"I know," Mason interrupted. "Anyway, you heard enough to make you determined you were going to learn more. When your husband went out, you followed him."

She started to say something, then checked herself.

Mason said, "Lynk was murdered up in Lilac Canyon. Your sister knows something which makes her think you did it."

"That I killed Lynk?"

"Yes."

"She wouldn't think that."

"Either that, or there's some bit of evidence which makes her think the police will arrest you."

The woman on the bed said nothing, but stared past Mason with a look of almost dreamy abstraction.

"Can you tell me what it is?" Mason asked.

"No."

"Did you kill Lynk?"

"No."

Mason said, "Lynk had some stock

which he was holding as collateral security — stock in the Faulkner Flower Shops."

"No, that's a mistake. He didn't have that."

"He didn't?"

"No."

"Who does have it?"

"I do."

"Where?" Mason asked.

"As it happens," she said, "I have it with me."

Mason pursed his lips in a silent whistle. "So that's it," he said after a moment.

"What is?"

"You got that stock from Lynk."

"Don't be silly. I had it all the time."

"Remember," Mason went on, "Lynk had a partner. Clint Magard put screws on Lynk yesterday afternoon, and found out everything that had been going on."

"I don't see what that has to do with me."

"A great deal. Magard knows that Lynk had that stock with him last night when he went to Lilac Canyon."

"He's mistaken, Mr. Mason."

He said, "I'm afraid I can't help you, Mrs. Lawley. I don't defend murderers. If I handle a case, I want some assurance that my client is innocent."

161

She stirred uneasily on the bed. Mason said, "I'm sorry. I'm not going to put you to any more strain. I'd like to help you, but the way things are now, I can't."

She sighed, closed her eyes, interlaced her fingers, and said wearily, "I'll tell you . . . how it happened."

"Cut out all the trimmings, just give me the bare facts."

"After Millie left, I wanted to ask Bob some questions, but I didn't want him to know I'd been listening. I went back to my room and dressed. I heard Bob moving around downstairs. He did some telephoning. He talked with a friend of his named Coll, and he kept dialing some number that didn't answer. About eleven-thirty, I heard him go out. I hesitated for a while, wondering whether I dared. Then I decided to take a chance. My coupe was in the garage. I didn't turn the lights on. I pulled out before he'd gone two blocks and managed to follow him."

"Where?" Mason asked.

"Lilac Canyon."

"You followed him?" Mason asked.

"Without any difficulty. He was completely engrossed. I didn't have any trouble until he got up to Lilac Canyon. Then the road twisted and turned so much I couldn't see which way he turned."

"So you lost him?" Mason asked, keeping his eyes and voice without expression.

"I knew from what I'd overheard of his conversation over the phone that a man named Lynk had a place up at Lilac Canyon."

"So you went to Lynk's place?" Mason asked.

"Yes."

"How did you find it?"

"I made inquiries."

"Where?"

"There's a little store and service station, just a neighborhood affair, down by the foot of the grade. I remembered having passed that. Lights were on and a lot of cars in front. They were having a birthday celebration for the man that runs it. Of course, I didn't know that at the time. I just knew the lights were on. . . . They told me when I went in. . . . I asked him if they knew where Mr. Lynk's place was. . . . I asked indirectly."

"They told you?"

"Yes. One of the guests knew."

"And you went up there?"

"Yes."

"Now approximately how much of an interval had elapsed from the time you lost sight of your husband until you arrived at Lynk's cabin?"

"Ten minutes."

"All right, go ahead."

"I went to the cabin and knocked. There was no answer. The door was slightly ajar — open perhaps an inch."

"You went in?" Mason asked.

"Yes."

"And what did you find?"

"You know what I found — a man — I suppose it was Lynk — slumped over against a table. He was dead — shot."

"What did you do?"

She indicated that she wanted to rest. For more than a minute she lay with her eyes closed, breathing heavily. At length she said, "The shock should have killed me, but, strangely enough, I didn't have any shock — not then. . . . For some reason, I was as detached as though I had been watching a mystery play on the screen."

"You weren't frightened?"

"I seemed to be without any emotion whatever. My feelings were completely numbed. The shock — that is, the emotional shock — came later."

"Go ahead," Mason said.

"I knew, of course, that Bob had been

out there, that they'd had a quarrel, and Bob had shot him."

"How did you know that?"

"For one thing," she said, "my gun — that is, Millie's gun, the one that she gave me — was on the floor."

"How did you know it was that same gun?"

"Because there's a little corner chipped off of the mother-of-pearl handle."

"Where was the gun?"

"Lying on the floor."

"What did you do?"

"Picked it up."

"Were you wearing gloves?" Mason asked.

"No."

"Then you got your fingerprints all over it?"

"I suppose so."

"You didn't think of that at the time?"

"No."

"Then why did you pick up the gun? Did you think you might have to defend yourself?"

"No, of course not. I thought it was evidence Bob had left. I was protecting him. I . . . love him. I'm his wife."

"All right, you picked up the gun. What did you do with it?"

"Put it . . . in the pocket of my coat."

"And then what?"

"There were papers on the table," she said.

"You looked through those papers?"

"No, I didn't. But something caught my eye. The stock in the Faulkner Flower Shops."

"How did that happen to catch your eye?"

"It's distinctive, the lithography on the stock certificate. I saw this stock certificate, picked it up — saw what it was."

"And what did you do with that?"

"I put it in my purse."

"Then what?"

"Then," she said, "I walked out."

"Did you leave the door ajar behind you?"

"No, I didn't. There was a spring lock on the door. I pulled the door shut."

"Get your hands on the doorknob?"

"Yes, of course."

"And no gloves?"

"No."

"Then what?"

"I got in my coupe and drove away."

"Where?"

"I went directly home. I realized, of course, what Bob had done. I wanted to hear his side of it."

"Then what?"

"I waited for a while, and Bob didn't show up, and then I got in a panic. I began to realize what a horrible thing it all was — the numbing effect of the shock had worn off and left me with the realization of what it meant. My heart got bad. I took some of my medicine. It helped a little."

"Then what did you do?"

"I felt that I simply had to see Bob. It was the most awful feeling I've ever had in my life to realize that the man I love — the man I married — and then seeing that body . . . I guess that was the first time it really struck me — the force of it. Bob was a murderer."

She again closed her eyes and lay for a minute or two simply resting.

"Did you go anywhere in search of your husband?" Mason asked after a while.

"No. I realized he wasn't the sort to face things like that. I knew he'd run away. I felt I'd never see him again. I knew I didn't want to, and yet I knew that I loved him."

"What did you do?"

"I needed someone in whom to confide. There was only one person."

"Your sister?"

"Yes."

"Did you see her?"

167

"No. I knew I couldn't stay in that house by myself. I threw just a few things into an overnight bag, got in my car, and drove by Millie's house. She wasn't home. Her car wasn't in the garage. I knew she worked quite frequently at the office in the Broadway shop — you know, the Faulkner Flower Shops, the Broadway Branch."

"So you went there?"

"Yes."

"And she wasn't there?"

"No."

"Then what?"

"Then was when the reaction set in."

"What did you do?"

"I was pretty sick for a while. I went into the lobby of a hotel and sat down. I may have been unconscious. A bellboy asked me if I wanted some water, and asked me if I was ill. I told him that I'd overtaxed my heart a little, and if he'd let me stay there for a few minutes, I'd be all right."

"You finally got to feeling better?"

"Yes."

"So the net result of what happened is that you picked up the gun with which the murder had been committed, carried it to your house and left it on the dresser of your room with your fingerprints all over it?"

"I'm afraid so, yes."

Mason said, "Your husband seems to have skipped out."

"Yes. He would."

"Where," Mason asked, "is that stock?"

"You mean the Faulkner Flower Shops certificate?"

"Yes."

"In my bag."

Mason handed her the bag. "I'm going to take charge of that."

She opened her handbag, gave him the folded stock certificate.

The telephone rang. Mason said, "That's probably Dr. Willmont," and picked up the telephone. He said, "Hello," and heard Dr. Willmont say, "What is it this time?"

Mason said, "Another patient, Doctor."

"Violence?"

"No, I want you to come to the Clearmount Hotel in a rush. I'll be waiting for you in the lobby. Can you do it?"

"An emergency case?"

"In a way."

"I'll be right over."

"How's Miss Dilmeyer?"

"Still sleeping."

"Can't you hurry that up a bit?"

"I can, but I'm not going to. Too many people are going to pounce down on her as soon as she regains consciousness. I'm going to see she stays quiet just as long as she can. Where did you say you were? The Clearmount Hotel?"

"Yes. That's a little hotel on . . ."

"I know where it is. I'll be there in about ten minutes."

Mason crossed over to the writing desk, took out an envelope, fitted the stock certificate into it, addressed the envelope to himself at his office address, and took some stamps from his billfold.

Mrs. Lawley watched him silently.

"The doctor," Mason explained, "will be here in about ten minutes. I'll go down to the lobby and meet him. What have you done with your car?"

"I gave it to the hotel people to put in the garage."

"You have a claim check?"

"Yes."

"Give it to me. I'm going to do something with your car. I don't want you to ask any questions."

She gave him the claim check. "You know, Mr. Mason, I'm beginning to feel better. Telling you has lightened the burden. You're very competent and reassuring. There's one thing you don't need to worry about."

"What's that?"

"About *my* connection with it."

"Why?"

She said, "Bob wouldn't have enough courage to face the music, but he wouldn't let me get the blame. He'll write the police a letter or something, and tell them, and then he'll . . ."

"Then he'll what?" Mason asked as her voice faded.

"Then he'll be a fugitive."

"What's he going to do for money? Do you have a joint account?"

"He has my power of attorney. Come to think of it, most of my income has been going into *his* account. I don't know. I haven't bothered with business. The doctor told me I mustn't even think of it. I put it all onto Bob's shoulders."

"What's the status of your finances?"

"I don't know, Mr. Mason. . . . After what Millie intimated about Bob and the horses — I just don't know."

"You have enough money to pay your bill here?"

"Oh, yes. I have a hundred dollars or so in cash, and a book of travelers' checks."

"The travelers' checks are with you?"

"Yes. I always keep them in my purse."

"How many do you have left?"

"Almost a thousand dollars — I think

it's exactly nine hundred and twenty. I have some twenty-dollar checks, some fifty-dollar checks, and some hundred-dollar checks."

Mason said, "I'm going to take them off your hands."

He walked over to the writing desk, took out a sheet of hotel stationery, tore off the top of the sheet, and wrote, "For value received, I hereby sell, transfer, set over, and assign to Della Street the travelers' checks hereinafter described and the funds evidenced thereby. I hereby empower the said Della Street as my agent to sign my name to the said checks, cash them, and turn over the money to Perry Mason. I hereby appoint the said Della Street as my agent and attorney-in-fact to cash each and all of said checks at such time, place and manner as may seem expedient."

Mason took the paper over to her, said, "Read it, sign it, and then put down in your handwriting the description of the travelers' checks, the numbers, and amounts. You mention that the document is being executed for a valuable consideration. You'll want some money here to tide you over. You can't cash checks as Carlotta Lawley while you're registered as Mrs. Dunkurk. Here's some cash now, and I'll give you more as you need it."

Mason opened his wallet and counted out three hundred dollars in ten-dollar bills.

"I'm afraid I don't understand. I don't need so much money in cash, and if you're going to be my lawyer, you'll need a fee. You can take those checks as a retainer, and . . ."

"Your sister said she was going to take care of my fee. That can wait. Right now, I have a definite plan. I need these checks to put that plan in operation. I want a receipt for the three hundred dollars which I have paid you."

Once more he went over to the hotel writing desk, and drew up a receipt which he handed to Mrs. Lawley. "Now then," Mason said, taking his fountain pen from his pocket, "don't try to understand what I'm doing. Don't ask questions because I won't tell you. I'm taking you on faith. You'll have to take me the same way."

"But, Mr. Mason, why can't I simply tell my story? Why can't I . . ."

Mason interrupted her, "Circumstantial evidence is frequently the most convincing perjurer that ever took the witness stand. You've stuck your head into a noose. You were protecting Bob. It seems entirely natural to you. It won't seem so natural to someone else. You're overlooking the most damning bit of evidence in the entire case."

"What's that?"

"You stopped at that service station and neighborhood store. There was a party going on. You asked for directions to Lynk's cabin. Someone knew the way and told you. Under the circumstances, a whole flock of witnesses can identify you. You were excited, laboring under a great strain, your heart was bothering you, and your appearance must have been rather conspicuous."

"You mean that they'll think I did it?"

"They'll be so certain about it," Mason said grimly, "that unless I can do something to get them on the trail of the murderer, they'll quit working on the case just as soon as they uncover that bit of evidence."

She closed her eyes and thought for a moment, then said, "Well, why not? After all, Mr. Mason, I'm not kidding myself. This heart condition has been bad. What happened last night hasn't made it any better. Bob is — well, he wants to live, and what he did, he did for me. I can never forgive him for doing it, but I can understand

174

why he did it. Why not just let me take the responsibility?"

Mason said, "We'll find out more about that heart of yours in a few minutes. Now you sit back and relax. List the numbers on those travelers' checks, write them on the power of attorney, and then sign both of these documents. While you're doing that, I'll go down to the lobby and wait for Dr. Willmont. When I come back with him, hand me the documents and the travelers' checks. Don't let Dr. Willmont know what they are. Simply hand me the papers and the checks all folded up together."

He got up and stood looking down at her, his smile reassuring. "It isn't going to be as bad as it seems," he said, "just getting things straightened out. You'll find Dr. Willmont very competent."

He stepped out into the corridor, pulled the door closed, and went down to the lobby. He had been there less than two minutes when Dr. Willmont arrived.

"What is it this time?"

"Woman who needs a careful check-up."

"Who is she?"

"The name," Mason said, "is Mrs. Charles X. Dunkurk. She's from San Diego."

"What do you want me to do?"

"There are several things I want you to do. First, I want you to confine your questions to bare essentials. Don't ask her about herself."

Dr. Willmont shot him a keen glance. "That's rather a large order," he said.

"I think you'll realize it's reasonable when you see her."

"You mean I'm not to ask where she lives, whether she's married, or anything?"

"That's right. If you ask her any personal questions, it will call up a series of memories which will result in a nervous shock. If you feel she can stand it, go ahead. But it's your responsibility."

"All right. What else?"

"Make a complete examination. When you finish, tell me exactly what you find. I don't want you to shade it one way or another."

"What do you mean?"

Mason said, "If that woman can stand the shock of being dragged to the district attorney's office, interviewed, perhaps arrested, I want to play the game that way. If she can't, I've got to play it an entirely different way."

"All right," Dr. Willmont said, "let's take a look at her. What is it? Her nerves?"

"Her heart."

"That," Dr. Willmont said with relief in his voice, "should simplify matters a lot. I was afraid you were just making me the goat for a hide-out."

"No, this is on the square."

"All right, let's take a look at her."

They went up to Mrs. Lawley's room. Mason introduced Dr. Willmont. "Now then," he said, "Dr. Willmont is going to prescribe for you. He'll only ask questions which are absolutely necessary."

Dr. Willmont bowed and smiled.

Mason nodded, turned toward the door. "I'll be waiting in the lobby, Doctor."

It was twenty-five minutes later that Dr. Willmont walked over to sit down beside Mason. He took a cigar from his pocket, clipped off the end, and lit it.

"I'll try to give you the picture as clearly as I can without using technical terms. The average man thinks of heart disease as something very serious which will prove speedily fatal. As a matter of fact, the heart is an organ. It's composed of muscles, nerves, valves, arteries, and a heart lining. Any one of these parts is subject to derangement, and when that happens, we have a condition known as heart disease, or a weak heart.

"Now, without going into details, I can

177

tell you this: That woman's heart shows every evidence of having been badly impaired. I would say that she had an endocarditis, that she had made a partial recovery, that she had been subjected to a nervous shock which had thrown an unusual strain on her heart, that she has, therefore, suffered a temporary set back, that with proper care and treatment she will gain back the ground she has lost. I would say she was on the mend."

"How about subjecting her to the strain of appearing before the district attorney, or perhaps . . ."

Dr. Willmont shook his head. "You keep that woman right there in that hotel bedroom," he said. "Keep her quiet. Have her meals brought in. Keep her cheerful. Keep her from worrying. Give her the proper medicine, and, inside of a few days, she'll be back out. As a matter of fact, Perry, I didn't inquire as to what had happened. I can tell she's had some shock, but, in the end, the result may be beneficial."

"What do you mean by that?"

"There's a mental condition involved. There nearly always is in cardiac cases. This woman was trying to keep a stiff upper lip, but she'd been warned so much about excitement and shock and impressed with the necessity for keeping quiet that she'd resigned herself to invalidism. She was trying to be brave, but subconsciously she felt she'd never be any better. The fact that she was able to stand what she's recently been through has proven a surprise. It will be beneficial — if she gets proper care now."

Mason said, "That's all I wanted to know. She stays here."

"Who is she?" Dr. Willmont asked.

Mason said, "Make no mistake about that, Doctor. She's Mrs. Charles X. Dunkurk of San Diego."

Dr. Willmont nodded.

"What have you learned about Esther Dilmeyer?" Mason asked.

"It was veronal all right," Dr. Willmont said. "Five grams to a candy center."

"Fingerprints?"

"None."

"Any other clues?"

"None that I know of."

"When will she wake up?"

"Perhaps tonight, perhaps tomorrow morning, perhaps not until tomorrow night. I'm not going to hurry it any. She's coming out of it nicely. She's having now what you might call a normal sleep."

Mason said, "I guess that's about as

good a job as you can do for her. I'd like to talk with her, but I'd probably be trampled to death in the rush. I suppose the police and the D.A.'s office are camping on the doorstep."

"Worse than that," Dr. Willmont said. "They think the patient should be restored to consciousness, that heroic means should be used, and . . ."

"And *you* do not, I take it?" Mason interrupted.

"I," Dr. Willmont said, regarding him with twinkling eyes, "*definitely* do not."

Mason said, "I'll walk down the street a way with you."

"I have my car here. I'll give you a lift."

"No, I'm going only a short distance."

"I have a couple of prescriptions for her."

"Give them to me. I'll pay for them and have them sent up."

Mason took the prescriptions, strolled out of the lobby, watched Dr. Willmont into his automobile, and then went to the garage where he surrendered the claim check, got Mrs. Lawley's coupe and drove it down to the business district. He found a parking place, carefully polished the steering wheel, the handles on the door, the gear shift lever, and the back of the rear

180

view mirror with his handkerchief. He locked up the car and walked away. After two blocks, he dropped the ignition key through a steel grating in the sidewalk.

9

It was after ten when Perry Mason opened the door of his private office. He hung up his hat and coat, said, "Hello," to Della Street, and she brought in the mail.

"Sit down a while, Della. Let the mail go. I'm in a jam."

"What is it?"

"I don't know how bad it's going to be. You've seen the papers?"

"Yes. Is it about Lynk's murder?"

"It's connected with that."

"Mildreth Faulkner?"

"No, her sister, Carlotta Lawley."

"The paper doesn't say anything about her."

"The police aren't ready to do anything about her yet. For one thing, they think they have a better case against Mildreth Faulkner, and, for another thing, there's a lot they don't know about Carlotta yet."

"Will they find out?"

"Yes."

"When?"

"Probably today."

"I thought you were representing Miss Faulkner."

"No. I don't want her case, and I don't think she wants me."

"Why doesn't she want you?"

"Because she wants me to represent her sister, and she's smart enough to know that if I'm representing her sister, I can't have any strings tied to it."

"Does the sister know that?"

"No."

"Why are you in a jam over it?"

Mason offered her his cigarettes. She shook her head. He took one, scraped a match on the sole of his shoe, lit up, and sat for a moment gazing at the flame of the match before he extinguished it. Then he said, "She could be guilty."

"Who?"

"Either one of them, Carlotta or Mildreth."

"You mean of the murder?"

"Yes."

"Well?" she asked.

He said, "'I've always tried to represent clients who were innocent. I've been lucky. I've taken chances. I've played hunches, and the hunches have panned out. Circumstantial evidence can be black against a client, and I'll see something in his demeanor, some little mannerism, the way he answers a question or something, which makes me believe he's innocent. I'll take the case, and it will work out. I'm not infallible. My percentage should run about fifty-fifty. So far I've always been on the black side of the ledger. That's luck. Now I have a feeling things may turn, and the debits may catch up with me."

"How much difference would it make?" she asked.

"I don't know," Mason said frankly. "I do know that a lawyer can't simply sit back and refuse to take any case unless he thinks his client is innocent. A client is entitled to legal representation. It takes the unanimous verdict of twelve jurors to find a person guilty. It isn't fair for a lawyer to turn himself into a jury, weigh the evidence, and say, 'No, I won't handle your case because I think you're guilty.' That would deprive an accused person of a fair trial."

She watched him with solicitous eyes. "Are you whistling in the dark to keep your courage up?"

He grinned at her. "Yes."

"I thought so."

Mason said, "The hell of it is she's got a

weak heart. She's been through a lot, and the pump has gone bad. It will take a long spell of rest, medicine, and recuperation before it gets back into any sort of shape.

"If she's accused of crime, taken before a grand jury, interrogated by the district attorney, or even hounded by newspaper reporters, she's not going to make it."

"Make what?"

"She'll kick off."

"Oh."

After a moment, Mason said, "That's the same as a death penalty. If you know a person will die as the result of being accused — well, you just can't do it, that's all."

"What's the alternative?" she asked.

Mason rubbed his fingers along the angle of his jaw. "That," he said, "is the tough part of it. The law doesn't recognize a situation such as this. I could probably go to court and get an order putting her in a sanitarium under a doctor's care with no visitors permitted until the doctor said so. But the doctor would be someone appointed by the court. He would be more or less subject to influence by the district attorney. The main thing is that the minute I go to court I have to prove my case. I can bring in a doctor who testifies to what *he* found. The district attorney would want *his* doctor to check on mine. The judge would probably want to see her personally. She'd have to know something of the nature of the proceedings. She'd know they were going to charge her with murder when she got well enough to . . . No, I can't go ahead that way. I can't let that hang over her head."

"Where does that leave you?" Della Street asked.

Mason said, "I've got to take the law into my own hands. I've got to fix it so they can't find her."

"Isn't that a pretty large order if they really want her?"

Mason said, "That's what bothers me. There's only one way to really keep them from doing it — and at the same time accomplish something else I want."

"What's the something else?"

"I want the police to get Robert Lawley."

"Aren't they looking for him?"

"Not very hard. So far, he's just a missing witness who skipped out to save his own bacon, and the police can prove everything they want by other witnesses."

"So what are you going to do?"

Mason grinned. "I've already done it," he said. "I'm just looking back to see the

186

thing in its proper perspective — like climbing a mountain. You keep looking back to see how far you've climbed."

"Or how far you have to fall?" she asked.

"Both," he admitted.

There were several seconds of silence, then Della said abruptly, "Well, you've done it. Why worry about it?"

"That isn't what I'm worrying about."

"What?"

He said, "I've got to drag you into it."

"How?"

He said, "I hate to do it. I don't see any other way out. If you follow instructions and don't ask any questions, I can keep you in the clear, but . . ."

"I don't want to be kept in the clear," she said impatiently. "How many times must I tell you that I'm part of the organization? If you take chances, I want to take chances."

He shook his head. "No dice, Della."

"What do you want me to do?"

"Just follow instructions and not ask any questions."

"What are the instructions?"

"I have a book of travelers' checks. The name on those checks is Carlotta Lawley. Practice that signature until you're pretty good at it — not *too* good, because I want someone to get suspicious; but I don't want it to happen until after you've cashed some of the checks."

Her eyes were alert. Anxious to miss no detail of his instructions, she sat perfectly motionless, watching and listening.

Mason said, "You'll need to make a build-up on the first checks. Go home and put on your glad rags. Go to a pawn shop, get some secondhand luggage, have the initials 'C.L.' put on it. Go to a hotel, say you don't know whether you're going to get a room or be with friends, that you'll know in half an hour. Go over to the cashier's window, say you'd like to cash a check for a hundred dollars, but that you can get along with a smaller check if they'd prefer. You won't have much trouble there. Explain that you're waiting to see about getting a room.

"Then go over to the telephone, and tell the clerk you're going to be staying with friends, and go out. Do that at a couple of hotels. Then go to a department store, buy a little stuff, and cash a small travelers' check in payment. All of that is going to be easy."

"What's the hard part?"

"You'd probably better do it in a department store," Mason said. "Order about five dollars' worth of merchandise and try to cash a hundred-dollar check. The cashier will be tactful but suspicious. She'll ask to see your driving license or some identification. You look in your purse, then get in a panic, and say you left your coin purse together with your driving license in the ladies' restroom. Tell the cashier you'll be back. Now get this. As you leave, call back over your shoulder, 'There's over three hundred dollars in that coin purse.' "

"Then what?"

"Then duck out, and don't come back. Get out and stay out."

"The travelers' check?"

"You leave that with the cashier."

"And don't try to claim it?"

"No. That's where the catch comes in."

"How so?"

"The cashier will wonder why you don't come back. She'll also wonder why you're trying to cash a hundred-dollar travelers' check for a five-dollar purchase if you had three hundred dollars in your coin purse. The cashier will start looking at the signatures a little more closely. Then the cashier will call the police."

"All right," Della said. "When do I start?"

"Now."

She walked over to the coat closet, put on hat and coat, paused to powder her face, and touch up her lips in front of the mirror. "Okay, Chief. Give me the checks."

Mason smiled. "You haven't asked me whether you were going to jail."

"This isn't my day to ask questions."

Mason got to his feet, slid his arm around her waist, and walked to the door with her. "I hate to do this, Della. If there'd been anyone else I could trust . . ."

"I'd have hated you the rest of my life," she said.

"If things don't go just right, call me, and I'll . . ."

"What will you do?"

"Get you out."

"In order to do that you'd have to give away your plan of campaign."

He shook his head. "If you get pinched, my plan of campaign is all finished . . . and so am I."

"Then I won't get pinched."

"Ring me up and let me know how things are coming. I'll be anxious."

"Don't worry."

He patted her shoulder. "Good girl."

Her eyes were eloquent as she flashed him a quick smile, then slipped out into the corridor. Mason stood listening to the sound of her heels on the tiled corridor. He was frowning and thoughtful. Not until after the elevator door had clanged shut, did he walk back to his desk.

At eleven-thirty-five Harry Peavis called, and Mason told the receptionist to bring him in.

The lawyer studied the tall, lumbering figure of the florist as Peavis came marching across the office, his manner indicating a dogged determination.

"How are you, Mr. Peavis?" Mason said, and shook hands.

Peavis had been freshly shaved, massaged, and manicured. His suit showed a despairing effort on the part of the tailor to mask the toil-worn slouch of the shoulders. His six-dollar tie and fifteen-dollar custom-made shirt seemed incongruous against the weather-checked skin of his neck. His powerful, gnarled fingers circled Mason's hand and gripped — hard.

Mason said, "Sit down."

There was that in Peavis' manner which indicated a scorn of diplomacy and hypocrisy. "You know who I am," he said, and it was not so much a question as a statement.

Mason said, "Yes."

"You know what I want."

Again Mason said, "Yes."

"Do I get it?"

Mason's lips softened into a smile. "No."

"I think I do."

"I think you don't."

Peavis took a cigar from his pocket, extracted a knife from his vest pocket, carefully clipped off the end of the cigar, then raised the eyes under his shaggy iron-gray brows, and said to Mason, "Want one?"

"No, thanks, I'll stay with the cigarettes."

Peavis lit the cigar. He said, "Don't think I'm making the mistake of underestimating you."

"Thanks."

"And don't make the mistake of underestimating me."

"I won't."

"Try not to. When I want something I get it. I'm a slow-wanter. I don't see something, say all at once, 'I want that,' and try to get it. If I want something, I look it over for a good long time before I decide I really want it. When I decide I want it, I get it."

"And right now you want the Faulkner Flower Shops?"

"I don't want Mildreth Faulkner out."

"You want her to stay in and work for you?"

"Not for me. For the corporation."

192

"But you want to control the corporation?"

"Yes."

Mason said, "When Mrs. Lawley got sick, you had her husband pretty well sized up. You knew you could play on his weakness, didn't you?"

"I don't have to answer that question."

"You don't. That's right. It might save time if you did."

"I've got lots of time."

"I suppose that you knew Sindler Coll — or was it the blond lure, Esther Dilmeyer, that you had for a point of contact?"

Peavis said, "Go to hell."

Mason picked up the telephone, said to the girl at the switchboard, "Get me the Drake Detective Agency. I want to talk with Paul Drake."

While he waited, Mason glanced across at his visitor. Peavis sat with an absolutely expressionless face. He might not have heard, or, if he had, failed to appreciate the significance of the call. He puffed thoughtfully at the cigar, his deep-set eyes of glacial blue glittering frostily from beneath the bushy eyebrows.

After a few moments, the switchboard operator said, "Here's Mr. Drake," and Mason heard Paul Drake's voice on the other end of the line.

"Hello, Paul. This is Perry. I have a job for you."

"Thought you might have," Drake said. "I read about Lynk's murder in the paper and wondered if you were going to get mixed up in it."

Mason said, "A man by the name of Harry Peavis, a florist, controls a large part of the retail flower shops in the city. He's been trying to get a controlling interest in the Faulkner Flower Shops. There are three of them. It's a closed corporation. One of the principal stockholders got sick, turned the stock over to her husband. Peavis saw a chance to get that stock. I don't know whether he knew Lynk, or whether he knew some people who knew Lynk. Two people may have figured in the deal, a Sindler Coll, who lives in the Everglade Apartments in two hundred and nine, and an Esther Dilmeyer, who's in the Molay Arms Apartments. Someone sent the Dilmeyer girl a box of poisoned candy last night — filled with veronal. She ate some of the chocolate creams, and passed out. She's in the hospital now under the care of Dr. Willmont. She probably won't wake up for another twelve hours. Incidentally, Harvey Lynk had a partner, Clint

194

Magard. I don't know whether Magard was in on it or not."

"Okay," Drake said.

"Got those names?"

"Yes."

Mason said, "Get busy. Find out whether Peavis knew Sindler Coll or Esther Dilmeyer. Or he may have been working through Lynk. Anyway, investigate Peavis and find out his connection with it."

Peavis smoked in stony silence.

"Anything else?" Drake asked.

"Yes," Mason said. "Get what dope you can on Peavis. If there are any weak points in his armor, I want to know them. Put a bunch of men on it, and get results."

"Starting now?" Drake asked.

"Immediately," Mason said, and hung up.

Mason pushed the phone away from him and settled back, tilting his swivel chair to a reclining position.

Harry Peavis crossed his legs, knocked ashes from the end of his cigar, and said to Mason, "Very dramatic. It might bother some people. Doesn't bother me. It isn't going to get you anywhere."

"It's just routine," Mason said. "I'd never forgive myself if I overlooked it."

Peavis said, without reproach, "You must think I'm a damn fool."

Mason said, "I'll tell you more about that when I get Drake's report."

"When you get ready to quit kidding and act grown-up, I'll talk," Peavis said.

"All right, act grown-up."

Peavis said, "Money will do lots of things."

"It will for a fact."

"You have money, and I have money. We can both spend it."

"What are you leading up to?"

"It might be better if we saved it."

"Why?"

"You could use your money to better advantage. So could I. You've hired detectives. I can hire detectives. I can hire just as many and just as good ones as you can."

"Well?"

"If I have to put it in words of one syllable, I can show that Mildreth Faulkner went out to call on Lynk. She found the door slightly open. She went in and found the body. She found that certificate of stock. She figured that Lynk came by it wrongfully. She picked it up and went out. Now then, by the time I've finished proving that, where is that going to leave Mildreth Faulkner?"

"It's your party," Mason said. "Go ahead and serve the refreshments."

"All right. I will. It leaves her in jail. It leaves her charged with murder, and it's going to take a damn sight smarter man than I am, a damn sight smarter man than you are, to get her off. That isn't going to do either of us any good. The reason I'm interested in the Faulkner Flower Shops is because they're money-makers, and because I want Mildreth Faulkner working for me."

"Why?" Mason asked curiously.

Peavis met his eyes then, and said slowly, "That's another one of the things I want."

Mason stared thoughtfully at the blotter.

"You get my point," Peavis said.

"Yes."

"What are you going to do about it?"

"I don't know."

"When will you know?"

"I can't even tell you that."

Peavis got to his feet. "All right," he said, "I'm a businessman, and you're a businessman."

"One question," Mason said.

"What?"

"Does Mildreth Faulkner know what it is you want?"

The bluish-green eyes met Mason's with the force of a physical impact. "No," he said, "and she isn't to know until *I'm* ready to tell her. I tell her at my own time and in my own way. What I told you was simply to explain my position."

"Thanks for dropping in," Mason said.

"My telephone number's in the book," Peavis remarked. He started for the door, turned, and stared steadily at Mason. "I'm not so damn certain," he observed calmly and impersonally, "but what you and I are going to have trouble. If we do, it isn't going to be like any other fight you ever had. Good morning."

"Good morning," Mason said.

At twelve-thirty-five Della Street telephoned. "Hello, Chief. I'm in a telephone booth at the hotel. Just cashed one of the hundred-dollar checks."

"Any difficulty?"

"No."

Mason said, "I'm having my lunch sent in here. I'll be at the end of the telephone. If you have any trouble, call me. I won't leave the office under any circumstances until I hear that you're finished. Try and clean it all up by three o'clock."

"How many do I cash?"

"Four or five, then try to let someone get suspicious."

"Okay. I'll keep you posted."

Mason telephoned a restaurant to send

198

up sandwiches and coffee.

At one-thirty Della Street telephoned again. "Two department stores, twenty bucks each. Okay. I'm ready to try for a big one now."

"Go ahead. I'll be right here."

Mason called the switchboard operator and said, "I won't see any client this afternoon. Keep my line open. I'm expecting Della Street to call in. It may be important. I don't want her call to run into a busy signal."

He hung up and lit a cigarette, smoked four puffs, and threw it away. Thirty seconds later, he lit another one. He got up and began pacing the office floor. From time to time, he looked at his wrist watch.

There was a timid knock at the door of the outer office, and the switchboard operator opened the door and eased herself into the room. "Mr. Clint Magard is out there," she said. "He says he has to see you, that it's important, that . . ."

"I won't see him. Get back to the switchboard."

She backed out of the room.

A moment later, she returned. "He said I was to give you this note." She ran across the office, dropped the note into Mason's palm, and dashed back.

Mason read:

You have a duty to your client. If you don't see me right now, it will be just too bad for that client. Think it over.

Mason crumpled the note into a ball, threw it down into the wastebasket, picked up the telephone and said, "He's called the winning number. Send him in."

Magard was heavy-set, bald-headed, with a fringe of red hair around his ears and the back of his head. He wore spectacles and had a triple chin. Mason recognized him at once as the man in evening clothes he had seen going into Sindler Coll's apartment.

"Sit down," Mason said. "Start talking. I've got something on my mind. I didn't want to be disturbed. I'm nervous as hell, and I'm apt to be irritable. If what you have to say will keep, it had better keep."

"It won't keep."

"All right then, spill it."

Magard said, "I presume you think I'm a heel."

Mason said, "It's a temptation to answer that question in detail. That's not an auspicious beginning."

Magard's face was as fat and placid as a

full moon on a summer evening. "I know how you feel," he said.

"What did you want to tell me?"

"I want you to know where I stand."

"I don't give a damn where you stand."

"Your client's interests . . ."

"Go ahead," Mason interrupted.

"Lynk and I are partners in the Golden Horn."

"You mean you were."

"All right, we were. We didn't get along too well together. I didn't have enough money to buy him out at the price he wanted, and I wouldn't sell. It's a good business. I had no idea Lynk was playing around with this stuff on the side."

"What stuff?"

"Sindler Coll, Esther Dilmeyer, crooked horse racing, a sort of glorified tout service."

"But you were friendly with Sindler Coll?"

"I never saw him in my life until last night — that is, this morning — when I called on him at his request."

"Why?"

"That's what I wanted to talk with you about."

"I'm listening."

"Coll thought we should get together. He

201

said you'd be representing the murderer, that you'd try to get her off, and . . ."

"Why do you say *her?* Why not *him?*"

"Because I think it was a woman."

"What makes you think so?"

"I have my reasons."

"All right, Coll sent for you. He thought that I was going to be representing the murderer. So what?"

"That you'd be clever as the very devil and would be trying to get your client off."

"That's natural."

"That in order to do it you'd pin the murder on someone else. Coll said that he'd long been interested in the way you tried cases. He said you never tried them by simply trying to prove your client innocent. You always tried to pin it on someone else. He said that it happened too often. He figured you framed someone, and then stampeded a jury."

"And he called you at that hour of the morning to tell you that?"

"No, to suggest that we take steps to see that we were protected."

"In other words, that I couldn't pin the murder on you or him."

"That's right."

Mason said, "It's an idea at that. Thanks for giving it to me."

"You're welcome," Magard said, and smiled a little.

"So you had this conference," Mason said, "then you come to me. Why?"

"Because I thought you should know what Coll was doing. He wanted me to give him an alibi, and then he'd give me one. We'd swear we were together."

"And you decided not to play ball with him?"

"That's right."

"Why?"

"Because," and this time Magard's smile was very much in evidence, "*I* happen to have an alibi."

"And Coll doesn't?"

"Not one that he thinks would stand up."

"Will yours stand up?"

"Absolutely."

"Why did you come to me?"

"Because I want something."

"What?"

"I'm not a fool, Mr. Mason. I know that when you start fighting, you rip things wide open. I know that Lynk was mixed up in a bunch of stuff. It isn't going to look good, no matter how it's dressed up. But you can — well, you can make it look like hell."

"And you want me to pull my punches?"

"No. But if you can get your client acquitted without making a stink about my business, I'll appreciate it."

"I'm not making any promises."

"I didn't expect you to."

"Won't the police close you up anyway?"

Magard's triple chin rippled as his lips twisted into such a broad smile that the pouches of fat on his cheeks pushed his eyes almost closed. "You leave that to me, Mr. Mason."

"I intend to," Mason said. "What's your proposition?"

"I'm interested in helping you get your client off *before trial*."

"So there won't be any publicity?"

"That's right."

"What do you want in return?"

"I want you to go easy with the newspapers. If there's a preliminary hearing, I want you to leave the Golden Horn out of it just as much as you can."

"No dice," Mason said.

"Wait a minute," Magard went on, holding up a pudgy forefinger. "There's one qualifying phrase I was going to add. I want you to leave the Golden Horn out of it as much as you can if you find it will be to the advantage of your client to do so."

"That's different."

"I thought it would be."

Mason said, "I won't hamstring myself one bit, Magard. I won't make any promises. I won't . . ."

Magard interrupted him by holding up his hand, making a waving motion of the wrist as though patting the words back in the lawyer's mouth. "Now, wait a minute, Mason. Keep your shirt on. If it's to the best advantage of your client not to burn me up, you won't do it. That's right, isn't it?"

"My client comes first."

"Then the answer is yes?"

"Yes."

"All right, I'm going to keep you posted on what's going on. I'm going to give you enough dope so that I'll be valuable to you. I'll keep coming in here and telling you things just as fast as I find them out — *as long as you don't throw mud on the Golden Horn.* Now you're not under any obligation to me whatever. You can go ahead and throw mud any time you want to, *but* the minute you do that, you've quit getting any information from me."

"Let's begin now," Mason said.

"What do you want?"

"How about Peavis? Did he work

through Lynk or through Coll?"

"Through Sindler Coll and Esther Dilmeyer. He knew both of them. He got them to work on Lawley so they could pick up that stock. He knew that Lawley would never sell it unless he got in a jam. He wanted them to get Lawley in a jam."

"Did they do it?"

"Yes."

"What sort of a jam?"

"I don't know."

"Was the girl mixed in it?"

"I think so."

"And then what?"

"Well, naturally, Lawley wouldn't deal directly with Peavis. He'd have gone directly to his wife or to Mildreth Faulkner if he thought Peavis was mixed in it. He thought he was dealing with Coll's employer, Lynk. He needed money. He wanted to put up the stock as collateral. Lynk wouldn't stand for that. Lynk told him he had to turn over the stock absolutely, but, he told him, he'd hold the stock for five days, and then let Lawley buy it back if Lawley made the clean-up he expected."

"Lawley expected to make a clean-up?"

"Yes."

"How?"

"On the horses."

"And after Lynk got the stock, he wouldn't turn it over to Peavis except at a much higher price than they'd agreed on?"

For a moment, Magard looked startled. "How did you know that?" he asked.

"I'm asking," Mason said.

"I can't answer that question — not yet."

"Why?"

Magard rubbed his hands together. His manner suddenly oozed bubbly good-nature. "Well, Mr. Mason, look at it from my viewpoint. You aren't obligated to me one bit. You're obligated to your client. As long as you can serve your client's best interests by . . ."

"You've covered that already," Mason said. "You don't need to go over it again."

"Well," Magard said, "I just wanted you to see it from my standpoint. I'd be a damn fool to give you too much information all at once."

"We might make a deal," Mason said.

"Not you," Magard observed. "I know you too well, Mason. You wouldn't make any agreement in which the best interests of your client didn't come first. If you did, you'd be a damn fool. I don't want to do business with damned fools. I had one dose of that. That's enough."

"And so you intend to dole out the information?" Mason asked.

"That's right."

Mason said, "I'm going to outsmart you on that, Magard. I'm going to take the information you give me, and take a short cut. I'll be two paragraphs ahead of you before you've made three visits to this office. Then I'll raise hell with you just on general principles."

"That's a chance I have to take," Magard said.

"You don't seem very much alarmed."

"I'm not."

"Suppose you tell me about *your* alibi."

Magard chuckled. "I've told that to the police."

He got to his feet. "I've told you enough for one interview, Mr. Mason. Good afternoon."

"When," Mason asked, "will I see you again?"

"Perhaps tomorrow, perhaps not for a week. I guess that's why I'm a gambler. I like to take chance. I like to play dangerous games."

"You're playing one now," Mason told him.

Magard's diaphragm rippled in a chuckle. "I am at that," he observed, and bowed himself out of the exit door.

Mason was less nervous now. He smoked a thoughtful cigarette, sat motionless in the swivel chair back of his desk, studying the pattern on the carpet. After a few minutes, he smiled; the smile grew into a chuckle.

The telephone rang. He jumped into activity, snaking his long arm out to pick up the receiver. "Hello," he said when the receiver was halfway to his ear.

He heard Della Street's voice, high-pitched with excitement. "Chief, I've done it. The cops are looking for me."

"Get up to the office quick."

"Coming," she told him, and hung up the telephone. He waited for her, pacing the floor, smoking nervously. When he heard her quick steps in the corridor, he flung open the door, circled her in his arms, held her close to him, and patted her shoulder. "I shouldn't have done it," he said.

Della pushed her body back a little so she had room to tilt up her head to look into his eyes. "Good Heavens, what's the matter?"

"It's all right for me to take chances," he said, "but I didn't realize what it meant to me to have you out on the firing line. I'll never do anything like that again, Della — not ever."

"Goose," she said, smiling, her lips half parted.

He kissed her tenderly, then hungrily, released her, walked abruptly back to the desk, said, "That's the trouble with me, Della. When I get working on a case, I subordinate everything to that case. I become hypnotized with a single purpose. I don't take any heed of consequences. I only want results."

"That's a darn good way to be," she told him, taking off the little narrow-brimmed hat which perched jauntily on one side of her head, surveying her face in the mirror, calmly applying a touch of lipstick.

"Tell me about it."

"Nothing to it," she said. "The hotels were a cinch. The department stores were almost as easy. Then I tried for the big play — and something went wrong."

"What?"

"I don't know. I said I wanted to cash a check and pushed the book through the window. The cashier just took one look at the checks, then at me. She moved her right hand very casually. I saw her shoulder move as she pressed a button. She said, 'All right, Mrs. Lawley, just sign your name.' "

Mason's eyes glinted. "What did you do?"

"I said, 'Oh, I've forgotten my fountain pen,' grabbed the book of checks, and beat it. The cashier called out to me that she had a fountain pen, but I pretended not to hear.

"I went down in the elevator. It seemed to take ages. On the main floor there was a commotion. Two men were running for the elevators. One of them pulled back his coat to show a star. He said, 'I'm an officer — get me up to the cashier's office, quick.' "

Mason said abruptly, "Did you ever set a grass fire, and have it get away from you?"

"No. Why?"

"It gives you the damnedest feeling of surprised impotence. You think you're going to burn a little patch of grass. You touch a match, and all of a sudden a whole hillside explodes into flame. You dash madly around the edges, trying to trample out the fire, and it laughs at you."

"What," she asked, "does that have to do with what happened at the store?"

"Have you ever met Lieutenant Tragg?"

"No."

"Not quite as tall as I am," Mason said, "about my age, black, wavy hair, wears a gray, double-breasted suit, has a promi-nent, clean-cut nose with thin nostrils, and

211

when he's excited, has a habit of tilting his head back so that his chin is up and his nostrils . . ."

"That's who it was," she interrupted.

Mason sighed. "Too fast for me," he said moodily. "I tried to build a little fire to smoke someone out into the open, and the fire got away from me."

"What do you mean?"

"Don't you see what I was doing, Della?"

"Trying to make them think that Carlotta Lawley had been robbed?"

"Not robbed. Murdered."

Her eyes widened.

"It's logical," Mason said. "Her husband was held to her by one bond — the bond of money. She loved him, but to him she was merely a convenience, a meal ticket, a source of income. Mildreth always had hated him. Probably he looked on his wife's sickness as a godsend. At first, he felt it would give him an opportunity to prove himself, to show Mildreth that he could be a shrewd businessman, a careful guardian of his wife's property, a faithful custodian of her income. And things didn't go so good. Probably an initial loss which couldn't have been foreseen, something which might have happened to anyone, but which, because he was lashed by the knowledge of Mildreth's contempt, magnified itself out of all proper proportion in Lawley's mind.

"There was only one thing for him to do. He must recoup that loss. He must change it into a profit. Spurred by the whiplash of his own impatience, he didn't have time to wait for sound investments. He had to do something quick. He had to gamble.

"From the fact that he went so far, I presume that that first desperate chance turned in his favor. He gambled and won. It was that easy."

She said, "But you don't even *know* him, Chief."

"Yes, I do. You don't need to see a man, look in his face, shake his hand, and hear him talk, in order to know him. You can watch the things he does. You can see him through the eyes of others."

"But the eyes of others are distorted by prejudice."

"You make allowances for that prejudice when you know the others. You can then judge the extent of their distortion. That's the only way you can solve cases, Della. You must learn to know the characters involved. You must learn to see things through their eyes, and that means you *must have sympathy and tolerance for crime."*

She nodded.

"He had won," Mason went on, "and he was jubilant. What he didn't realize was that he was like the lion that has tasted meat. He could never go back. He could never forget that full-bodied flavor. He made other losses. He tried to recoup them by gambling, and that time he wasn't so successful."

"You mean gambling at the wheel?"

"No, not that — not at first," Mason said. "It probably was a sure-thing tip on the horses. A friend in whose judgment he had learned to have confidence, someone who apparently knew all the inside facts."

"Sindler Coll?" she asked.

"Probably."

"And then," she said, "I suppose he was decoyed along . . ."

"He got in so deep," Mason said, "that there was only one way out, and that was to plunge. He plunged and lost, and lost again. Then came the time when he took stock of the situation. For the first time he really saw the position in which he'd placed himself. And then was when they dangled the real bait in front of his eyes. Then was when they had a sure-thing tip, something that was so absolutely certain that he became hypnotized with it. But you can't gamble without money, and on this sure-thing, lead-pipe cinch which they dangled in front of his eyes, they demanded cash. So he had to raise cash, and Lynk wouldn't *lend* him any money on securities as collateral. He pointed out that the loan was for a gambling stake, that there could be too many complications. Instead, he offered to buy the stock outright, that within five days Lawley could buy it back.

"By that time Lawley was so completely engrossed with the possibilities of once more turning his losses into profits that he didn't bother to consider the cost of the step he was taking. That's the difference between a good businessman and a bad businessman. The good businessman wants something and weighs the cost of what he wants against the utility of the article he desires. That's the way Peavis plays the game. The poor businessman sees something that he wants, and he *must* have it. The price represents only an obstacle which stands between him and possession."

"But what's that got to do with Lieutenant Tragg?"

Mason dismissed it all with a gesture, smiled, and said, "I get to reconstructing

215

what Lawley must have done, and how he must have felt, and I find it too fascinating. . . . Well, anyway, Lawley's next move, once he found that he had lost out, would be — well, you can realize for yourself."

"What do you mean?" she asked.

"Murder," Mason said simply. "He wouldn't come to it all at once. It wouldn't be the first solution that would come into his mind, but he'd fling himself against the bars of his predicament as a caged animal would try out the iron bars, trying to find a weak point."

"And so he murdered Lynk?" she asked.

"Not Lynk," Mason said impatiently, "— not unless he could have gained by it, not unless he could have secured that stock."

"Didn't he?"

"If he had, he'd have gone back home. He'd have waited for his wife with an air of calm routine. No, if Lawley had murdered Lynk, it was a murder done either for revenge or to get the stock back. That would have been the purpose of it."

"But the stock has disappeared."

"If Lawley had murdered Lynk for the stock, the stock would be missing," Mason said. "Someone murdered Lynk. The stock *is* missing. That doesn't necessarily mean

Lawley did it. We must guard against that mental trap. Perhaps Lawley did it, perhaps he didn't. But what I'm getting at is that if he didn't murder Lynk, his mind would turn elsewhere."

"You mean his wife?" Della Street asked.

"Yes."

"But . . . I don't see . . ."

"His only out," Mason said. "His wife still had money. There were other securities. If she died, Lawley wouldn't have to account to her. He wouldn't have to account to Mildreth Faulkner. Her death wouldn't get him back the property he'd lost, but it would give him the stake for another gamble, and, above all, it would save his face. With a man of Lawley's type, the saving of face is the thing of paramount importance."

"But they'd certainly suspect him. He being the one to profit . . ."

"No," Mason interrupted. "That's where the man could be diabolically clever. You see, the stage is all rigged. He could commit the perfect crime. She's been struggling with a weak heart. Doctors have warned her that excitement might prove fatal. It would only be necessary for Lawley to face her with some terrific shock, something that would throw a strain on her heart, and the death would be due to natural causes."

"You think he'd do that — that any man would do that to his wife?"

Mason said, "It's done every day. Wives kill husbands. Husbands kill wives. Mind you, Della, it takes a powerful motivation to lead to murder. That's why people don't usually murder comparative strangers. The more intimate the relationship, the more devastating the results which come from it. That's why, taken by and large, more wives kill husbands than kill strangers. More husbands kill wives than kill persons outside the family."

"I didn't know that was true," she said.

"Look at your newspapers. Why, those husband-wife killings are so common, they aren't even front-page stuff. Usually there's no mystery. They're drab, sordid crimes of emotional maladjustment. A husband kills a wife and commits suicide. A woman kills her children and commits suicide."

She nodded.

"And so," Mason said, "I wanted to call Tragg's attention to what would probably happen next. I wanted him to realize that whoever killed Lynk, Carlotta Lawley was in danger. The best way I could do that was to make him think that it had actually happened."

"Why? He wouldn't protect a woman who was already dead."

"I didn't want him to protect her," Mason said. "I've already done that. I wanted him to turn the police force upside down to catch Bob Lawley, and put him behind bars."

"And that's the reason you had me cash the checks?"

"Yes."

"So that the police would think Lawley had some female accomplice, that he killed his wife and took her travelers' checks, that the accomplice is going about cashing those checks?"

"Exactly."

"Well, it worked all right, didn't it?"

Mason said, "It worked, Della, too damned well. Lieutenant Tragg was watching for it. He's looking for Carlotta Lawley, and he's asked department stores . . . Good Lord!" Mason exclaimed. "What a fool I was not to have realized it!"

"What, Chief?"

Mason said, "Carlotta Lawley must have an account at that department store where you tried to cash the check. The cashier probably didn't know her personally, but she knew her signature, and Lieutenant Tragg knew she had an account there. He'd told the cashier to notify him at once if any new charges went on the account."

Della said, "Yes, that would account for it."

Mason said, "Put your hat back on, Della. You're going places."

"Where?"

"Places. I don't want Lieutenant Tragg to come walking in and say, 'Miss Street, were you, by any chance, the person who tried to cash a travelers' check this afternoon by signing the name of Carlotta Lawley?' "

"You mean he suspects?" Della Street asked.

"Not yet," Mason said, "but he'll get a detailed description of the woman who tried to cash the check, and he'll come to the office to see me. Then, if he sees you while the description is fresh in his mind — he's too shrewd a detective not to tumble."

"So I'm to hide out?" Della Street asked, picking up her hat again and adjusting it in front of the mirror.

"No," Mason said. "We can't have that. That looks like flight, and flight looks like guilt. No, Della, we're going to go out to take some depositions or work on a case. You're going to stay on the job. I'm going to come back and forth to the office. In that way, you won't be available, yet your absence will have been explained."

Her eyes lit up. "That," she said, "won't be hard to take. I can think of half a dozen places which would be simply swell for a vacation."

He nodded and said, "And, by the way, Della, if the mailman delivers an envelope addressed in my handwriting with the return address of the Clearmount Hotel, *don't open it*. It might be a lot better if you didn't know what was inside of it."

Della Street's eyes narrowed. "Would it," she asked, "be a certificate of stock?"

"You and Lieutenant Tragg," Mason said firmly, "are getting too damn smart."

10

Della Street, moving with the swift rapidity of one who is accustomed to accomplishment, stepped into the outer office to instruct the receptionist. Perry Mason, standing by his desk, hat and coat on, was scooping legal papers into the brief ease which he intended to take with him.

Suddenly the door from the outer office was pushed open. Della entered Mason's office, jerked off her hat, tossed it to the shelf above the washstand in the closet, opened her locker, took out a comb and brush and started changing her hair.

With bobby pins held in her mouth so that her words sounded jumbled, she said, "He's there. . . . Only seen me with my hat on just for a minute. . . . Gertie looked to me when he asked for you . . . said he had to see you right away . . . claims he can't wait . . . I'll change my appearance as much as I can. . . . Wouldn't do for me to skip out *now*."

Mason watched her brush the curls out

of her hair, make a part in the middle, slick her hair down on each side. Her fingertips dipped into water from the open tap, smoothing out the curled ends.

"Lieutenant Tragg?"

She nodded, her mouth bristling with bobby pins.

Slowly, Mason took off his coat, hung it up, carefully placed his hat on a hook just behind Della, said, "He won't wait."

"I know it," she muttered. . . . "Told him you had a client but would be free in two or three minutes."

Mason opened a drawer in his desk, pulled out the papers from his brief case, dropped them into the drawer, closed it, and kicked the brief case back into the footwell under the desk.

Della swept the last of the bobby pins from her lips, looked at herself appraisingly.

"Let's go," Mason said.

Wordlessly, she vanished into the outer office, returning with Lieutenant Tragg in tow.

"Hello, Lieutenant," Mason said casually.

Tragg wasted no time in preliminaries. "Mason," he said, "I hand it to you."

"To me?"

"Yes."

"For what?"

"You caught me napping. The thing impressed me at the time. I guess it stuck in my subconscious, but I was too preoccupied to notice it. You drew a red herring across the trail, and I went barking off on a false scent."

Mason said, "Sit down, Lieutenant. Have a cigarette. My secretary, Miss Street."

"How do you do, Miss Street." Tragg took a cigarette, sat down in the big armchair, accepted Mason's match, and seemed somewhat embarrassed.

"I don't get you," Mason said.

"Last night while I was all hot and bothered about that gun Mildreth Faulkner had, and about the way she'd managed to pull the trigger so that a paraffin test wouldn't give me any results which couldn't be explained, you went out to your car. You're a damn good driver, Mason, but when you turned around, you clashed gears, raced the motor, backed and twisted."

"I must have been excited."

"Yes. Crazy like a fox. Any time Perry Mason gets so excited he fumbles the ball, it's a long, cold day. You know why the chief took Holcomb off Homicide and put me on?"

"No. Why?"

"He got tired of having you walk into court and pull rabbits out of the hat. It was up to me to make a better showing than Holcomb."

"That shouldn't be exceptionally difficult."

"Not if I'm going to let my attention get distracted while you set the stage for your little sleight of hand tricks," Tragg said ruefully.

"I don't know what you're talking about."

Tragg didn't even bother to look up from his cigarette. "Carlotta Lawley," he said.

"What about her?"

"She drove up to her sister's house. You heard the car and knew who it was. I was too occupied trying to get some damaging admissions out of Mildreth Faulkner. You walked out and stole the whole bag of tricks right from under my nose."

"What," Mason asked, "are you intimating I did?"

"Told Carlotta Lawley that I was in there, that things didn't look so good for her, that you had managed to coach Mildreth Faulkner so she'd draw our fire for a while. That idea of having the 'accidental' discharge of the gun was a masterpiece."

"Was it the murder gun?" Mason asked.

"It was the murder gun."

"Do you know where she got it or how she got it?"

"Of course. She got it from Carlotta."

"Is that what Miss Faulkner says?"

"Naturally not. Miss Faulkner acts more guilty than she would if she were guilty. She's doing her job too well. She's overacting. She's helping her sister by playing red herring."

Mason said, "You seem to have rather a high opinion of her intelligence."

Tragg met his eyes. "Damned high. She has what it takes, that woman."

"But you don't think she's guilty?"

"No. Not now."

"What's brought about the sudden change?"

"Sindler Coll."

"Don't let him fool you," Mason warned. "He sent for Magard last night. He said that if Magard would give him an alibi, he'd give Magard one. Suggested that they . . ."

"I know," Tragg interrupted. "Magard wouldn't play ball because he already had an alibi. Coll is frightened stiff. He has an idea the police might frame him for the murder if we can't turn up a good suspect.

I'm acting as though I was toying with that idea. That makes him wild. He's frantically trying to find out who really did it to save his own neck."

"I wouldn't trust him," Mason said. "I'd figure anything he'd bring in would be a phony."

"He found Mrs. Rockaway," Tragg said.

"Who's she?"

"She and her husband run the service station and grocery store down near the mouth of Lilac Canyon."

"What does she know?"

"Right around midnight a woman drove up to the place. She seemed very nervous, and her lips were a little blue. She asked several questions about streets, where different streets turned off, and did they know where a Mr. Horlick lived and wasn't there a Mr. Smith who had a place that was for sale, right near a cabin owned by Mr. Lynk?"

Tragg stopped talking to study Mason's face.

"Go ahead," Mason said.

"Well, Mrs. Rockaway walked right into the trap all right. She said there was a Smith living up near the top of the hill, but he didn't live anywhere near Mr. Lynk's place, that she didn't know any Mr.

Horlick, and she hadn't heard about Smith's property being for sale, that there were some other places around there for sale, but she hadn't heard about the Smith place being for sale."

"I suppose," Mason said, "by the time she gets to court, she'll swear this woman was Carlotta Lawley."

Tragg's smile was triumphant. "Don't worry, Mason," he said. "The Rockaways were having a birthday party. There were a dozen guests there. They all got a good look at the woman. It was Carlotta Lawley all right."

"A woman going out to commit a murder would naturally drop in on a birthday party and ask directions so they could remember her afterwards," Mason said.

The smile faded from Tragg's face. "Now then," he admitted, "there's the rub. That bothers me. But notice that she didn't walk right in and ask where Lynk lived. She beat around the bush and got the information so skillfully that if Coll hadn't given me the tip, they probably never would have reported. Of course, they might have recognized Mrs. Lawley's picture in the paper, but, without that tip, Mrs. Lawley's picture might never have been in the paper."

"How did Coll find out about it?"

"Just leg work."

"I don't think much of it," Mason said. "You wouldn't be letting Coll be such a mother's helper on your murder case that you overlooked him as a possible suspect on the candy. That *might* be Coll's game, you know."

"Don't worry. I don't have any more confidence in Coll than you have. He's in the clear on the candy business. That was sent by someone in the Golden Horn."

"How do you figure?"

"The wrapping on the box was paper they use at the Golden Horn. The address was typed on a sheet of paper of exactly the same kind they use as stationery. Then the portion which contained the type-writing was cut off and pasted on the wrapper with glue such as they use at the nightclub. Now, here's a significant clue. The glue was very hard. It had completely set. The chemist in our crime laboratory says it's over forty-eight hours old. See what that means? Whoever sent that candy had been planning the thing some time in advance, then waited for a propitious moment."

"What determined that moment?"

"When Mildreth Faulkner sent those orchids. The card dropped to the floor when the Dilmeyer girl took the orchids out of the box. The poisoner picked up the card, put it in the candy, and called a messenger."

Mason thought that over. "Sounds goofy. Have you located the messenger?"

"Oh, yes. That was easy. A woman walked up to the counter of a messenger service in the theatrical district during the rush hour, slid the box over on the counter, and walked out. The box had a note pinned on it, 'PLEASE SEND,' and a two-dollar bill attached. Evidently the poisoner watched through the window from the sidewalk to see that the box was taken by the sending clerk."

"Any description?" Mason asked.

"None whatever. It was while the place was jammed with late evening package deliveries. The clerk remembers she was a woman, and that's all."

"Or a man dressed in a woman's clothes?"

"Not likely. I figure it's a woman's crime. Poison is a woman's weapon, anyway. A man will use a gun, knife, or club."

"Fingerprints?"

"Only those of Esther Dilmeyer. The

poisoner wore gloves."

"You're certain of the identity of the paper with that at the Golden Horn?"

"Absolutely. What's more, the label with the address glued on was typewritten in Lynk's own office. His typewriter wrote the address, beyond any doubt."

Mason frowned. "Damned strange," he said. "Esther Dilmeyer could have told about that card and cleared Miss Faulkner."

"You forget Esther was supposed to go to sleep and never wake up."

"Yes. I guess that must have been it," Mason agreed, but his voice showed he was dubious. "It's a clumsy crime, and yet it isn't. . . . Lynk could have done it very easily."

"Well," Tragg said, "I think the murder is more important. This candy was sent by a woman who has access to various places in the Golden Horn. She knows very little about poisons, hates Esther Dilmeyer, and was there when the Faulkner orchids came in. The card dropped out. Perhaps Esther didn't see it. This woman picked it up. When Esther wakes up, she'll be able to give me the low-down. In the meantime, I want to get this murder cleaned up."

"Well, don't let me detain you."

"You're not," Tragg said, smiling. "I'm

just getting warmed up with you. I have some other questions to ask."

"Go right ahead," Mason said. "Take up all of my time you want. I haven't a thing to do when you leave except make out a social security report, a workman's compensation insurance report, and dig up some information the government wants on my income tax. Then I write the state about a social security question, and it will be time to go home. I wish someone could persuade the government its cut out of my income would be greater if it left me with a little time to do some work for myself."

Tragg laughed. "I figured it out from the evidence I had that Mrs. Lawley was skipping out. I decided she hadn't had sufficient time to pack up many of her personal belongings. I felt certain that she'd buy at least some articles of clothing because she'd be afraid to go back to the house.

"I thought she'd either go to her bank to get a check cashed, or to some department store where she had credit. I located her bank and her department store early this morning, and put a man on the job at each place. Now then, a short time ago a woman went into the department store where Mrs. Lawley has an account, and instead of buying something and having it charged as I had anticipated, went directly to the cashier's window to have a travelers' check cashed. The cashier gave the pre-arranged code signal which was to summon my man to the office. As it happened, I was in the store at the time. In some way, the woman got wise and beat it. Now then, Mason, here's the significant thing. *That woman wasn't Carlotta Lawley.*"

"You're certain?" Mason asked, keeping his eyes away from Della Street.

"Yes. The signature on the check is a forgery. The woman's description doesn't answer that of Mrs. Lawley at all. Mrs. Lawley is older, has heart trouble, moves slowly, and is a little flabby. This girl was young, attractive, fast-moving, quick-thinking, alert, and on her toes."

"Indeed," Mason muttered.

"You don't seem much interested," Tragg said.

"Should I be?"

"Yes," Tragg said. "Bob Lawley murdered his wife."

"I don't follow you, Lieutenant."

"His wife evidently had a book of travelers' checks which she carried in her purse. If she wanted to raise money for an emergency, she'd go cash those checks anywhere. The fact that they're in the hands of another woman who is signing Mrs. Lawley's name is a pretty good indication that something has happened to Carlotta Lawley."

Mason said, "That's a pretty tall deduction from one bit of evidence."

"Well, there's one other thing."

"What?"

"An officer tagged a car for overtime parking this morning. The officer took a look at the registration certificate. It was Carlotta Lawley's car."

"Find out anything from the car?" Mason asked.

"Yes. I fingerprinted it. I found out that someone had parked the car and then carefully wiped off every fingerprint on it."

Mason raised his eyebrows.

"You can figure what that means. *She'd* never have done that."

"Why?"

"It was her car. It was registered in her name. There was no reason for her to rub off *her* fingerprints. Her name was written on the registration certificate."

"I see."

"But, if her husband had killed her, taken the body out, and dumped it some place, and brought the car back, he'd have wiped off *his* fingerprints. That's the instinctive reaction of a guilty man these days."

"Yes," Mason said thoughtfully, "there's an element of logic there. How about that alibi of Magard's? Is it good?"

"Magard was with Peavis from right around eleven o'clock until about five minutes to twelve. Peavis remembers the time because the appointment was made at ten-thirty and was for eleven o'clock, which, of course, was rather unusual. They talked until nearly midnight, then Magard left."

"No one knows the exact time?"

"No. Peavis remembers hearing the clock strike midnight, and thinks it was just about five minutes after Magard left."

"What time did Magard get into the Golden Horn?"

"Around a quarter past twelve."

"When was the murder committed?"

"Just about midnight."

"And Coll?"

"Coll was trying to find Bob Lawley. Bob had telephoned him an SOS earlier in the evening."

"Did he find him?"

"No."

"Why not figure he was looking up in Lilac Canyon?"

Tragg said, "I'm sorry, Mason, but you

235

can't divert my suspicions. There's too much evidence the other way. For another thing, if Coll had done it, he'd have had a better explanation of what he'd done with his time."

Mason was thoughtful for several seconds, then said, "I don't like him, Tragg. I figure he had something to do with that poisoned candy. He could have had an accomplice — a woman. He's the sort who would work through a woman."

"I'm not giving him a clean bill of health," Tragg said. "I'm just using him."

"How long would it have taken Magard to get to Lilac Canyon from the place where he left Peavis, and how long would it have taken Coll?"

"From Peavis' apartment to Lynk's place, six and a half minutes. From Coll's apartment, fifteen minutes. I timed it with a stop watch."

"How long from Peavis' apartment to the Golden Horn?"

"Twenty-one minutes."

The telephone rang. Della Street said, "Hello. . . . Yes . . ." glanced at Perry Mason, and said, "I think he'll want to talk with you himself. Hold the line, please."

She gave Mason a significant glance and

pushed the telephone over to him.

Mason said, "Hello," and heard Mildreth Faulkner's voice, high-pitched with excitement, saying, "Mr. Mason, can you come at once?"

"What's the matter?"

"I must see you. I must! I must! I've heard from Carlotta."

"You have?"

"Yes. She telephoned me. Bob was with her . . . and her heart went bad while she was talking on the telephone. I heard her gasp, and I heard Bob say, 'Oh, my God,' then he hung up the telephone."

Mason said cautiously, "You're certain about the identity of the various parties?"

"Absolutely. I'd know her voice anywhere — and his, too."

"Where are you now?"

"At the Broadway Flower Shop."

"I'm engaged right at present, but I can get away within a few minutes if you'll wait there."

"Please hurry," she said. "I feel certain that you know where she is."

"I'll do the best I can," Mason said.

He hung up the phone, and Tragg got to his feet. "Well, there's no need for me to interfere with your work, Mason."

Mason said, "Get your book, Della."

"Sounds like an emergency," Tragg drawled.

"We're going to make a will," Mason said, "and we're racing against time."

Della walked along the corridor at Mason's side, her feet beating a quick tattoo on the flagged floor as she strove to keep up with Mason's long strides.

"Think he suspects?" she asked.

"Damn him, yes," Mason said. "I tell you the man's clever."

"But what will we do?"

Mason held his thumb against the elevator button. "We'll cross that bridge when we come to it."

She said, "I'm certain I didn't leave any clues that would point to you."

"It's my fault," Mason said. "I've been dealing with Sergeant Holcomb so long that I'd begun to take the police pretty much for granted. Tragg is a fast thinker. It occurred to him that she might use her credit, and he had a man staked out. If you hadn't been so quick-witted . . ."

A red light came on, and the elevator slid to a stop. Mason and Della entered, and Mason, taking a quick glance at the other occupants, warned her to silence with a glance.

"Suppose he's got a man waiting here to

shadow you?" Della asked as they reached the lobby.

"Probably. However, it won't make any difference. They'll be certain to have someone watching Mildreth Faulkner so Tragg will be notified the minute we show up."

Lois Carling, behind the counter at the flower shop, looked at them curiously as they entered. "Something I can do for you?" she asked. "Did you wish . . ."

Mildreth Faulkner came running out of the office to greet them. Lois Carling fell back to watch them with ill-concealed curiosity.

Mildreth said, "Take me to her at once, Mr. Mason. You must."

Mason said, "Your line may be tapped. Della, go into the drugstore on the corner and telephone the Clearmount Hotel. Ask to talk with Mrs. Dunkurk. When you get her on the phone, tell her who you are, ask her if she called her sister recently."

"Oh, but she did," Mildreth insisted. "I'd know her voice anywhere."

"Just check on it," Mason said to Della Street.

She walked rapidly down the aisle, and out of the door. Mason glanced curiously through the office windows at the array of potted flowers.

"Just atmosphere," Mildreth explained. "We fill our orders from . . ."

"How sound-proof is this glass?"

"It's all right."

"I notice that that girl behind the counter seems to be taking quite an interest in us."

"Oh, she's all right — a little curious, that's all."

"She was friendly with the girl that worked here before — the one who had the five shares of stock?"

"Yes."

"Seen her since she was married?"

"Oh, yes. They're great cronies."

"Then she's probably met Peavis."

"Oh, she knew Peavis long before that. Peavis used to try to pump her about the business. He'd bring her candy, and try a little flattery, but he never got very far. Peavis always tries to bribe the girls with candy. He's crude and naïve — and dangerous, and that girl is too high-powered for this job — that's all."

Mason said, "I don't want to go to your sister until I know more about this. I'm afraid it's a trap. Lieutenant Tragg is clever."

"But, good heavens, I know my own sister's voice. I heard . . ."

She broke off as Harry Peavis, accompanied by a weasel-faced, narrow-shouldered man in a flashy suit, opened the door and started rapidly toward the enclosed office.

"That's Peavis. He . . ."

"I know," Mason interrupted.

Peavis reached the door of the office, opened it, said, "I'm sorry to do this, Mildreth." He turned to the little, nervous individual at his side. "That's her."

The man stepped forward. "Mildreth Faulkner, as president of the Faulkner Flower Shops, Inc., I hand you this complaint, summons, order to show cause, preliminary injunction and restraining order."

Mildreth shrank back.

"Go ahead and take them," Mason instructed her, and to Peavis, "What's the suit?"

"Civil suit," Peavis said, watching Mildreth's face. "I don't want anyone else to show up with that stock certificate before I've had a chance to present my claims."

"What *are* your claims?" Mason asked as Mildreth Faulkner uncertainly extended her hand to receive the documents which the bright-eyed, nervous man was holding out to her.

The process server said glibly, "An action to declare a certificate of stock lost or destroyed, and have a new one issued in its place; an indemnity bond protecting the corporation and the officers thereof against any liability in the event the old certificate, properly endorsed, should be presented; a summons and order to show cause returnable at two o'clock tomorrow afternoon with the defendant corporation having the right to have a continuance at its option; a restraining order preventing the corporation from transferring the stock in the meantime to anyone except Peavis. That's all for now, Miss Faulkner."

Mildreth Faulkner seemed dazed at the barrage of legal phraseology.

"Sounds complicated," Mason said to her, "but don't worry about it."

"It's really simple," Peavis explained. "I own those shares of stock. Something happened to the stock certificate. The man who held it for me was murdered. The stock certificate seems to have vanished."

"He was your agent?" Mason asked.

"Read the papers I've just served."

Mildreth Faulkner said, "Harry Peavis, do you mean to stand there and admit that you hired gamblers to entice my brother-in-law . . ."

"I didn't hire anybody to entice anyone,"

Peavis said doggedly. "I found out that Lawley was playing the ponies, running into debt, and cutting a wide swath. I found out he'd hocked everything your sister had given him once before in order to get out of a financial jam. He'd come out on top of the heap that time, and had kept right on with his gambling. I knew that it would be only a short time before he'd do it again. Someone was going to be lucky and get this flower shop stock. I decided it might as well be me."

Mildreth said scornfully, "That was setting a trap."

"All right," Peavis said, "have it your own way. I may have baited it, but he set it himself."

Mason, looking toward the door, saw Della Street returning. "All right, Peavis, you've made your service. We'll be in court and thresh the matter out there."

Peavis said, "We might be able to work out some sort of a settlement."

"No," Mildreth Faulkner exclaimed indignantly.

Della Street, standing outside the door, took a notebook from her purse, scribbled a brief note, and entered the office. Peavis said, "Good afternoon, Miss. Looks as though I'd interrupted a conference."

"You did," Mildreth told him.

Della handed the folded sheet of note-book paper to Mason. He opened it and read, "Mrs. Dunkurk checked out. A man called for her about an hour ago."

Mason passed the message on to Mildreth.

She read it, glanced swiftly at Mason, then averted her eyes.

Peavis said, "I'm sorry, Mason, but I can't leave yet because I'm not finished."

"Why not?"

"I'm waiting for some more papers. Here they come now."

The door of the flower shop swung open. Lieutenant Tragg, accompanied by a woman in the middle forties, entered.

"No," Peavis said, "my mistake. I'm waiting for a messenger."

"What are those other papers?" Mason asked.

Peavis smiled and shook his head.

Della Street, moving closer to Mason, squeezed his arm — hard. Mason, feeling the force of those digging fingers, flashed her a smiling reassuring glance. At what he saw on her face, he turned quickly to study the woman who was being escorted into the shop by Lieutenant Tragg.

She had high cheekbones, stiff, lackluster,

black hair, and a rather wide mouth with thin lips. Her eyes looked out through large-lensed spectacles with calm competence.

"The cashier?" Mason mumbled.

"Yes."

"Any other door out of here?" Mason asked, moving casually so that he interposed his shoulders between Della and the door.

Mildreth Faulkner shook her head.

Peavis studied Mason curiously.

The office was in the back of the store. Two of its sides were the side and back walls of the flower shop. The other two sides were of wood to a height of about three feet from the floor, the rest being composed of glass windows divided into panes of about ten inches by twelve.

Tragg's progress down the long aisle of the store was utterly devoid of haste, nor did he seem to pay the slightest attention to the group that was gathered in the office. There was, in the very calmness of his unhurried approach, the element of remorseless pursuit. Nothing Tragg could have done could have been more calculated to upset the nerves of anyone who had a guilty conscience than the even-paced, ominous rhythm of his march.

He reached the door of the office, held it open for the woman. She entered.

Tragg said, "Hello, you seem to have a little gathering here."

No one said anything.

Tragg said, "I had a matter I wanted to take up with Perry Mason, and I . . ."

"That's the woman!"

The startled voice of the cashier, raised in high-pitched accusation, showed that Lieutenant Tragg had not advised her of what he expected to find.

Mason slipped his arm protectingly around Della Street's shoulders, held her to silence by the pressure of his hand on her arm. "Meaning the woman who tried to cash the travelers' check?" he asked conversationally.

"Let's let Miss Street tell about that," Tragg said.

Mason shook his head. "There's no need for that."

Tragg's face showed his irritation.

"That is she," the cashier said in a lower voice this time, but with the ring of conviction.

"Of course it is," Mason remarked casually.

"I'm afraid," Tragg said, "that unless Miss Street can explain matters, I'll have to arrest her."

"On what ground?"

"Intent to defraud and forgery."

Mason said, "You'd better read up on your law before you get your fingers burnt, Lieutenant."

Tragg was unable to keep some of the irritation out of his voice. It was plain that he had hoped to get some admission directly from Della Street. "You're a pretty good lawyer, Mason," he said. "I don't know much law. I'm just a dumb cop. I suppose that there's a section in some law some place providing that your secretary can walk into a store, say she's Carlotta Lawley, and forge Carlotta Lawley's name to a check on which she gets money without violating any law in the world."

Mason said calmly, "In the first place, Della didn't get any money. In the second place, she didn't say she was Carlotta Lawley. She said she had a travelers' check she wanted to cash. Get this, Tragg. A travelers' check is different from any other check. There isn't any such thing as a valid travelers' check issued without any funds. The checks are paid for when they're purchased, and the money remains on deposit."

"And I suppose it's quite all right for her to go around signing Carlotta Lawley's name," Tragg said.

Mason casually took the folded paper,

which Carlotta Lawley had signed, from his pocket. He handed it to Tragg.

Tragg read it, and for a moment, there was a grim tightening of the line of his lips. Then an expression of triumph glittered in his eyes. He folded the document and pushed it down into his pocket. "All right, Mason," he said, "the swap is satisfactory."

"What swap?"

"You've got Della Street out of it at the expense of getting yourself in."

"In what way?"

"This document shows on its face that it's either a forgery or else you had a contact with Carlotta Lawley this morning."

"I had that contact," Mason said. "The document was signed then."

"You realize what that means?"

"What?"

"You've been aiding and abetting in the commission of a felony."

"I don't think she committed any felony."

"Well, she's a fugitive from justice."

"I wasn't so advised."

Tragg strove to keep his temper. "Well, you're advised of it now. I want her."

"For what?"

"*I* think she's committed a felony."

"What?"

"Murder."

"That," Mason said, "is different."

"All right. Now, I'm going to ask you where she is."

Mason said, quite calmly, "I don't think she's guilty, but, in view of your statement, I have no recourse except to tell you that last night while you were talking with Mildreth Faulkner, I heard a car drive up. I went out to the curb. It was Carlotta Lawley. I realized that the condition of her health made it imperative that she get immediate rest, that the strain of a long questioning might prove fatal. I instructed her to go to the Clearmount Hotel, register as Mrs. Charles X. Dunkurk of San Diego and wait for me, getting as much rest as she could in the meantime."

Lieutenant Tragg's eyes showed surprised incredulity which gave place to hot anger. "Dammit, Mason," he said, "is this a story you're making up out of whole cloth in order to put me off on a false trail? If it is, I'll swear out a warrant for you myself and drag you down to headquarters."

"You won't drag me anywhere," Mason said ominously.

"Where is she now?" Tragg asked. "Still at the hotel?"

Mason shrugged his shoulders and said, "I've told you all I know. When I entered this office, *so far as I knew*, Mrs. Dunkurk was still in the Clearmount Hotel."

A uniformed figure came hurrying through the door of the flower shop. A messenger boy walked rapidly to the office, jerked the door open, and said, "Is Mr. Peavis here?"

"Here," Peavis said with a grin.

The boy handed him some folded documents which Peavis in turn handed to the process server. The process server said, "Mr. Mason, I hand you herewith a subpoena *duces tecum* ordering you to appear in court at the time set for the restraining order, and order to show cause in the case of Peavis versus Faulkner Flower Shops, Inc. You'll note that by this subpoena you are ordered to bring into court any stock certificate in your possession or under your control, covering stock in the defendant corporation issued to one Carlotta Faulkner who subsequently became Mrs. Robert Lawley."

The anger left Tragg's face. He smiled, and the smile broadened into a grin. He looked across at Peavis approvingly, then at Mason. "And what a sweet fix that leaves *you* in, Counselor!"

He strode over to the telephone, dialed a number, and said, "This is Lieutenant

Tragg of Homicide. I want some action. Get through to Sergeant Mahoney. Tell him to sew up the Clearmount Hotel. Do it fast. Get a couple of radio cars on the job first. There's a Mrs. Dunkurk of San Diego registered there. I want her, and want her bad."

He slammed up the telephone, said to the cashier, "That's all, Miss Norton. You can return to work."

He gave Mason one quick glance. For a moment, the triumph in his eyes changed to sympathy. "Tough luck," he said, "but you asked for it." Then he pushed open the door of the glass-enclosed office and all but ran down the long length of the store.

11

Lieutenant Tragg and Detective Copeland sat in the back room of the drugstore. Bill Copeland was reading one of the *True Detective* magazines he had filched from the newsstand. An old-timer, Copeland took everything in stride. He frequently said, "I've seen 'em come, and I've seen 'em go. I've been publicly praised for catching 'em, and given hell for letting 'em slip through my fingers. It's all in the day's work, and you can't work yourself into a stew over it. You gotta take 'em as they come."

Lieutenant Tragg was nervous. At frequent intervals he peered through the square of colored glass which enabled the prescription clerk to look out into the brightly illuminated store. Tragg carefully studied every customer, and between times nervously paced the floor or stared at the doors as though he could entice his prey simply by visual concentration.

The drug clerk, putting up an order of capsules, said, "No need to worry, Lieutenant. I know him personally. If he comes in, it'll be for a prescription. You'll have all the time in the world."

Bill Copeland looked up from his magazine, surveyed Tragg with the expression of interrupted contentment with which a grazing cow studies a moving object. He seemed utterly incapable of understanding Tragg's nervousness.

For the second time within five minutes, Tragg consulted his wrist watch. "Well, I can't waste time waiting here. After all, it's just a hunch."

Copeland marked his place in the magazine with the nail of a stubby, thick forefinger. He said, "I'll handle 'm, Lieutenant. Keep in touch with a phone, and you'll know it within thirty seconds of the time I get him."

Tragg said wearily, "I guess I'll have to do that. I did want to . . ." He broke off as a man in a pinstriped, double-breasted blue suit walked quickly into the store, shook his head at the young woman who moved up from the cigar counter to wait on him, and said, in a voice plainly audible to those in the back room, "I want the prescription clerk."

Tragg said to the clerk, "Take a look at this, will you?"

The clerk looked over Tragg's shoulder, then gently pushed him aside in order to get a better view.

"That's your man," he said simply.

Tragg released a long-drawn sigh. Copeland started to close the magazine, then thought better of it, and laid it face down on a corner of the table used for filling prescriptions, leaving it spread open at the page he had been reading.

Tragg gave his orders quickly. "I'll slip out the side door. Give him his prescription right away. Don't keep him waiting. As soon as he starts for the door, Bill, you come out from behind here and start following. You have your car outside. I have mine. Between us he shouldn't get away, but don't take any chances. As soon as we get an idea where he's headed, I'll move on ahead. If he sees you, or starts acting as though he was suspicious, toot your horn twice. At your signal, I'll swing in front, and we'll grab him for the pinch."

Copeland said, "Okay."

The drug clerk walked out to the counter, came back in a few moments with the number of a prescription. "This is a re-fill on a powerful heart stimulant. He's in a hurry, says it's very urgent."

Copeland adjusted his tie, straightened his coat, and patted the bulge over his hip. The prescription clerk said, "Take that magazine along if you want, officer," and Copeland picked it up quickly. He rolled it up, shoved it under his left arm, holding it clamped against his side, and said, "Thanks." Lieutenant Tragg slipped out of the shipping door into the alley, and walked around to the front of the drugstore, and got in his car.

He had less than two minutes to wait. His man jumped into a Buick sedan, and stepped on the starter. Behind him, Copeland, carrying his magazine clamped under his arm, appeared in the door of the drugstore, walked over to the curb, and wormed his broad shoulders in behind the steering wheel of a close-coupled coupe.

Tragg was the first away. In the rear-view mirror, he saw the Buick pull out next, and from the manner in which the car edged over to the left, decided the driver was going to make a left-hand turn.

Tragg gave a left-hand signal, and ventured timidly into the intersection, waiting for oncoming traffic to get past. This brought the car behind him up close to his bumper, and he saw his man hold out a left arm. Behind the Buick, Bill Copeland, plugging along in his light coupe, made the turn without bothering to signal.

Bob Lawley was in a hurry. He kept trying to get ahead of Tragg's car, and at last Tragg let him go, following along closely behind. Copeland, taking his cue from the changed conditions, tagged along behind Tragg's car.

Tragg, watching the man in the car ahead, saw that he apparently gave no thought of being followed. A dozen blocks down the street, Tragg had an opportunity to pass again. Lawley fooled him with an abrupt right-hand turn shortly after that, but Tragg, heading on down the street, saw that Copeland was tagging right along behind their quarry.

Tragg swung his car to the right at the next intersection, went to the first cross street, looked up and down the street, saw no sign of the cars he wanted, drove another block, and saw Copeland's coupe parked in the middle of the block. There was no sign of the blue Buick.

Tragg swung his car into a sharp turn and drove up on the other side of the street, parking his car almost directly opposite the coupe.

Copeland got out and sauntered across.

"Get him?" Tragg asked, trying to keep

nervousness out of his voice.

Copeland said casually, "He's in there."

"Where?"

"That bungalow. He swung his car into the driveway, and drove up to the garage. I stopped my car fifty feet back and waited to see if he was wise. I don't think he was."

"Where'd he go?"

"Inside, through the back door."

It was that quarter hour after sunset when cool shadows merge imperceptibly into gathering dusk. Here and there in the block, lights had been switched on, but there were no lights showing in the windows of the little bungalow.

Tragg said, "Take the rear. Knock on the door, and tell him you want to look at the wiring. Say you're from a radio station, and there's a leak somewhere in the neighborhood. I'll go to the front door and ring the bell hard just about the time you're doing the talking. That should bring him up to the front. He'll probably leave the back door unlocked. You walk in. If I have any trouble, grab him, and when you grab him, make a good job of it."

"Okay," Copeland said.

Tragg gave him ten seconds, then walked down the sidewalk, climbed the steps to the porch of the dark bungalow, and listened. He could hear steps and thought he could hear the rumble of voices in the back.

Tragg pressed the bell button, waited a second, then pressed it again, long, insistent rings.

Steps approached the door. Tragg loosened the gun in his shoulder holster. He was adjusting his tie when the door opened and Bob Lawley said, "What do you want?"

"You've just moved in, haven't you?"

"That's none of your business."

"Oh, yes, it is, brother. I'm from the assessor's office."

"Well, this place is furnished, and was rented furnished. I don't want to be interrupted, and . . ."

Tragg looked past Lawley, saw Bill Copeland cat-footing down the corridor, just a few steps away.

"I haven't any time to talk now," Lawley finished, and started to close the door.

Tragg put out a foot, nodded over to Copeland, and said, "All right, Lawley, you're under arrest."

The man recoiled, then, as Tragg pushed through the door, turned to run. The maneuver brought him up against Bill Copeland's thick bulk. Copeland clamped his arms around Lawley, holding him as in a vise. "Okay, Lieutenant," he said without emotion.

Tragg slid handcuffs from his hip pocket, and, as Bob struggled to free himself, snapped them about his wrists.

At the bite of cold steel on his skin, Bob Lawley flung into a wild, hysterical struggling, and Tragg, grabbing the chain of the handcuffs, gave it a jerk which brought a bone-crushing pressure to bear on his prisoner's wrists.

As Lawley subsided, white-faced with pain and futile rage, Tragg said, "Let's be reasonable about it, Lawley. Where's your wife?"

"In . . . in the bedroom."

"All right," Tragg said, "let's go talk with her."

"What are you going to say to her?"

"I want to ask her some questions."

Lawley was panting from his struggle. His eyes were sullenly defiant. "You can't."

"Why not?"

"She . . . she can't talk with anyone."

Tragg thought for a moment, then said, "I'll tell you what I'm going to do with you, Lawley. I'm going to give you a break."

Lawley's face showed sneering disbelief.

"I'm going to take these bracelets off you," Tragg went on, "and we're going into that bedroom. You're going to introduce Copeland here and me as a couple of buddies of yours you happened to meet while you were gone for the medicine. You're going to tell her that I'm a man who can help you out of your scrape, and then you're going to keep quiet, and let me ask questions."

"What do I get out of it?"

"I'll see that you get a square shake, no framing, and no rough stuff."

"That's not enough."

"All right, I've offered you the easy way. I'll do it the hard way if I have to."

"How's that?"

"You'll find out. You aren't in any position to drive a bargain."

Bill Copeland stooped down to pick up the detective magazine which had fallen to the floor when he circled Lawley with his arms.

Lawley cursed, launched a savage kick at Copeland's face. Copeland took the kick on his shoulder, started to straighten up, then changed his mind, picked up the magazine, and doubled his right fist.

Tragg stepped between them. "Not now, Bill. Just watch him. Keep him quiet."

Copeland sighed, let his fist turn into

fingers which brushed off the shoulder of his coat, and said, without rancor, "Okay, Lieutenant."

He shoved Lawley back against the wall, hard. Tragg took the package of medicine from Lawley's pocket.

"What are you going to do?"

"Shut up," Copeland said, taking a handful of Lawley's shirt near the collar, and twisting the cloth.

The second door Tragg tried opened into a bedroom. The drapes were drawn over the window, and it was dark. Tragg stood just inside the door waiting for his eyes to adjust themselves to the dim light of the room. He could hear the sound of labored breathing. A woman's voice said gaspingly, "Bob."

Tragg stepped forward. "Your husband asked me to rush this medicine to you," he said.

"Where . . . where's he?"

"He had to attend to some business which came up unexpectedly. He'll be along directly, but he wanted you to have the medicine right away."

"Yes . . . an emergency medicine. . . . Took all I had last night . . ."

Tragg found a light by the bedside. He switched it on, and unwrapped the medi-

261

cines. There were two of them, one an ampule to be crushed and inhaled, the other in capsule form. The directions said to take two and thereafter to take one every thirty minutes until six had been taken, then one every two hours.

Tragg got her a glass of water from the bathroom, gave her the capsules. She swallowed them one at a time. He found a towel in the bathroom, crushed the ampule, and held it under her nose.

For five minutes nothing was said. Tragg stood there watching her. She began to breathe easier. She smiled bravely up at him, and her mouth had the flabby-lipped look of weakness. She said, "It's a complication of various troubles. I suppose a lot of nerves are mixed in with it. I feel better now. Thank you."

Tragg helped himself to a chair, drew it up by the bedside. "I don't want to bother you, Mrs. Lawley," he said.

She looked at him in some surprise.

"I have to ask you a few questions. I don't want you to strain yourself."

"Who are you?"

He said, "I'm trying to get at the truth of what happened last night. I suppose you know that a warrant has been issued for your husband."

"I — I didn't know."

"If your husband is guilty or if you're guilty," Tragg went on, "I don't want you to talk. If you're feeling too weak, I don't want you to try. But if you can answer just a few questions, it will help a lot."

"Help who?" she asked.

"Your husband, if he's innocent," Tragg said. "Your sister, you."

She nodded.

"But," Tragg hastened to assure her, "don't misunderstand me. You don't have to answer my questions."

She moved uneasily on the bed.

From the hallway where Copeland was holding Lawley, there was the sound of a brief struggle, a half-articulate cry, then silence.

Tragg thought fast. "The furniture men moving in some things that your husband bought."

"Oh," she said, and settled back against the pillow, her eyes closed. "He shouldn't have bought anything. He's just an overgrown boy. Money burns a hole in his pocket." Her face had a creamy tint to the skin, but beneath that was a faint bluish tinge which Lieutenant Tragg had seen before.

As her breathing grew easier, she seemed

to sleep, and Tragg tiptoed from the room to where Copeland was holding Lawley. Lawley's left eye was swelling shut. "Take him out to the car, Bill," Tragg said.

Copeland took a tighter grip on the shirt collar. "Okay, buddy," he said. "You heard what the boss said. On your way."

There was no more resistance left in Lawley. He permitted himself to be taken out to the car quietly.

Tragg went back to the room and sat down.

He had been there some fifteen minutes when Mrs. Lawley opened her eyes. "I feel better now. Are you a doctor?"

"No," Tragg said. "I'm an investigator."

"You mean a private detective?"

"I work for the people," he said.

She thought that over for a while. "You mean the police?" she asked.

"Yes."

She started to struggle up to an upright position. Tragg said, "Take it easy, Mrs. Lawley. I'm only trying to find out the truth."

"What do you want to know?"

He said, "How did it happen that you took that stock certificate from the scene of the murder, Mrs. Lawley?"

Her eyes closed again. "What murder?"

264

Tragg clenched his hands. He took a deep breath, hesitated for a moment, then said, "We've found that stock certificate in Mr. Mason's possession. He says you gave it to him."

She opened her eyes — coughed. "Did he say that?"

"Yes."

"It was his own suggestion."

"I know. Why did you take it?"

"It was mine."

"Was Lynk dead when you walked into the house?"

"Yes."

Her eyes opened, then fluttered closed. "I'm very tired," she said.

"Suppose you rest for a few minutes," Tragg suggested.

She said drowsily, "You seem like such a nice man. Clean-cut. I'd imagined the police were different. . . . You're . . . nice."

He said, "Take your time, Mrs. Lawley." His hands clenched until his fingers ached. Sweat made his skin moist. Damn it, he was only doing his duty. When you were solving crimes, you had to play the game according to the way the cards fell.

"A very . . . nice . . . gentleman . . ." the woman on the bed muttered.

12

As they walked out of Mildreth Faulkner's flower shop, Della Street said to Mason, "Do you suppose he knew all the time it was I who tried to cash that check?"

Mason said, "He evidently had considered that possibility. He trumped my ace — damn him!"

They got in Mason's car. Mason started the motor and savagely slammed the gear shift back.

"But *how* did he know?"

"He put two and two together. He knew I was trying to cover Mrs. Lawley until the situation clarified itself. He knew that I was trying to drag Bob Lawley into it."

"Suppose Lawley will talk if Tragg finds him?"

"Him?" Mason asked, contempt in his voice. "Of course, he'll talk. I know the type. He'll make a grandstand about what he's going to do and what he's not going to do. He'll tell them they can beat him up, or drag him with wild horses, but that he won't say a word. Then he'll cave in, spill everything he knows, and try to pin the crime on his wife."

"Why did Mrs. Lawley leave the hotel?"

Mason said, "You're full of questions, aren't you? . . ." He slid the car to a stop at a street intersection and motioned to a newsboy who was selling the late afternoon papers. "Here's where we answer this one."

"You mean she advertised?"

"No," Mason said. "He did, the heel!"

"I thought you kept all papers away from her."

"I told her not to read any. But giving instructions to a woman is something like putting money on roulette."

The signal changed. Mason handed the boy a quarter, grabbed the newspaper, passed it over to Della, and said, "Look in the ad section under TOO LATE TO CLASSIFY."

Mason drove slowly through traffic while Della Street looked through the newspaper. "Here it is," she said.

"What does it say?"

"Carla, I am worried sick with anxiety for you, dearest. Telephone Grayview 6-9841, and tell me you are all right. That's all I want to know. I can face the music if only you are all right."

"How's it signed?" Mason asked.

"Honeybunch."

"The Goddamn rat!"

Mason saw a chance to put his car in a parking place at the curb. He slid in just beyond a fire plug, and said to Della, "There's a drugstore on the corner. Ring up the Drake Detective Agency. Tell them we want to know who has the telephone listed in Grayview 6-9841."

"Couldn't I handle it by calling the number of perhaps . . ."

"No," he interrupted. "Drake specializes in that sort of stuff, and knows how to go about it."

"How long will it take him?"

"Not over a few minutes probably."

"Then do we go to the office?"

"We do not. We'll pay Mr. Sindler Coll a visit."

Della jumped out of the car, walked rapidly into the drugstore, and was back in a few minutes. "He's on the job," she reported. "And there's a report ready on the other stuff you wanted. I took it down in shorthand."

"All right, read it to me as we're driving along."

He started the car. Della opened her notebook, translated the various pothooks and slanting lines. "Peavis, a tough, two-fisted go-getter. Got into the flower business in nineteen-twenty-eight. Before that had been in the liquor-running business. In the liquor business he had some trouble with a man named Frank Lecklen who tried to hijack some of his stuff. Lecklen went to the hospital with two bullets in him, and wouldn't talk. He told police he shot himself. Peavis called to see him, hired a special nurse and doctor. Lecklen is now going under the name of Sindler Coll.

"Esther Dilmeyer, twenty-three, a come-on girl at a nightclub and gambling joint. She's had a spotted history. Was discharged from the Rockaway Candy Company for insubordination and violation of rules — seems she ate more candy than her wages amounted to. Worked for the Ease-Adjust Shirt Company. The boss' wife got jealous. Then Irma Radine, who works at the Golden Horn, met her. Irma had worked at the Rockaway Candy Company with Esther. Irma introduced her to Lynk. Lynk fell for her, and Esther went to work on a percentage basis. Coll started getting friendly about three months ago. She fell hard. Lately Coll has been cooling off. He's supposed to have another flame, but he's being very secretive about it. No one seems to know just who she is.

"Paul Drake said that was all he had to date, but he was keeping on the job. Does any of that help, Chief? That is — much?"

Mason said, "I'm damned if I know, Della. It'll all fit in. . . . That Irma Radine knows her pretty well. . . . That's why she acted so queerly when Tragg was questioning her at the Golden Horn. Think she's pretty strong for Coll, too. He seems to be a riot with the ladies. . . . We'll see what we'll see." And Mason devoted his attention to the traffic.

At Sindler Coll's apartment house, Mason said, "You'd better wait here, Della," and rang the bell opposite Coll's name.

There was no answer.

After a few minutes, Mason rang the bell marked MANAGER. The buzzer signaled the door was open. Mason entered, crossed the lobby, turned to the left, and rang the bell on the door of the manager's apartment. Mrs. Farmer opened the door and, as she recognized him, smiled effusively. She had evidently spent some time at a beauty parlor, and her tightly girdled, snappily dressed figure was entirely different from the loose-muscled body which had been wrapped in a kimono the night before.

Mason let her see his surprise. "You look — *wonderful!*"

Her smile barely missed being a simper. "You're so nice," she said coyly.

Mason traded on the prestige of his former association with Tragg.

"Do you know where Coll is?"

"I don't think he's in."

"Neither do I. He doesn't answer."

"I don't think he's been in all day. He went out around nine o'clock this morning."

"Alone?"

"No. Some man was with him."

"You don't know where he went?"

"No."

Mason said, "I'd like to take a look in his apartment. You have your passkey?" He made the request sound quite casual, and she didn't even hesitate.

Coll's apartment was a typical example of the moderate-priced, furnished, single apartment. The room had nothing about it to reflect the personality of its tenant, nor was there anything in the apartment which would give a clue as to where Coll might have gone.

"Maid service?" Mason asked.

"Yes. He has a daily maid service."

"And evidently hasn't been in since the maid cleaned the place up."

The manager looked at the cleanly polished empty ash trays and nodded.

"Smokes cigarettes?"

"I believe so, yes."

Mason noticed a telephone on a stand near the door, and casually noted the number. It was Southbrook 2-4304.

Once in the apartment, the manager seemed to realize that the situation might prove embarrassing should Coll return, and that she had carried her co-operation rather far. "Of course," she said hurriedly, "I presume you just wanted to look in. I wouldn't want to have you touch anything."

"Oh, no," Mason assured her. "Certainly not. I thought perhaps he might have — well, that something might have happened to him."

"I understand."

She made it a point to hold the door open for him, and coughed significantly when she thought he had remained long enough in the apartment.

Mason took the hint, walked out into the corridor. She pulled the door shut. "I suppose," she said, "it won't be necessary to mention anything about this to Mr. Coll. He wouldn't like it."

"You don't need to mention it to anyone," Mason said, "because I won't."

In the lobby, he thanked her again, said, "I have a call to make," and went into the booth. He dialed the number of the Drake Detective Agency. Paul Drake had been called out, but his secretary was on the job, and said, "We have that number for you, Mr. Mason."

"What is it?"

"The phone's listed in the name of Esther Dilmeyer in the Molay Arms Apartments."

Mason gave a low whistle, then said, "Okay. Thanks."

He hung up and called Dr. Willmont at his office. "Where's that patient, Doctor?" he asked.

"Which one, the heart case? I haven't seen her since this morning. I didn't know you wanted . . ."

"Not that one. The poisoned-candy case, Esther Dilmeyer."

"Still in the hospital."

"You're certain?"

"Yes."

"She wouldn't have left the hospital without your knowing it?"

"Absolutely not."

Mason said, "You wouldn't, by any chance, be letting someone slip something over on you, would you?"

"Not in that hospital," Dr. Willmont said positively. "It's run like clockwork. As far as I know, Miss Dilmeyer is still sleeping. I left word that I was to be notified if there was any change in her condition."

"Perhaps you'd better call up and verify the fact that she's there."

Dr. Willmont said testily, "I don't need to. She's right there. I'll take the responsibility for that."

"She couldn't have sneaked out and . . ."

"Not a chance in the world. . . . I'm going out there just as soon as I finish with my office patients. You can call me then if you want."

"How soon will that be?"

"Just a minute," Dr. Willmont said. "I'll see how many more patients are in the office. . . . Oh, nurse. How many have you? . . . Two. . . . Hello, Mason. It shouldn't be over fifteen or twenty minutes."

Mason said, "All right, I may meet you there."

He hung up and rejoined Della Street in the car. "Got the address on that number, Della."

"Where?"

"Esther Dilmeyer, Molay Arms Apartments."

"Why, I thought Miss Dilmeyer was still unconscious. . . ."

"She is," Mason said. "She's sleeping it off. Dr. Willmont says so."

"Then what does it mean?"

"It means," Mason said, "that I've been asleep at the switch."

"I don't understand."

Mason said, "It stuck out like a sore thumb. We knew that Bob Lawley was playing around. We knew that he'd been mixed up in an automobile accident, and that Esther Dilmeyer had been with him. She's a come-on blonde at a nightclub. She was working with Lynk and Sindler Coll, and they, in turn, were working for Peavis. There was big money involved. Get the sketch? Naturally, she wouldn't have been standoffish with Bob Lawley."

"You mean he had a key to her apartment?"

"Sure, he did," Mason said, "and when he realized he was in a jam last night, he naturally *went to her apartment*. It was the logical thing for him to do. I should have known that's where he'd have been. He's just the type who would want some woman to stroke his forehead and comfort him and tell him that it was all right, that she'd sacrifice herself for him and a lot of that hooey."

"Yes," Della Street said thoughtfully, "everything he's done seems to fit in with that type."

Mason said, "Well, he went to the apartment. Esther wasn't there. So he made himself at home. He telephoned the ad into the newspaper, charged it to Esther's telephone, and sat back and waited. Carlotta violated my instructions, got a newspaper, read it, and looked in the classified ads. She and her husband may have had some understanding like that. In case of any emergency, they'd communicate with each other that way. Some people do. Or she may just have looked. Anyway, she got the telephone number. She called Bob."

"And what did he do?"

"Went out and got her."

"And then what?"

Mason stroked the angle of his chin. "There's the rub. Let's go out there and see what we can find, Della."

They drove out to the Molay Arms. Mason tried the bell of Esther Dilmeyer's apartment, got no answer, and called the manager. He said, "You'll remember me. I was out here last night on that poisoning matter. . . ."

"Oh, yes," she said, smiling.

"I want to get some things out of Miss Dilmeyer's apartment, and take them to her at the hospital. Would you give me the passkey please?"

"I can hardly do that," she said, and hesitated, "but I'll go up with you while you get what you want."

Mason said, without letting her hear any change in his voice, "That's fine."

They walked up the stairs. Mason managed to slide in close to the wall, so that when she started to open the door, he was the first into the room.

There was no one in the apartment.

"What was it you wanted?" the manager asked.

Mason said, "Her nightgown, bedroom slippers, and some of her toilet articles. I'm rather helpless about those things, but I guess I can find them."

"Oh, I'll be *glad* to help! I think there's a suitcase in the closet. Yes, here it is. You can just sit down if you wish, and I'll get the things together. How is she?"

"You're very kind. She's doing nicely."

Mason looked around the apartment. Police had dusted articles — the telephone, the table, some of the doorknobs — for the purpose of bringing out latent fingerprints. The ashtrays were well filled with cigarette stubs. Mason had no means of knowing whether the police had remained in the apartment for some time collecting evidence, and had left those cigarette ends, or whether they were indicative of a more recent occupancy.

While the manager was neatly folding garments into the suitcase, Mason made a detailed study of the cigarette ends. There were three of the better-known brands. One brand invariably had lipstick on the stubs. The other two did not. There were only four stubs which Mason found with lipstick on them. There were fifteen of the second brand, and twenty-two of the third. Those had evidently been consumed by nervous smokers. Seldom had more than half of the cigarette been smoked before it was ground into the ashtray.

"Was there anything else?" the manager asked.

"No, thank you. That's all. You don't know whether anyone's been in here today?"

"Today? No, I don't suppose so. No one said anything to me."

"The police?"

"No. They finished last night — early this morning."

"Maid service here?"

"Once a week is all. She takes care of her own apartment save for the regular weekly cleaning."

"When's that due?"

"Not until Saturday."

"Thank you very much," Mason said. "I'll tell Miss Dilmeyer how helpful you were."

He walked out of the apartment house carrying the suitcase, tossed it into his car, and said to Della Street, "Well, I guess I go to the hospital."

It was twenty minutes past five when he reached the hospital. Dr. Willmont was already there.

"Patient still here?" Mason asked.

"The patient," Dr. Willmont said, "is still here. She wakened about forty minutes ago, and while she's a little groggy, her mind is clearing up very nicely."

"Do the police know?"

"Not yet."

"I thought they left instructions they were to be notified as soon as . . ."

"They did. I left instructions that I was to be notified of the patient's condition, that no information was to be given to anyone else, and that no visitors were to be received until I personally had checked up on the patient's condition. In a hospital, the doctor is boss."

"That," Mason said, "makes it nice. How much trouble would it cause if I sneaked in and had an interview before the police arrived?"

"It would cause a lot of trouble," Dr. Willmont snapped. "You know that as well as I do. It would put me on a spot, and would make trouble for the hospital. Within certain limitations I can countermand police instructions when I personally assume the responsibility and the orders are for the good of my patient."

Mason smiled. "I appreciate your position and your professional ethics, Doctor. Now, you know the mechanics of the hospital, and I don't. How can I get to see Esther Dilmeyer in advance of the police *without* making trouble for you?"

"You'd have to do it without my knowledge," Dr. Willmont said promptly.

"And without the knowledge of the nurse in charge?"

"That's right."

"And, I take it, your instructions have been very definite that nothing like that is to happen?"

"That's quite correct."

Mason lit a cigarette.

Dr. Willmont said, "I'm going to call the special nurse into the office for the purpose of checking over the patient's chart. The patient is in room three-nineteen. Then I'm going to send the nurse down to the dispensary to get a prescription filled. It will be a prescription that will take a little time to fill. Sorry I can't let you interview the patient, but it's absolutely impossible. Step this way, please."

He took Mason's arm, escorted him over to the desk, and said to the woman in charge, "There are to be absolutely no visitors for Miss Dilmeyer until after the police have talked with her, and the police aren't to talk with her until I give permission."

"That's my understanding," the woman said.

Dr. Willmont turned to Mason. "I'm sorry, Mr. Mason, but you see how it is."

Mason said, "Thank you, Doctor. I appreciate your position. Will you tell me when I *can* see her?"

Willmont shook his head in crisp negation. "I have nothing whatever to say about that, sir. I am acting merely as physician. As soon as it becomes advisable for her to see *anyone*, I will notify the police. From that point on, unless her health becomes affected, I will have absolutely nothing to say about who sees her. That will be entirely in the hands of the authorities. Good evening, Mr. Mason."

"Good evening, Doctor," Mason said, and turned away.

Dr. Willmont marched with quick, springy strides toward the elevator. Mason started toward the door, detoured into a telephone booth, waited until the attendant at the desk had her back turned, took the elevator to the third floor, and located Esther Dilmeyer's room. He walked on past and waited in the corridor until he saw the nurse go out carrying a card fastened to a clip. Then Mason walked down the hallway and pushed open the swinging door.

Esther Dilmeyer was sitting up in bed, sipping hot coffee. She looked up at him and said, "Hello."

"How are you feeling?" Mason asked, walking over and sitting on the edge of the bed.

"I don't exactly know yet. Who are you?"

"I'm Mason."

"Perry Mason?"

"Yes."

"I guess I owe you one. You saved my life, I understand."

"I did the best I could," Mason said.

"Did you have a hard time locating me?"

"I'll say."

"Gosh, that hot coffee tastes good. I guess I'm caught up on my sleep for quite some spell now."

"Any idea who sent you the candy?" Mason asked.

She hesitated.

"Go on," Mason prompted.

"Well, I thought it — you know, I'm not accusing anybody, but . . ."

"Go on."

"Well, I met a young woman who seemed very much on the up-and-up — a squareshooter, you know."

"That was Miss Faulkner?"

"Yes, that was Miss Faulkner. She runs the Faulkner Flower Shops."

"I know."

"Well, she told me I should have some orchids to go with my dress and sent them over."

"Then what?"

"I got fed up with the whole business and decided to walk out on the joint. I was working over at the Golden Horn. They call me a hostess, but, you know, I was supposed to give the boys the spending urge, and let the management cash in."

Mason nodded.

"Well, I went on home, and when I had been there about ten minutes, a messenger brought a box of candy. I opened the candy, and it had exactly the same sort of card in it that had been with the orchids."

"The same handwriting?" Mason asked.

"I didn't make a detailed comparison, but it certainly looked like it, and the initials and everything were the same."

"So what did you do?"

She smiled and said, "Chocolate creams are one of the things I am fondest of. I was feeling low, and I went to town."

"Then what?"

"I began to feel funny. I thought at first it was just drowsiness, but I had a one o'clock appointment at your office so I knew I couldn't go to sleep. If it hadn't been for that, I'd probably have drifted off without knowing anything about it, but, as it was, I kept fighting myself trying to keep awake. And then suddenly I realized it wasn't just being sleepy. I'd been doped. I had an awful time keeping myself awake long enough to talk with you over the telephone. I can just remember hearing your voice. I kept trying to talk, and I'd go to sleep in between words, wake up with an awful effort, and then I'd go off to sleep again. It seemed as though I'd been talking with you for ages and ages."

Mason said, "Now this is highly important. It may make a lot of difference. When you were talking with me, I heard a crash. It sounded as though you'd fallen out of the chair to the floor."

"I can't help you on that, Mr. Mason. I can't remember."

"I understand that, but when we arrived at your apartment, the telephone was lying on the floor, and *the receiver had been put back into place.* Now I can't figure that you'd have put the receiver back."

"I don't think I could have."

"Then someone must have been in your apartment, *after* you became unconscious and before I arrived."

"And found me lying on the floor and gone off and left me without trying to help?"

"Yes."

"That would be strange," she said. Her eyes glinted with sudden anger.

"It would. Who else has a key?"

She took a deep breath. "Now get me straight, Mr. Mason. I'm no tin angel, but I strut my stuff at the nightclub. When I go to my apartment — well, I'm all finished. That's the only way a girl can play my racket and have any self-respect left. No one at the nightclub even knows where my apartment is. Irma Radine's one of my best friends there. Even she doesn't know. The men who run the place don't know."

"You're certain?"

"Abso*lute*ly, posi*tive*ly, definitely certain."

"Robert Lawley for instance?"

"Robert Lawley," she said, with a grimace of distaste, "a weak-chinned, spineless wise guy. He's what the boys call 'half smart.' He thinks he's so la-de-da he's a pain in the neck."

"How did you meet him? Did Peavis ask you to get in touch with him or . . ."

"Sindler Coll," she said.

"You've known Sindler?"

"Not so very long."

"Well?"

"I was strong for Sindler," she said. "I liked him. He got tired of me, and tried to run another jane in on the business when it looked as though there was going to be some gravy. I didn't like that."

"I don't blame you."

She said, "You're certainly asking a lot of personal questions," finished the coffee, and Mason took the empty cup and set it with the saucer on the table.

"What has Sindler said about me?" she asked, after a moment.

"Nothing."

She studied her fingernails. "You're certain of that?"

"Why, yes, of course. What is there to say?"

"Oh, you know, a man can shoot off his face sometimes. I thought perhaps he'd make some crack about the poison."

"No. He seemed very solicitous."

"He's a good egg, at that."

Mason took the handkerchief he had found in the telephone booth from his pocket. "Is this yours?"

She looked at it. "Why, yes. Don't tell me I've been leaving handkerchiefs around in men's apartments."

"That handkerchief was found in the telephone booth at Sindler Coll's apartment house."

She said, "I wasn't going to tell you about that."

"About what?"

"I went around to Sindler's apartment before I went home — that is, I tried to, but — well, he came out in the hallway to meet me. He told me he was having a business conference and couldn't see me, to come back later on."

"That was right after you left the Golden Horn?"

"Yes."

"And what did you do?"

She said bitterly, "A business conference! His hair was mussed, his tie was pulled over to one side, and there were lipstick smears on his mouth."

"So what did you do?"

"I went right back downstairs. I tried to telephone Miss Faulkner. I was willing right then to go out to Bob Lawley's place and spill everything. I wanted to tell her I'd go to your office and tell you the whole business — everything, or do anything else she wanted."

"Did you get her?"

"No. There was no answer at her house, or at the shops."

"Then what?"

"So then I gave up telephoning and went to my apartment, and the messenger came with the candy, and you know the rest."

Mason said, "It'll help a lot if you don't remember having seen me. You're not supposed to have visitors. The police are narrow-minded about such things."

"Oh, the bulls," she remarked contemptuously. "Well, don't worry about them."

"You'll tell your story to them just as you told it to me?"

She laughed. "Don't be silly. I'll tell the cops nothing. I don't beef to the cops. I handle my own grief."

Mason said, "Get any ideas about Miss Faulkner out of your head. She wanted you as a witness. If you'd been poisoned and died, she'd have been in a fix. Your candy was sent by some other person."

"Okay, Mr. Mason. If you say so, it's so."

Mason said, "Good girl. Here's luck for a speedy recovery."

"Recovery, hell!" she cried. "I'm so recovered right now, I'm going to wreck this joint if they don't let me out."

Mason laughed. "You can talk with Dr. Willmont about that."

"Who's he?"

"The doctor I got for you."

Her eyes suddenly became suspicious. She looked at him and looked around the hospital. "Say," she said, "I can't afford to hang around in any private rooms in a hospital. I should be in a ward."

Mason said, "The room and the doctor are on me."

"Say, you're a white guy! Maybe there's something I can do for you some day."

"Who knows," Mason said, and tiptoed out of the room.

Seated in his car, Mason opened the afternoon newspaper, and read through the classification of "HOUSES FOR RENT — FURNISHED." He listed five which were not too far from the Molay Arms Apartments. From a telephone booth, he started calling the numbers given in the ads, stating in each instance that he was interested in a furnished house, asking briefly about the rent, and so on. When he called the third number, a woman's voice advised him rather shortly that the house had been rented that afternoon, and the phone connection was unceremoniously severed.

Mason stopped at the office to pick up Della Street. "Want to take a ride?" he asked.

"Yes. Where?"

"Out to a furnished house."

"To see whom?"

"Carlotta Lawley perhaps."

"Why the perhaps?"

"Because," he said, "Lieutenant Tragg has had all the police facilities working for him. My only chance was to play a hunch. I couldn't compete with his organization when it came to following a cold trail. I had to jump at conclusions and take a short cut."

"And you think he's beaten you to it?"

"If he hasn't, it's his own fault."

Della sat beside him in the automobile without so much as asking a question until Mason arrived at the address of the furnished bungalow which had been for rent.

An ambulance was just pulling away from the door. Ahead of the ambulance, in a police sedan, Lieutenant Tragg was shifting his car into speed. Two men sat in the rear seat. Their close-huddled stiffness indicated that one was handcuffed to the other.

Mason didn't even bother to stop at the bungalow. He kept right on going.

"Now where?" Della Street asked. "Police headquarters?"

"No," he said, "dinner."

"Aren't you going to try to get her out?"

Mason shook his head. "The more I stir things up now, the more damage I do. If I'm tugging one way and Lieutenant Tragg is pulling the other, with Mrs. Lawley in between . . ."

"But, Chief, couldn't you keep her from talking?"

"What about?"

"Oh, her connection with — well, perhaps what she said to you, or . . ."

"Evidently," Mason said dryly, "you didn't notice the expression on Lieutenant Tragg's face as he went by us."

13

Judge Grosbeck, who had called court to order, looked over the tops of his spectacles at Perry Mason. "Peavis versus Faulkner Flower Shops," he said. "Order to show cause. Frank Labley of Labley & Cutten for the plaintiff. Perry Mason for the defendant."

Frank Labley said promptly, "Ready for the plaintiff," and glanced across to where Mason was seated.

"And ready for the defendant," Mason announced. Labley showed surprise. "You mean you're ready to go ahead on the order to show cause?"

"Exactly."

"The notice," Judge Grosbeck pointed out to Mason, "was rather short. You are entitled to one continuance as of course, Counselor."

"Thank you, Your Honor. I'm ready."

Labley slowly got to his feet. "Your Honor, this comes as a distinct surprise. It's almost a matter of routine where the notice given is so short for the defendant to ask for a continuance."

Mason seemed completely disinterested.

Judge Grosbeck said sternly, "However, Counselor, this is the time heretofore fixed for the hearing of the restraining order. The defendant is entitled to one continuance as of course, but you are not."

"I understand, Your Honor, but — well — Very well, I'll do the best I can."

"Have any counter affidavits been filed?" the judge asked Mason.

"No, Your Honor. I wish to call some witnesses."

"How long will it take you to examine those witnesses?"

"Some little time."

"The court would much prefer to have the matter submitted upon affidavits and citation of authorities."

"In view of the short time which was given me, Your Honor, it was impossible for me to prepare affidavits."

"I will grant you a continuance to enable you to prepare counter affidavits."

"But I don't care for a continuance, unless counsel stipulates the restraining order may be vacated in the meantime."

Frank Labley jumped to his feet, his manner indicative of indignation. Judge

Grosbeck waved him down to his chair, smiled, and said, "Very well, Mr. Mason. The court will hear your witnesses."

Labley said, "I'll stand on my affidavits and the verified complaint in the case for my showing, except that I may bring matters out on cross-examination of the witnesses called — and, of course, reserving the right to put on rebuttal testimony."

"Very well. Proceed, Mr. Mason."

Mason said, "I will call the plaintiff, Mr. Peavis."

Peavis slouched forward, held up his right hand, was sworn, and took the witness chair, where he sat regarding Mason with calm hostility.

"You're the plaintiff in this action, Mr. Peavis, are you not?"

"Just a moment," Labley interposed, jumping to his feet before Peavis could answer the question. "Before any questions are answered, I feel I am entitled to know whether Mr. Mason has produced in court the stock certificate in response to the subpoena *duces tecum*."

Mason bowed. "I have it here," he said.

"That identical stock certificate?" Labley asked with surprise.

"Yes."

Labley sat down, looking rather dazed.

A plain-clothes officer, sprawled out in the back row of chairs, suddenly straightened, got to his feet, and tiptoed from the courtroom.

Judge Grosbeck regarded Mason with thoughtful silence. "Answer the question," Mason said to Peavis.

"Yes, I am."

"You have been trying to buy an interest in the Faulkner Flower Shops for some time, have you not?"

"I have."

"You knew that certain shares of stock were in the name of Carlotta Lawley?"

Peavis said, "Let's save a little time, Mr. Mason. I'm a businessman. I saw there was an opportunity to get control of the Faulkner Flower Shops. I knew that I couldn't buy the stock myself. I approached Harvey J. Lynk and told him that I'd pay a certain price for the stock if he could get it."

"Mr. Lynk was a gambler?"

"I don't know, and I don't care. I made him an offer for the stock. He advised me that he had it."

"Ah," Mason said, his tone showing his interest. "Let's have that answer again, Mr. Reporter."

The court reporter read the answer.

Peavis said hastily, "That is, I told Lynk to get it for me."

"Now, let's get this straight," Mason said. "Did you tell him you'd pay a certain price for the stock, or did you tell him to get it for you?"

"Objected to as incompetent, irrelevant, and immaterial. It's argumentative, a mere question of splitting hairs."

Mason smiled. "It goes to the very gist of the action, Your Honor. If Mr. Peavis hired Mr. Lynk to get the stock for him as his agent, then the moment the stock came into Mr. Lynk's possession, the title really vested in Mr. Peavis."

Peavis nodded vehemently.

"If, on the other hand," Mason went on, "Peavis merely communicated to Lynk a willingness to pay a certain price for the stock, and Lynk secured the stock, but it was taken from his possession before he had an opportunity to sell to Mr. Peavis, then Peavis had no title. He *hoped* to buy the stock. He had no vested interest in it."

"That," Judge Grosbeck ruled, "is quite apparently the law."

Peavis said, "I'll gladly answer that question. I hired Mr. Lynk as my agent to get the stock."

"Did you give him any money?"

"Well, no. But he knew that the money would be forthcoming as soon as he had reason to call for it."

"You mean as soon as he had the stock?"

"Well —" Peavis glanced at his lawyer, then glanced hurriedly away.

"Can't you answer that question?" Mason asked.

"No," Peavis said. "The stock didn't have anything to do with the payment of money. I hired him to get the stock. He was my agent."

"And how did you get in touch with Mr. Lynk?"

"Objected to," Labley said promptly, "as incompetent, irrelevant, and immaterial. It makes no difference how the plaintiff made his contacts with Mr. Lynk. The point is that he made them."

"Of course," Judge Grosbeck pointed out, "this man is an interested party, a hostile witness, a . . ."

"If the court please," Mason interrupted, "I'll be willing to hold the question in abeyance. I don't wish to take up the court's time unduly. I'll let Mr. Peavis step down, and call another witness.

"If subsequent testimony makes it necessary for me to examine Mr. Peavis on this point, I think the court will appreciate, by that time, the relevancy of the facts sought to be ascertained."

"I don't see how they can be pertinent," Labley insisted.

"Well, we'll let the question remain in abeyance as Mr. Mason has suggested," Judge Grosbeck ruled.

Mason said, "Step down, Mr. Peavis. Mr. Coll, will you take the stand please?"

Sindler Coll took the oath as a witness with manifest reluctance. He seated himself on the witness stand and appeared very ill at ease.

"How long have you known Mr. Peavis?" Mason asked as soon as the witness had given his name and address to the court reporter.

"Almost ten years."

"What's your occupation?"

"I'm a sharpshooter."

"What do you mean by that?"

"Well, I speculate. Wherever I see an opportunity to make a profit, I pounce on it."

"And Peavis approached you with reference to getting this stock?"

"He did."

"And you had a conversation with Peavis as to what he was ready to do, and then you passed that word on to Mr. Lynk, did you not?"

"That's right."

"In other words, you acted as the go-between?"

"Yes, sir."

"Now, so far as you know, Mr. Peavis never met Mr. Lynk."

"Well . . . yes, sir, I think he did."

"Oh, he did?"

"Yes, sir."

"When?"

"Well, that was the night of the tenth."

"The night Lynk was murdered?"

"Well, he was murdered early — no, I guess that's right. I guess he was murdered at midnight of the tenth."

"How do you fix the time?"

"On what I've read in the papers."

"When did you last see Mr. Lynk?"

"On the afternoon of the tenth."

"About what time?"

"About three o'clock."

"What did he tell you?"

"He said he wanted to talk with Peavis."

"And what did you do?"

"I got Peavis."

"Did you sit in on the conversation?"

"I did."

"What was discussed?"

Coll shifted uncomfortably in his chair. "Well," he said, "Lynk told Peavis that he could get, or was getting the stock, and for Peavis to be there with his money to pick it up."

"What do you mean by there?"

Coll said, "I didn't mean to say that. I just meant that Harvey wanted Peavis to have the money all ready."

"In other words, without the money, Lynk didn't intend to deliver the stock?"

"I don't know. I . . ."

"It's hearsay anyway," Labley said.

Mason shook his head. "No, Counselor, it calls for a conclusion of the witness. I'll withdraw it."

Judge Grosbeck smiled.

"So," Mason said musingly, "Lynk told Peavis to be there with the money."

"That's right."

Labley cleared his throat. "I am wondering if the witness understood that question."

"We'll have it read to him," Mason said.

The court reporter read the question and answer, and Coll said quickly, "No, no, that isn't right. I didn't mean that. I didn't say that Lynk told him to be *there* with the money. That's a word that the lawyer has put into my mouth."

Mason smiled. "In any event, Mr. Coll," he said, "Lynk wanted Peavis to be out there at Lilac Canyon with the money, didn't he? Whether it was to be given as compensation for services performed or as the purchase price of stock?"

"I . . . well . . . I don't know what he wanted. I can't remember exactly what *was* said."

Mason said, "That's all."

Labley said, "In *Lilac* Canyon, Mr. Coll?"

Coll jumped as though a pin had been stuck into him. "No, no," he said. "I didn't mean that. No, certainly not. He didn't say anything about Lilac Canyon. He just said — well, he said Peavis had better get his dough ready because the stock was in his hands."

"Did Mr. Lynk tell Mr. Peavis where to bring that money?" Labley asked.

"No, sir. He did not."

Labley hesitated a moment, glanced dubiously at the frankly skeptical face of Judge Grosbeck, and said, "That's all."

The judge settled back in his chair and half closed his eyes, knowing that the preliminary having been laid, it would be good procedure for Mason to clamp down on Coll and rattle him with a running fire of cross-examination before he could recover his self-possession. The judge, who had every intention of giving Mason plenty of leeway, composed his features into an expression of judicial impassivity.

But Mason surprised everyone by saying, "That's all, Mr. Coll."

Coll avoided Labley's eyes as he left the witness stand.

"Esther Dilmeyer," Mason said.

She came forward and held up her hand to be sworn — very chic in a soft black wool jacket dress and a tiny black hat. The only touch of color was a gold pin at her throat and a matching bracelet on her left wrist.

Judge Grosbeck looked at her curiously. Labley seemed somehow ill at ease.

Mason said, "Your Honor, this young woman has just been discharged from the hospital. An attempt was made to poison her, and her recovery was . . ."

"The court understands the facts generally," Judge Grosbeck said, looking at Esther Dilmeyer.

She gave her name and address to the court reporter, and smiled at Mr. Mason.

"Miss Dilmeyer," Mason said casually, "you're acquainted with Mr. Peavis?"

"Yes."

"And have been for some time?"

"Well, a few weeks."

"And, at his suggestion, you made it a point to become acquainted with Mr. Robert Lawley?"

"No."

"No?" Mason asked, raising his eyebrows.

"No, sir."

"Who did make that suggestion?"

Labley jumped to his feet. "Your Honor," he said, "it is incompetent, irrelevant and immaterial."

Judge Grosbeck looked at Mason curiously. "I'd be glad to hear from you on that point, Mr. Mason," he said.

Mason's manner was quietly matter-of-fact. He said, "Your Honor, there are two horns to the dilemma which confronts the plaintiff in this action. Either he can appear in the role of holding himself out as a prospective purchaser for the stock in question, in which event the fact that Lynk died before the stock could be sold leaves the plaintiff with no right whatever to maintain his action; or he can adopt the position that Lynk was his agent, purchasing the stock for the plaintiff in this action. That is the only theory on which he can maintain the present action. The minute he adopts that theory, he becomes responsible for everything which Lynk, *as his agent,* did. Now then, in place of seeking a legal remedy, he has sought an equitable remedy. He is now in a court of equity. It is an axiom that he who comes to equity must come with clean hands. If the actions of his agent, Lynk, in obtaining this stock were such as to shock the conscience, if he employed illegal means, or if he resorted to entrapment, fraud, or oppression, then the plaintiff is not entitled to an equitable remedy because the courts of equity won't let him cross the threshold."

Judge Grosbeck nodded.

Labley jumped to his feet. "Why, Your Honor, I don't understand such to be the law."

"It is," Judge Grosbeck said, with calm finality.

"But Peavis didn't know anything about what Lynk was doing."

"If Lynk was his agent," Judge Grosbeck said, "it was his duty to notify Peavis of everything he was doing. His actions were for the benefit of Peavis. Peavis can't accept the benefit of those actions and refuse to assume the responsibility."

Labley sat down slowly, cautiously, as

though after what had happened, it would not have surprised him if the chair had suddenly been jerked out from under him.

Mason said, "I'll put it this way, Miss Dilmeyer. You were told that Mr. Lawley owned some stock in a company which Peavis wanted. You were, therefore, asked to be nice to Lawley and . . ."

"No one told me any such thing," she said.

Mason raised his eyebrows. "They didn't?"

"No."

"How did you get acquainted with Mr. Lawley?"

"I was told to cultivate his acquaintance."

"By whom?"

"By Mr. Coll," she said.

Labley smiled triumphantly.

"And Peavis had nothing whatever to do with Mr. Coll. Coll was not *his* agent," Labley said to the judge.

"That," Judge Grosbeck remarked, "remains to be determined."

"Now then," Mason said, "on the night that Mr. Lynk was murdered, did you hear any conversation between Lynk and Coll about the stock?"

"Not that night. That afternoon."

"What did Mr. Lynk say?"

"Lynk said that he had the stock in his possession, that if Peavis wanted to get hold of it, he'd have to meet him before midnight with cold, hard cash, that Lynk didn't want any checks. He wanted cash."

"You heard that conversation?" Mason asked.

"Yes, sir."

"Where did it take place?"

"In the Golden Horn."

"That's a nightclub?"

"Yes, sir."

"Where in the Golden Horn did the conversation take place?"

"In an upstairs — well, in an upstairs suite of rooms."

"And after you had heard that conversation," Mason said, "an attempt was made on your life, is that right?"

"I object," Labley shouted. "That is an attempt to prejudice the court. It is a plain intimation that my client has resorted to an attempted murder in order to enable him to buy a few shares of stock in a corporation."

Judge Grosbeck looked at Mason with cold, judicial impassivity. "Counselor," he asked ominously, "is it your contention that there is a connection between the two events?"

Mason said, "If the court will bear with me, I think that perhaps we will uncover some rather valuable evidence. The question relates only to a point of time. Your Honor is far too experienced to be influenced by insinuations which are not substantiated. It is not as though a jury were trying the case."

Judge Grosbeck nodded. "Proceed," he said.

"Answer the question," Mason ordered Esther Dilmeyer.

She said, "Yes," in a very low voice.

"Now," Mason said, "your manner of eating candy is rather unusual, isn't it? You eat piece after piece, very rapidly?"

"Well, perhaps, yes."

"How long have you had that habit?"

"Ever since I was nineteen when I had a job in a candy factory," she said with a smile.

"You learned to eat candy in that way while employed there?"

"Yes," she said, and laughed lightly. "The girls weren't supposed to eat any of the candy on which they were working, but — well, I didn't like the boss and thought I was getting even with him."

"I see," Mason said with a smile. "Now, someone must have known of your propensities for eating one piece of candy right after another."

She hesitated, then shook her head.

"You'll have to speak up," Judge Grosbeck said, "so the court reporter can take down your answer."

"No," she said, "I don't think anyone — oh, perhaps some of my intimate friends . . . Irma Radine for one."

"And is Mr. Lawley an intimate friend?"

"No," she said quickly.

"Mr. Coll?"

"No," and her tone was sharply defiant.

"Mr. Magard, perhaps?"

She said, "Mr. Magard is an employer rather than a friend."

"But he knows about the way you eat candy?"

She hesitated, disliking to give an affirmative answer which would make a plain implication. Judge Grosbeck was leaning across the big mahogany desk now, looking down at the witness, studying her facial expressions. Frank Labley, plainly puzzled, apprehensive of the manner in which the hearing was developing, quite apparently afraid to try to stop the proceedings by objections, sat forward on the edge of his chair, turning his head from the witness to Mason, then back to the witness.

"Answer the question," Mason said.

"Mr. Magard knew that I had worked in a candy factory."

"How did he know that?"

"He hired me."

"That is, you were working in the candy factory when Mr. Magard hired you to work in the Golden Horn?"

"No. He looked up my record."

"And you don't consider Mr. Coll an intimate friend?"

"No."

"He was at one time?"

"Well . . . well, it depends on what you call a friend."

"And how about Mr. Lawley? He was at one time?"

"Well, not — oh, I guess so."

"Did Mr. Peavis ever give you candy?"

"Yes. Several times. He's nice."

"And saw you eating it?"

"Yes."

Mason said, "I think, Your Honor, that now I will ask for a continuance until tomorrow morning. I am, of course, aware that it is a matter addressed to the discretion of the court and . . ."

"No objection on our part," Labley interposed hurriedly.

"Very well," Judge Grosbeck ruled.

"Pursuant to stipulation of counsel the matter is continued until tomorrow morning at ten o'clock."

For a moment it seemed that Judge Grosbeck wanted to ask a question of Esther Dilmeyer, then he quite evidently changed his mind and decided to continue in his rôle of judicial impassivity. He rose and walked into his chambers.

Magard walked down the aisle of the courtroom from the seat where he had been an interested spectator. He went directly to Mason. His manner was truculent. "What," he asked, "is the idea of trying to drag *me* into that candy business?"

"I didn't," Mason said, standing up at the counsel table, pushing documents down into his brief case. "I merely asked questions. The witness answered them."

"Well, you asked them in a funny way."

Mason smiled, "It's a habit I have, particularly when I'm dealing with people who try to dictate to me."

Magard moved a step closer. His appraisal of the lawyer was coldly hostile. In such a manner might an expert hangman survey a condemned prisoner, studying his build, his weight, the muscles of his neck.

"Well?" Mason asked.

Magard said, "I don't like it," turned abruptly on his heel, and walked away.

Mildreth Faulkner walked over to put her hand on Mason's arm. "I probably don't appreciate the fine legal points, but it seems to me you have them guessing."

Mason said, "I think I'm on the track of something. Did you see Carlotta?"

The animation left her face. She nodded, and tears glistened in her eyes.

"How is she?"

"Pretty bad. After they got her to the receiving hospital, the doctor took charge. He said that for at least forty-eight hours she was to have no visitors. He made an exception in my case because she kept asking for me, and he thought it would make her feel better. He warned me I mustn't talk about the case."

"Did you?"

"Not exactly. But she had some things to tell me. I tried to stop her at first, but then decided it was better for her to talk and get it off her chest. It seemed to be worrying her."

"What in particular?" Mason asked.

"They trapped her into admitting that she'd given you the stock certificate. They told her that you'd put yourself in the clear by turning it over to the police. Mr.

Mason, how can police be so absolutely brutal, so utterly unscrupulous?"

"They figure they're dealing with criminals and the ends justify the means."

"Well, that's no way to cope with crime. They lie and resort to brutality. They can't ever get people's respect doing that. They're almost as bad as the criminals."

Mason said, "You're bitter now because it's been brought so close to home — and after all, it's an exceptional case."

She said, "It's going to be touch and go with Carla now. I don't know whether she'll pull through. She looks infinitely worse than I've ever seen her — and she was getting along so well."

"I know," Mason said sympathetically. "This is the very situation I was trying to avoid."

"Well, it isn't your fault. If she'd followed your instructions, she'd have been all right. She realizes that now."

"And she hasn't told them anything else — only about the stock?"

"That's all, but with the evidence they have against her, that's enough. Mr. Mason, she just can't go ahead with this. . . . And if they should convict her . . . Perhaps it might be better . . . better if . . ."

"She didn't pull through?" Mason asked.

She tried in vain to blink back the tears, but nodded. Mason said, "Something one of the witnesses said this afternoon gave me a new idea."

"You mean there's hope?"

"Lots of it."

"If Bob would only be a man," she said, "and tell the truth, he could save her. If he'd just admit that he was out there, and that she followed him. . . . But Bob killed him, so naturally he won't say anything that would risk his precious neck."

"Bob probably doesn't know that she followed him," Mason said.

"He most certainly does," Mildreth said indignantly. "Remember that Bob came to the Clearmount Hotel and got Carla. He drove her away, and they talked a lot. And do you know, Bob lied to her? He absolutely wouldn't admit that he'd ever surrendered the stock or that he went out there to see Lynk? Can you imagine that — after she followed him herself, saw him with her own eyes going up to Lilac Canyon?"

"How does he account for that?"

"Well, you know Bob. He always has the most wonderful explanations. He says that before he'd gone ten blocks from the house, he picked up a friend of his. He won't tell the friend's name. He says that he drove the friend uptown, that the friend wanted to borrow the car for about an hour, and Bob stepped out and let him take the car."

"Your sister believes that?"

"Of course she believes it! She'd believe anything he told her. She makes me sick."

"Could that have happened?"

"I don't see how. Carla was following him all the time. Of course, there were a few times when she got behind in traffic. Bob was shrewd enough to ask her first about the times she'd temporarily lost sight of the car. Then he had this changing of drivers occur at one of those times — the big fourflusher."

"Did you point out to Carla that . . ."

"Oh, I tried to, but what's the use. I could see that she was very weak. She wanted to tell me these things because she wanted you to know them. That Lieutenant Tragg! If I ever get a chance to give him a piece of my mind, I . . ."

"You will," Mason said. "Here he comes now."

She whirled to face the door of the courtroom where Tragg, having just entered, smiled at the deputy, then pushed his way through a little knot of people gathered in the aisle, and came walking rapidly toward them. His smile was cordial. "Good afternoon," he said.

Mildreth Faulkner tilted her chin and turned so that the point of her shoulder was toward him.

Tragg said, "Come, come, Miss Faulkner. Don't take it that way."

She said icily, "I don't like lies, and I hate liars."

He flushed.

Mason put his hand on her arm. "Take it easy," he cautioned.

Tragg shifted his eyes to Mason. "No hard feelings, Mason?" he asked.

"No hard feelings," Mason said. "I can dish it out, and I can take it. But I can't help feeling concerned about my client."

Tragg said, "I want to talk with you about that."

"Go ahead."

"First, however, I have a disagreeable duty to perform."

"Yes," Mildreth Faulkner said icily, "you want to carry water on both shoulders. You want to be friendly with people, but you betray their confidences and . . ."

"Easy," Mason interrupted. "Let's see what the lieutenant has to say."

Tragg's face was a shade darker than

usual. He addressed his remarks entirely to Mason, carefully leaving Mildreth Faulkner out of the conversation. "I'm sorry, Mason, but you made an admission in open court that you had this stock certificate. I have no alternative but to demand that you turn it over to me, and am also notifying you that you're going to be called in front of the grand jury."

"Why?"

Tragg said, "You know Churchill, don't you?"

"You mean Loring Churchill, the deputy district attorney?"

"That's the one."

"What about him?"

"He doesn't like you."

"That's nothing," Mason said promptly. "I don't like him. He's an egotistical, academic nonentity. He has the brains of an encyclopedia, and the personality of a last year's almanac."

Tragg laughed. "Well, anyway, he sent me up here to get that stock."

"How did he know I had it?"

"As soon as you made the statement in open court, we were advised. Churchill was waiting for that."

Mason said, "Well, you don't get the stock."

"Why not?"

"Because I've been served with a subpoena ordering me to bring that stock into court."

Tragg said, "Don't adopt that attitude, Mason. It won't get you anywhere."

"Why not?"

"You're in a jam."

"Why?"

"Because you've suppressed evidence."

"What's the evidence?"

"That stock certificate."

Mason said, "I stood up in open court and admitted that I had it. That doesn't sound like concealing it."

"You wouldn't have made that admission unless you'd been served with a subpoena, and, even then, you wouldn't have admitted it unless I'd trapped Mrs. Lawley into admitting she gave it to you."

"Yes," Mildreth Faulkner interrupted, "you should feel very proud of yourself for that — a brave police officer!"

Mason said, "Well, Tragg, that's a matter of opinion — whether I'd have admitted it or not."

"Well, I have my opinion," Tragg said, his lips tightening.

"You're entitled to it," Mason told him.

"I'm also entitled to the stock."

"Not unless you get an order of court. I was ordered to be in court as a witness and have that stock certificate with me. I'm here. I have that stock certificate."

"Judge Grosbeck would understand the situation."

"If he does, he can make an order."

"That will take time."

"So it will."

"And when I try to serve that order on you, how do I know I'm going to be able to find you?"

"You don't."

Tragg said, "Churchill will go up in the air over this. He won't like it a bit."

"Too bad," Mason said. "I suppose I'll spend a sleepless night now, knowing that Loring Churchill doesn't like me."

Tragg said, "Listen, Mason, you're on one side of the fence. I'm on the other. I get a kick out of you. You fight hard, and at times you fight dirty, but you're always fighting. If you turn over that stock certificate, Churchill probably won't go ahead with this grand jury business. I'd like to see you keep in the clear."

"To hell with Churchill."

"That's your final answer?"

"No. If he turns Mrs. Lawley loose within an hour, he'll get that stock certificate. Otherwise, he'll get it when I get damn good and ready to give it to him."

Tragg said, "I'm afraid Mrs. Lawley is going to face a jury."

"What charge?"

"First-degree murder."

"Decided to pin it on her, have you?"

"We have no alternative. Her husband made some damaging statements."

"Damaging to him or her?"

"Her."

Mildreth Faulkner forgot her animosity for Tragg in the shock given her by that information. "You mean Bob Lawley said something which made the case bad for Carla?" she asked incredulously.

"Yes," Tragg said, and then hastened to add, "I'm not supposed to be telling you this, I guess, but — well, to tell you the truth, Mason, I'm not very happy about it."

"Why not?"

Tragg said, "Bob Lawley impressed me as being a rat, a heel, and a fourflusher. His wife seems a dead game square-shooter."

"What did Bob tell you?" Mason asked.

Tragg hesitated. "Look here, Mason, you have a fast mind. You're usually able to get your clients out, one way or another. I suppose Churchill would give me the devil for this, but . . ."

"Well, go on."

Tragg said suddenly, "I'm a servant of the people. I'm a cog in a big system. I play the game to get results. I'm dealing with criminals, and I have a job to do."

"Why the prelude?" Mason asked.

"Because I'm sorry that I did what I did with Mrs. Lawley. If I'd realized how grave her condition was, I wouldn't have done it. I'll tell you that frankly."

"You've done it," Mason said.

Tragg said, "That's right, I've done it, and I'm not backing up on it. She's going to be treated just as any other prisoner would be treated. Only — well, this is a situation the law doesn't provide for. A woman who's dangerously ill. The slightest excitement may prove fatal."

"Let's hear what Bob Lawley told you," Mason said by way of answer.

"Lawley," Tragg said bitterly, "seems all broken up over his wife's condition. He cries and whimpers about it, and we let him in to see her, and he got down on his knees and kissed the sleeve of her nightgown."

"Go on."

"Well, just before that, he'd broken down and told the police everything he knew."

"What did he know?"

"He said he'd taken his car out, that he'd picked up a friend, that the friend wanted to borrow the car. Lawley had some telephoning he wanted to do so he drove in to the curb down by Coulter Street, that he let the friend drive the automobile away, that his wife was following him, that the car went to Lilac Canyon, that his wife went there after the car, and went to Lynk's house."

"How does he know all this?"

"Because she told him."

"And he told the officers that?" Tragg nodded.

"It's a privileged and confidential communication," Mason said. "No one should ever have inquired into what his wife told him."

Tragg said, "At first he was shaking his fists at the ceiling, swearing that he'd never divulge one single thing she had told him. Ten minutes later he was sobbing and spilling everything he knew."

"He would," Mildreth Faulkner said bitterly.

Mason said, "You know what he's doing, don't you, Tragg?"

"Trying to save his own bacon," Tragg said.

"Not that."

"What then?"

"Figure it out. His wife's in a precarious position. Excitement is bad for her. Strain and worry are worse. Not quite as spectacular in their effects, but more deadly in the long run."

"What are you getting at?"

"Who's the sole beneficiary under her will? Bob. Who is the beneficiary of her life insurance? Bob. Who would inherit her property? Bob."

Tragg pulled his brows together in a frown. "Mason, do you mean to say that he'd plan to kill his own wife?"

"Why not? Other men have killed their wives. It isn't completely unheard of in the annals of crime, you know, and this is a perfect setup. All he has to do is egg you folks on, and when her ticker stops, you'll be the ones who have to take the rap. He'll be smugly smiling to himself with all of the benefits."

"You don't sketch him in a very flattering light."

"Why should I?"

"What's your basis for making any such insinuations?"

"They aren't insinuations," Mason said. "They're charges. I'm telling you that's his game."

"The police wouldn't hound her so that

there'd be — well, fatal complications."

"The hell you wouldn't," Mason said. "You've already come pretty close to doing it."

"We haven't hurt her any."

"Don't kid yourself. She was getting along pretty well, then . . ."

"I'm not responsible for the excitement incident to committing murder."

"She didn't commit murder. She had some excitement, all right. That put her back. But I had her examined yesterday morning by a competent physician. You don't dare to let him examine her now and see what he has to say about what's happened in the last twenty-four hours."

Tragg said with some show of irritation, "We're not responsible for everything of that sort which can happen."

"You're responsible for your share of it — and look at Loring Churchill. That smug, beetle-browed, bookish nincompoop will nag her to death. Let Bob give him a few fresh facts to work on, and he'll keep trotting back and forth into Mrs. Lawley's room in the hospital until he's worn a groove in the floor."

"What," Mildreth Faulkner asked, "did Bob say besides that?"

Tragg said, "Not a great deal. What he

did say was more damning by implication than by direct statement."

Mason said, "Don't be a sap, Tragg. Use your head. Why would Mrs. Lawley have killed him?"

"Over that stock."

"Bunk! Bob might have killed him over the stock, but she wouldn't. She'd have found out how much money he wanted for it, paid through the nose, given Bob a spanking, listened to him cry and whine, then smoothed his hair, fixed his necktie nice and pretty, and given him some more money to play on the ponies."

Tragg stood silent for several seconds, his forehead creased in a portentous scowl. Suddenly he raised his eyes to Mason and said, "All right, Mason, you win."

"What?"

"I'm going to play ball with you. Dammit, that Bob Lawley doesn't ring true to me. I don't fall for him for a minute. I think he's a liar and a crook. I'd ten times rather figure he was guilty than his wife.

"He's a clever liar, and he's got Loring Churchill completely sold. I told Churchill I thought we should put some pressure on this guy, and Loring wouldn't hear of it. He thinks Mrs. Lawley is the one he wants.

Right now he's so busy trying to build up a case against her he won't listen to anything that doesn't have a tendency to prove her guilty. I don't like it."

Mason said, "Want to take a ride?"

"Yes."

"You?" Mason asked Mildreth Faulkner. She nodded.

Mason said to Della Street, "You'd better come along, Della."

"Where are you going?" Tragg asked.

Mason said, "I had a theory about this case that requires a little thought, and a few questions."

"You've asked the questions?"

"Yes."

"How were the answers?"

Mason said, "I'm pretty damn sure I'm right."

"Why not tell me first?"

Mason shook his head.

"Why?"

"Because the case isn't ripe. It isn't ready to pick. We haven't any evidence against the guilty person. All we have are certain things we can use to support a very logical theory.

"Now then, I know you. You hate to go off half cocked. You'll listen to what I have to say, think it over, and say, 'Gosh,

Mason, that certainly sounds like something, but let's not tip our hand until we have more than we've got now. Let's go to work on it and build up a perfect case.' "

"Well," Tragg said, "what's wrong with that? You don't want to flush the quarry too soon — not in this business."

Mason said, "The thing that's wrong with that way of playing it is that you'll keep Mrs. Lawley in confinement. You'll let her know that a charge is pending over her. You'll let Loring Churchill trot back and forth in and out of her room until she's worn to a shadow. She'll take a deep breath, and her heart will pop. Nix on it. We're going to get her out tonight. We're going to get that load taken off her mind."

"Suppose you upset the apple cart?"

"Then it's upset. Do you want to come, or don't you?"

"I don't approve of it."

"I knew you wouldn't."

Tragg said moodily, "Well, if you put it up to me that way, I'll have to come."

"Come on, then," Mason said.

14

Tragg parked his car in front of the Molay Arms Apartments. "Ring her bell?" he asked Mason.

Mason opened the rear door and assisted Mildreth Faulkner and Della Street from the car. "Better to ring the manager."

Tragg said, "Perhaps I can beat that. This passkey should do the work."

He took a key ring from his pocket, selected a key, tried it tentatively, shook his head, tried another key, and the lock clicked back.

"Locks on those outer doors are mostly ornamental, anyway," Tragg explained as they walked across the lobby. "Just what do you want with Esther Dilmeyer, Mason?"

"Ask her some questions."

"Look here, if you're getting anything hot, Loring Churchill should be here."

Mason said, "This may be only lukewarm."

"You're leading up to something."

"Uh huh."

Tragg said, "Okay, I'll ride along for a while, and see where you're going."

They walked down the thin carpet of the third corridor. There was a light coming from the transom over Esther Dilmeyer's door.

Mason said, in a low tone to Mildreth Faulkner, "Tap on the door. She'll ask who it is. Tell her."

"Then what?"

"I think that's all she'll want to know. If she should ask what you want, tell her you want to talk with her for a minute about something that happened today."

Tragg made one last attempt. "Listen, Mason, if you'd put your cards on the table, and tell us what you know, the department would . . ."

"Stall around until it got proof," Mason said, "and, by that time, *my* client would be dead."

Mildreth tapped gently on the door.

"Who is it?" Esther Dilmeyer called.

"Mildreth Faulkner."

"Oh, it's you. . . ." Noises from the apartment, the sound of slippered feet on the floor, the noise made by a bolt turning, and Esther Dilmeyer, attired only in underthings, opened the door to say, "I wanted to see you. I hoped you'd understand . . ."

She broke off as she saw the group in the corridor, then laughed, and said, "Well, excuse *me!* Why didn't you tell me there were men in the party?"

She said, "Just a minute," stepped back into the apartment, and picked up a robe which hung over the back of a chair. She slipped it on and said, "Come on in. You should have told me you weren't alone, Miss Faulkner."

Mason stepped forward. He asked, "You know Lieutenant Tragg?"

"Oh, yes. I saw him before I left the hospital. They wouldn't let me leave until I had permission of the police."

There was an awkward pause. Tragg looked at Mason, and Mason said abruptly, "Miss Dilmeyer, I think you're in some danger."

"I — danger?"

"Yes. Murder — so you won't get on the stand tomorrow."

"What makes you think so?"

He said, "Don't forget an attempt has already been made to murder you. Whoever tried then is just as anxious to get you out of the way now as he was a couple of days ago."

She laughed. "To tell you the truth, I hadn't thought much of anything about it."

"If some person had a desire to kill you forty-eight hours ago, I know of nothing which has happened in the meantime that would cause him to change his mind," Mason said.

Esther tapped a cigarette on the arm of the chair, and said, "You're probably more concerned about that than I am."

"Perhaps so. That's because I think that the person who sent you the candy is the same person who murdered Harvey Lynk."

She raised her eyebrows. "Well, isn't that a bright idea!"

Mason said, "We have several clues to work on. I don't know whether Lieutenant Tragg told you all of them."

"I didn't," Tragg said.

"To begin with," Mason observed as Esther Dilmeyer struck a match and held it to the end of her cigarette, "the address on the wrapper was typed on the typewriter in Mr. Lynk's office at the Golden Horn."

She shook out the match with a quick, nervous gesture. Her eyes showed that the statement came as something of a shock. "How in the world do you know that," she asked, "— unless someone saw the thing being typed?"

"Many people don't know that typewriters are more highly individualized than a person's handwriting," Mason said. "Any typewriter which has been in use for even a short time has a distinct individuality. The type gets out of line. An expert can compare samples of typing and tell absolutely whether they were done on the same machine."

Esther Dilmeyer said, "I didn't know that."

"That's one thing," Mason went on. "The other is that the paper was taken from Lynk's office."

"How do you know that?"

"Papers vary as to rag-content, weight, chemical composition, and trademark. Trademark is usually watermarked directly into the paper."

"Anything else?" she asked.

Mason said, "The label was pasted on with glue. The glue was similar in composition to some that is used at the Golden Horn, and, most important of all, the glue had set so thoroughly that the police were able to tell that the label had been put on at least forty-eight hours before the package was sent."

"Well," she said, "I guess the police are a lot smarter than I'd ever thought they were."

"They are," Mason commented dryly.

"Anything else?" she asked.

"Yes. Bear in mind that the label was prepared for the candy more than forty-eight hours before it was sent to you. Now, you've worked in a candy factory. You know something about what a job it is to tamper with chocolate creams, and then leave them so perfectly finished in appearance that there wouldn't seem to be anything wrong."

"Yes, I can appreciate that. It wouldn't be such a difficult job if one knew how, but it's no job for a bungler."

"Now also bear in mind that the card which accompanied the candy was one which had previously been enclosed with an orchid corsage sent to you."

"Either that or it's an exact duplicate," Esther Dilmeyer said, avoiding Mildreth Faulkner's eyes.

Mildreth laughed. "I certainly hope you don't think that *I* went back and sent the candy with another card."

Esther Dilmeyer didn't look at her.

She said to Perry Mason, "I'm only answering questions so we can help get the thing cleared up."

The smile left Mildreth Faulkner's lips. "Then you do think that *I* sent you the candy?" she asked.

Esther said, "I like to live and let live." She turned slowly to face Mildreth Faulkner. "I don't want to make any accusations or insinuations, but just the same that certainly looked like your handwriting on the card."

"Why, I never . . ."

"Easy, Miss Faulkner," Mason warned. "Let's develop the facts a little bit before we start looking for the person who sent that candy. Now then, Miss Dilmeyer, when you got that candy, and saw the card on the inside, you felt completely at ease. Is that right?"

"Yes, naturally. I'd met Miss Faulkner, found her very charming, and sympathetic — although she had grounds for being otherwise if she wanted to be — well, you know, narrow-minded about things and hold me responsible for things which were entirely beyond my control."

"I see, but that possibility hadn't occurred to you at the time you received the candy?"

"No. I thought she was a very nice person. She was going to give me a job, and I felt very friendly and — well, loyal."

Mason said, "Let's see where that leaves us. The person who sent the candy was someone who had access to virtually everything at the Golden Horn, someone who could use Mr. Lynk's typewriter, open the desk drawer, take out some of Lynk's stationery, use the glue pot, someone who knew something about the manner in which packages were handled at the package-delivery service during the rush hour; and, last of all, someone who was able to get that card which had been sent with the orchids and put it in the candy before the candy was delivered to the messenger service. That was an interval of less than thirty minutes. That calls for rather fast work."

"Unless," Esther Dilmeyer said, and then stopped.

"Unless what?"

"Unless Miss Faulkner was the one who sent the candy. If she did, there were *two* cards, and . . . and . . . well, that's all there is to it."

Mason said, "I've carefully investigated Miss Faulkner. She would have been unable to have sent the candy even if she'd wanted to."

"What do you mean?"

"She hadn't had sufficient experience with handling chocolates to have doctored the candy for one thing, and for another, she didn't have any access to the Golden

Horn forty-eight hours prior to the time the candy was sent. No, there's only one person who meets all of those requirements."

"Who?" Esther Dilmeyer asked.

"You," Mason said quietly.

She half rose from her chair, "Me! You mean . . ."

"I mean," Mason went on, "that you were the only one who could have sent that candy. You sent it to yourself."

"And then ate a lot of poison just to put myself in the hospital?" she asked sarcastically.

Lieutenant Tragg leaned forward, started to say something to Mason. Mason, without taking his eyes from Esther Dilmeyer, said, "Shut up, Tragg," and then to Esther Dilmeyer, "You didn't eat any drugged candy."

"Oh, I didn't?" she said. "I just wanted to get a ride to the hospital. I was pretending to be asleep and fooled the doctor, is that it?"

"No. You took a big dose of veronal, but you didn't get it in the candy."

She made a show of irritation. "Listen, I've got some things to do tonight. I understand that you saved my life. At any rate, you paid my hospital bill. I felt grateful to you, but you have bats in your belfry, and I haven't all night to sit here and listen to you spout a lot of theories."

"You see," Mason went on, "each piece of candy was held in a little brown paper cup folded and scalloped so as to fit around the piece of candy."

"Well?" she asked.

"In the box of candy which was on the table," Mason went on, "several pieces were missing, but the little paper containers were also missing, and those weren't anywhere in the room. You'd hardly have devoured the papers as well as the candy."

A swift flicker of expression showed on her face.

Mason followed up his advantage quickly. "But where you gave yourself away was when you told me that when you saw the card in the candy box, with the initials 'M.F.' on it, you were completely reassured. *If* you'd been telling the truth, that card would have made you suspicious, because, not thirty minutes earlier, you had received an orchid corsage with an identical card. You will even notice that on the card there were two pinholes, showing where the card had been pinned to the orchids. It's hardly possible that you could have failed to notice *that*."

"You're cuckoo," she said. "Why would I want to send myself poisoned candy?"

"Because," Mason said, "you wanted an alibi."

"An alibi for what?"

"For killing Lynk."

"Oh, so *I* killed *him*, did I?"

Mason nodded. "And then gave yourself away by trying to implicate too many people this afternoon in court. Magard, Peavis, Irma Radine. . . . You very adroitly suggested numbers of people who knew of your candy-eating propensities."

"Well, aren't you interesting!"

"You see," Mason said, "you wanted an alibi. It occurred to you that it would make a swell alibi if you could be drugged into complete unconsciousness at the time when the murder was committed. So you sent yourself poisoned candy, slipped out of your evening dress, put on more service-able and less conspicuous clothes, and drove up to Lilac Canyon.

"You probably telephoned Lynk to make certain he would be there. Then you stopped on the way to telephone me. You had to telephone me early enough to give yourself an alibi, but not early enough to enable me to locate your apartment and

338

get out here while you were still out on your murder mission. The best place you knew to telephone from was where Sindler Coll lived. You knew there was a booth in the lobby, that no one would be in the lobby to see you using the telephone, or to overhear the conversation."

"And just *why* did I telephone *you?*" she asked.

"For a very particular reason, Miss Dilmeyer. You wanted to have someone whose word the police would take. You wanted to have someone who knew something about you, but didn't know where you lived. You wanted someone, in short, who would make a good witness; but who wouldn't know where you lived or how to go about finding out.

"You'd planned your alibi and the murder for two or three days. You were wondering just how you could fix it so you would be found before you had been unconscious too long, but not soon enough to interfere with your alibi.

"You knew that I would have to get hold of Mildreth Faulkner to connect you with the Golden Horn. Even if I did, you weren't particularly concerned, because no one in the nightclub knew your address.

"You felt reasonably certain that I

wouldn't be able to get hold of Miss Faulkner until she came to keep her appointment at one o'clock, that then Miss Faulkner would give me the lead to the Golden Horn, that even then it would take me quite a while to locate your apartment.

"As a matter of fact, I almost got here too soon. Thanks to a little detective work on the part of my secretary, Miss Street, I connected you with the Golden Horn almost at once."

She said sarcastically, "Aren't *you* smart? I mean *real-l-ly!*"

Mason said, "You left Coll's apartment house after you had telephoned me, drove out to Lilac Canyon, killed Lynk, and then, after you killed him, took a big dose of veronal. Then you drove to your apartment, placed the telephone on the floor, taking care not to change the position of the receiver, and yielded to the drug which was beginning to make you sleepy. By the time I found you, you had just dropped off into deep sleep."

"That's your story?" she asked.

Mason nodded.

"Well, go jump in the lake. I suppose you'd like to have me be a nice fall guy so you could get your rich client out of a mess, but unfortunately for you I'm not going to do it. You'll have to find some other fall guy."

There was an interval of silence. Lieutenant Tragg looked across at Esther Dilmeyer, then looked away. He studied the carpet thoughtfully.

"Well," Esther Dilmeyer said, after more than a minute had elapsed, "what is this, a new kind of third degree, or are we just sitting here enjoying the scenery?"

"We're waiting," Mason said, "for you to tell us about the murder."

"*You* can wait until doomsday. Don't hold your breath until I start talking. I'm going out. And now if you folks will excuse me, I'll start dressing."

Tragg said, "You're not going out."

"No?"

"No."

"Why not?"

"Mason has built up a logical case."

"You mean *you* fall for that stuff?"

He nodded.

"You're nuts," she said, and then, after a moment, "All of you."

Again there was an interval of silence which seemed to make Esther Dilmeyer more nervous than when Mason had been accusing her of murder. "My God," she said, "don't all sit there looking at me in that tone of voice! Good Lord! This is *my* apartment. I want to dress."

"You're not going out," Tragg said. "You can consider yourself under arrest."

"All right, I'm under arrest. That doesn't mean that I have to sit here and look at a lot of sourpusses. And I suppose, since I'm under arrest, you're going to take me somewhere."

"Perhaps."

She flung open her robe. "In my undies, I suppose."

"No. You may dress."

"While you guys get an eyeful? No, thank you."

Mason lit a cigarette.

"Well, for God's sake, somebody say something. Won't you at least argue about it?"

"There's nothing to argue about," Mason said. "The evidence is conclusive against you, on the poisoned candy. If you didn't kill Lynk, you'd better start talking. You *might* have had some extenuating circumstances in your favor."

She said, "I know your game. You're trying to get me to talk. Well, brother, since you're so damn smart, I'll tell you something. Little Esther knows her rights. She's going to sit very quiet and not answer a single damn question. If the cops think they have enough to hold me on, they can take me up in front of a jury, and I'll get a lawyer who won't turn out to be a double-crosser. Then we'll see what happens."

Mason said, "That's fair enough if you deliberately murdered him in cold blood, but if you shot him in self-defense, or if it was an accident, you're going to have to say so now."

"Why now?" she asked.

"Because if you keep quiet now, and then try to make a defense of accident or justifiable homicide when you get to trial, it'll sound to a jury as though you were reciting something a lawyer had thought up for you. "

She said, "*You're* a big help."

"I am at that," Mason told her. "There are several weak points in your scheme. The police would have stumbled on them sooner or later. Then it would be too late for you to save yourself by telling what actually *did* happen."

"Oh, is that so? What are the weak points?"

"The missing paper cups in the candy box, the identical cards, your handkerchief, the telephone on the floor with the receiver in place — and the other things the police will find."

"What other things?"

Mason smiled. "Think back," he said, "on what you've done. Remember that the police now know exactly what happened. They only need to look for confirmation."

Her voice was defiant. "All right, let them look."

"By that time," Mason said, "it will be too late for you to tell your story."

"Why?"

"Newspapers will think it's something your lawyer thought up."

She regarded him with the thought-clouded eyes of one who is striving to reach a decision. "Suppose I tell it now?"

"The facts will sound a lot better coming all at once."

She studied the tip of her cigarette. "You may be right at that."

Tragg started to say something, but Mason's quickly imperative gesture motioned him to silence.

"Coll has a key to your apartment?" Mason prompted.

"Yes."

"Then he kept Bob Lawley here the day after the murder while you were in the hospital?"

"I suppose so. I wouldn't know about that."

"You're in love with Coll?"

"Not now. I was crazy over him. I'll get over it all right. It'll wear off. It has before, and it will again."

Mason looked at his watch. "Well, if you're going to . . ."

"Oh, all right," she said. "Here it is. I was color for the gambling house. It was my job to make men play, and keep them from quitting when they started losing. I got a commission. A while ago Coll and Lynk put it up to me that Bob Lawley was a rich playboy. I was to help them relieve him of some of the worldly possessions with which he was overburdened.

"I did my part.

"When things got ready for the payoff, they planned to doublecross me out of my cut, and plant Coll's new girl in on my job.

"That's all right. I was fed up with the life anyway, but I didn't propose to stand for a doublecross. I decided to do some calling on my own.

"Bob Lawley carried this gun in the glove compartment of the automobile. I don't think he even knew it was gone when I lifted it. Of course, I knew they'd suspect me first thing, and I needed an ironclad alibi.

"I decided to send myself some poisoned candy. I fixed it up four days ago — took a few pieces out of the box and put them in a paper bag which I could carry with me, poisoned the rest, wrapped the box and held it in readiness to send to myself by a messenger whenever Lynk gave me the chance to grab the stock. I was all set and waiting.

"The night he went out to Lilac Canyon I knew he'd have the stock with him. I thought the payoff was to be that night. Then Miss Faulkner got in touch with me, and gave me a lot of information I hadn't had before, also arranged for me to be at your office at one o'clock. I *had* intended to call the police to fix up my alibi, but you were a better bet. Coll knew where I lived and had a key to my apartment. I wanted to be certain he was out. I knew he'd be meeting Lynk out at Lilac Canyon. I shadowed Coll's place until I saw him leaving, then I went to the lobby, telephoned you I'd been poisoned, and started for Lilac Canyon. On the way, I ate the unpoisoned candy out of the paper bag, so the stomach content would show chocolate creams. Just before I went to Lynk's cabin, I took a big dose of veronal, put on a mask, and a raincoat.

"I knew Lynk was expecting a woman, from the way he answered my knock. When he saw my mask and the business end of the gun, he almost collapsed. I told him to get out that Lawley stock and put it on the table."

"Did you have any trouble with him?" Mason asked.

"Only that he was frightened and his hands were trembling so I was afraid he couldn't unlock the drawer that held the stock. Then, just as he did it, I heard a noise and looked back over my shoulder."

"The other girl?" Mason asked.

"That's right. You see I'd neglected to close the door behind me when I pushed Lynk back into the room. I'll say one thing: she was dead game. I swung the gun around and tried to bluff her. She didn't bluff. She came at me like a wildcat. She grabbed my right wrist with both hands and tried to wrench the gun loose. It was a double action. My finger was caught in the trigger guard. She kept pulling it back. I yelled at her to stop. She didn't stop. The gun went off. That scared her, and she jumped back. The gun fell to the floor. And then we saw Harvey Lynk.

"My mask was still on. She didn't know who I was. We made for the door. She left her overnight bag. I left the gun.

"I had an awful time getting home. The veronal was commencing to take effect. The last part of the drive I was having goofy ideas. I thought I'd dreamt the whole thing. I managed to get my car parked in the garage, got to my apartment where I'd left things all planted the way I wanted you to find them. I was asleep before I hit the floor. You know the rest of it.

"It wasn't until I regained consciousness in the hospital that I realized I'd left the raincoat and the mask in my car. That mask was a giveaway. I was going to destroy it tonight."

Mason nodded to Tragg. "All right, Tragg, go ahead."

The police lieutenant said, "Both of you women ran out without waiting to see how badly he was hurt?"

"We didn't need to examine him. He collapsed like a punctured tire."

"What was he doing while you two were struggling for the gun?"

"Trying to get the stock back in the drawer," she said. "He had his back turned toward us, but I saw he was fumbling with the drawer. Now I want you to do one thing."

"What?" Tragg asked.

"Get that other girl and make her tell her story before she knows who I am or what I've told you."

"Who is she?" Mason asked.

Her laugh was bitter. "That," she said, "is the payoff. An empty-headed little fool who thinks being a gambling-house decoy on a commission basis beats working for a living. She wants my job, and I want hers.

"That's the trouble with those empty-headed, high-spirited girls who have youth and looks. They think they'll always have youth. Age is something that leaves its mark on other people. I remember when I felt that way myself — and you lose quick in this game. When you're thirty here, it's the same as being forty in any other . . ."

"*Who* is it?" Tragg interrupted.

Esther Dilmeyer's laugh was harsh. "Lois Carling," she said, "— and that's the payoff."

Mason picked up the telephone and handed it to Lieutenant Tragg. "Call headquarters and tell them to release Carlotta Lawley," he said.

While he was waiting for the connection, he said, "And the next time you try to decoy me away from your sister, Miss Faulkner, don't have a gun go off accidentally and don't be such an obvious suspect.

You had me fooled for a while, but after I got to know you well enough to know what a bright mind you had, I realized you were over-playing your part. . . . Hello. Hello. Headquarters? Lieutenant Tragg of Homicide. We're releasing Carlotta Lawley. Perry Mason is arranging to put her in a private sanitarium. Rush it through and cut the red tape."

15

It was late that night when Della Street snuggled up beside Perry Mason in the lawyer's car and said, "Well, that's one thing about Lieutenant Tragg. When he promises to co-operate, he co-operates."

Mason nodded.

She wrapped her fingers around his right arm, a gentle, reassuring touch. "Did it occur to you, Chief, that Lieutenant Tragg is falling pretty hard for Mildreth Faulkner?"

"I'd have to be blind and deaf not to have had the thought occur to me."

"She seems to be interested in him."

"Why not? He's a pretty shrewd individual."

"I'll say he is. Having him on Homicide isn't going to be the cinch it was when Sergeant Holcomb was running things. You know, you're going to have to watch your step. Tragg is filled with co-operation this time, but if he ever *catches* you pulling one of your fast ones, I don't think he'd hesitate for a minute to throw the book at you."

"Let him throw —"

"Will they convict Esther Dilmeyer?"

"Probably not," Mason said. "Lois Carling came through and backed her story up. Of course, Esther went out there with a gun in order to perpetrate a felony, but — well, she's a darn good-looking girl, and . . ."

"And a good-looking woman can get away with murder?" Della asked.

"Homicide," Mason corrected, smiling. "There's a distinction."

"And you think Esther Dilmeyer's testimony will win the Peavis lawsuit for Miss Faulkner?"

"Sure it will. She knows that Peavis had only made Lynk an offer for the stock. It's a small point but damned important. And when I get done cross-examining Mr. Sindler Coll — well, I think Peavis will drop his suit."

Della laughed. "That's going to be a lovely cross-examination. Will you be able to show that the whole gambling thing was a crooked frame-up, in order to invalidate that transfer of stock?"

"Easy."

"Where will that leave Mr. Magard?"

Mason grinned. "Right out on the very tip end of a limb over a very deep pool. In case you're interested, we're on our way to the Golden Horn right now. We're going to order champagne, and I wouldn't doubt in the least if Mr. Magard comes down and falls all over us trying to square himself. Tragg wouldn't want much of an excuse to raid that place."

"Won't he do it anyway?"

"Probably."

"Then is it good policy for you to go down and promise Magard you'll . . ."

"I'm not going to promise Magard one single thing," Mason said, "and when it comes to dealing with the police, he can make his contact with Lieutenant Tragg."

She said uneasily, "I have a presentiment about Lieutenant Tragg."

"What?"

"I think he's going to be dangerous."

"The man's clever," Mason conceded. "Part of his instructions from the Chief's office are to keep an eye on me and hold me in line. I guess we'll have a lot of fun from now on."

There was no longer any good-natured banter in her voice. She said, "Says you. *I* don't like it."

"I'll appoint you my legal guardian if

you'll take the job, Della."

"No dice," she said. "You don't want a guardian any more than you want domestic ties — but try and get out of my sight, after this, for very long at a time. . . ."

He swung the car out toward the center of the road. "Look, baby," he said, "I was watching the way Tragg drives when he has the siren going. It's a technique all its own. You make your speed in between blocks, start to ride your brakes as you come to the intersection, then step on the throttle. . . . Watch."

She settled back against the cushions, watching his face, her eyes contented and amused as Mason sent the speedometer needle quivering up into the big figures.

The employees of Thorndike Press hope you have enjoyed this Large Print book. All our Thorndike and Wheeler Large Print titles are designed for easy reading, and all our books are made to last. Other Thorndike Press Large Print books are available at your library, through selected bookstores, or directly from us.

For information about titles, please call:

(800) 223-1244

or visit our Web site at:

www.gale.com/thorndike
www.gale.com/wheeler

To share your comments, please write:

Publisher
Thorndike Press
295 Kennedy Memorial Drive
Waterville, ME   04901

X